Bleeding Heart Yard

Also by Elly Griffiths

THE DR RUTH GALLOWAY MYSTERIES

The Crossing Places
The Janus Stone
The House at Sea's End
A Room Full of Bones
A Dying Fall
The Outcast Dead
The Ghost Fields
The Woman in Blue
The Chalk Pit
The Dark Angel
The Stone Circle
The Lantern Men
The Night Hawks
The Locked Room

THE BRIGHTON MYSTERIES

The Zig Zag Girl
Smoke and Mirrors
The Blood Card
The Vanishing Box
Now You See Them
The Midnight Hour

OTHER WORKS

The Stranger Diaries
The Postscript Murders

FOR CHILDREN

A Girl Called Justice
A Girl Called Justice: The Smugglers' Secret
A Girl Called Justice: The Ghost in the Garden
A Girl Called Justice: The Spy at the Window

Bleeding Heart Yard

ELLY Griffiths

QUERCUS

First published in Great Britain in 2022 by

QUERCUS

Quercus Editions Ltd
Carmelite House
50 Victoria Embankment
London EC4Y 0DZ

An Hachette UK company

A CIP catalogue record for this book is available
from the British Library

HB ISBN 978 1 52940 995 6
TPB ISBN 978 1 52940 996 3

This book is a work of fiction. Names, characters,
businesses, organizations, places and events are
either the product of the author's imagination
or used fictitiously. Any resemblance to
actual persons, living or dead, events or
locales is entirely coincidental.

10 9 8 7 6 5 4 3 2 1

Typeset by CC Book Production
Printed and bound in Great Britain by Clays Ltd, Elcograf S.p.A.

Papers used by Quercus are from well-managed forests and other responsible sources.

In loving memory of John Maxted

'Is my friend hearty,
   Now I am thin and pine,
And has he found to sleep in
   A better bed than mine?

Yes, lad, I lie easy,
   I lie as lads would choose;
I cheer a dead man's sweetheart,
   Never ask me whose.'

A.E. Housman
'Is my team ploughing?' From *A Shropshire Lad*

'The heart has its reasons of which reason knows nothing.'

Pascal, *Pensées*

Prologue

Cassie

Is it possible to forget that you've committed a murder? Well, I'm here to tell you that it is. Not entirely, obviously. But, day to day, it just doesn't register. Pete and I even had a phase of going to murder mystery parties. We'd get all dressed up and go to a friend's house and act out a script. There would be cue cards, props, even background music. The setting was usually a country house or a Mississippi river boat. Something like that. I progressed from playing Miss Ellie, high-spirited daughter of Black Jack Roulette, to Mrs Beacham the cook. We'd start off in character but, as the evening progressed, everyone would get drunk and forget the clues. This rather irritated me. I like following rules.

The kids used to love playing Murder in the Dark. It really was a very easy party game and kept them quiet for ages. They would all shut themselves in the downstairs bathroom, about ten of them. The detective would be left outside, sitting disconsolately on the stairs. After a few minutes of giggling, a blood-curdling scream would ring out and the door would open to reveal someone lying on the floor between the loo and the basin. The law-enforcer would then have to solve the crime, sometimes with a little help from me. 'That's not fair, Mum,' Lucy and Sam used to say.

The actual murder was so long ago that it genuinely seems to have happened to someone else. I suppose we all think of our eighteen-year-old selves as different people, but I could honestly look at pictures of the blonde, smiling girl and not recognise her. What did she think, who did she love, what music did she listen to? I simply couldn't remember. Dissociation is a word I remember from my psychology degree. I think I once wrote the definition on a cue card. 'A mental process where a person disconnects from their thoughts and feelings . . . often linked to trauma in childhood.' But I never thought that it was possible to live so happily with this condition. Who was the girl in the school photos? Nothing to do with me.

But I wasn't able to forget school completely. Pete went to Manor Park too and he was always going to reunions with members of the football and rugby teams. I even kept in contact with a few old schoolfriends. I didn't much want to see them; I just wanted to know where they were. Pete sometimes asked me to accompany him to his get-togethers, but I always refused. 'I don't want to look back,' I always said, 'I want to look forward.' Because the future was great. It meant the kids growing up, going to university, having families of their own. It meant Pete and me retiring, having more time and going on a round-the-world trip, doing the gap year that we couldn't afford at the time. I loved the future. I just wasn't so keen on the past.

'Cassie deserves to relax,' Pete's mother used to say. 'You

shouldn't nag her to go to the reunions. She's got enough on her plate. What with her job.'

And that's another thing you can do to forget. You can become a police officer.

Chapter 1

Harbinder

Saturday, 21 September 2019

Harbinder Kaur looks out of the window of her rented flat. London, she thinks. The word conjures up a potent cocktail of images. Day trips with school, the smell of plastic and vomit on the coach, colouring in worksheets on the Tower of London, posing with waxworks of TV stars. Weekends with various girlfriends, West End shows and meals in Soho restaurants where neither of them understood the wine list. The occasional visit for work, she and Neil standing in a publisher's office, bemused by books everywhere and by the existence of adults with names like Jelli. The London Olympics, the last time Harbinder had felt patriotic. The Fire of London. London Calling. Londinium. London Pride.

And now Harbinder lives in this enchanted, accursed place. She has a shared flat and a job as a detective inspector in the Criminal Investigation Department of the Metropolitan Police (Homicide and Serious Crimes Unit). To her not-so-secret delight she's in charge of a Murder Investigation Team (MIT) based in West Kensington, W10, an area mysteriously called Dalgarno. She still can't quite believe the speed with which all this has happened. One minute she was living with her parents in Shoreham, West Sussex, complaining about work and her colleagues, especially Neil, watching reruns of *Bones* every night and playing games on her phone. The next, she had passed her detective exam, applied for a new job, piled her few belongings into Neil's brother's van, and moved into the front bedroom of No 45 Barlby Road.

'You're a London girl now,' said her mother when she kissed her goodbye. There was real awe in her voice, spoiled only by her saying, with her next breath, 'You can always come back if it's too much for you.'

'Be careful in the big city,' said her dad. 'It's not cosy like dear old Sussex.' There was an edge of irony in his voice which wasn't surprising considering that Harbinder had been involved with several high-profile murder cases in the supposedly safe seaside town.

'I wouldn't live in London,' said Neil, who had kindly offered to drive the van.

'Why?' said Harbinder. 'Too many brown people for you?'

'No,' said Neil patiently. 'Too much crime.'

'We're police officers,' said Harbinder, already terrified by the traffic on the South Circular. 'We love crime.'

But she knew what he meant. London equals serious crime. Not just murder, which could be disappointingly mundane, but drugs, racketeering, gangs, human trafficking. The very worst of human nature, thought Harbinder, with a not unpleasurable shiver, as the van passed several boarded-up shops and a pub called Dr Crippen's. Which was why, after a month in her new job, she was rather disappointed that her work had so far mostly involved attending meetings and learning new computer programmes. At least she had her own office, though, with 'DI Harbinder Kaur' on the door. She'd tried to take a selfie for Neil but hadn't been able to get both her face and the sign in the picture. Her DS, Cassie Fitzherbert, sweetly offered to take a proper picture but the moment had passed.

Harbinder likes West London. Her flat is on the top floor of a solid terraced house in a long curving road leading down to Wormwood Scrubs. But there's a pleasant park nearby and a variety of shops, cafés and restaurants. She likes walking the streets at the weekends, catching sight of herself in shop windows, striding along in her jeans and leather jacket. It's September, a bright, clear autumn. Pumpkins are appearing in the shops and the tree outside Harbinder's window is turning from green to amber to red, like a traffic light in reverse.

Harbinder may have been teasing Neil but it's also nice to be in a multicultural city. The first time she saw Sikh men in turbans she thought that they must be her father or her brothers. It's refreshing, and rather strange, not to be the only person of colour on the bus to work. She's not the only woman of colour at the station either. Although she is the only DI.

Her flatmates are about as white as you can get though. Jeanne is Scottish, with red hair and almost translucent skin. Mette is Danish, tall and blonde, fearlessly riding a bicycle around the horror that is the Scrubs Lane Intersection. Jeanne is a teacher and Mette an architect. Harbinder doesn't know them very well yet but the flatmates have been out for a pizza together and chat whenever they coincide in the kitchen. There's no sitting room so they spend most of their time in their bedrooms. Harbinder doesn't mind this but, sometimes, playing Panda Pop by the open window at night and hearing music from the flats opposite she does catch herself thinking: is this all there is to London?

Now, it's Saturday evening and Harbinder is at her window again. She feels, not exactly homesick, she tells herself firmly, but slightly wistful. Yesterday, walking along the South Bank, watching the tourist boats going past and looking at the strange pieces of flotsam discarded by the Thames, she surprised herself by missing the sea. Harbinder is not a keen swimmer, or a beachcomber, like her friend Benedict, but she likes the way the sea is different every day, the way it doesn't care how she is feeling but just carries on with its own elemental ebb and flow. She misses not being able to see the horizon. The Thames is too narrow and London sometimes feels too big.

But, if she were in Shoreham, listening to her parents argue about *Britain's Got Talent*, she knows she would have felt trapped and rather pathetic. 'Harbinder Kaur,' the sardonic voice-over in her head would have intoned, 'still lives at home at the age of thirty-eight. She's gay but, although her parents know in theory, she has yet to introduce them to a girlfriend. Her main hobbies are arguing with her brothers and playing mindless games on her phone.' Now, at least, the narrative is: 'Harbinder Kaur, aged thirty-eight, is a detective in the London Met and shares a flat with two other female professionals.' It doesn't change the fact that she's alone on a Saturday night though, listening to Mette's TV through the wall, wondering whether it's too soon to change into her pyjamas. Jeanne is out with her boyfriend.

Harbinder has actually had an invitation of her own. Kim, one of her sergeants, mentioned that the team were going out for drinks to celebrate someone's retirement. 'You should come, boss. It'll be a laugh.' Harbinder should go, she knows. She wants to show her colleagues that she may be a diminutive Sikh woman, but she enjoys a pint as much as the next Met detective. She's also waiting for the right moment to come out to them. It's harder than you'd think. She doesn't want to make a big deal of it but if she leaves it any longer, they'll definitely assume that she's straight. The trouble is, she can't casually mention a girlfriend because she doesn't have one. The thought of an evening spent being the life and soul of the party whilst looking for an occasion to use the L word makes her feel depressed. She knows she won't go.

Should she ring her mother? But, if she does, Bibi will only try to persuade her to go home for Sunday lunch tomorrow. Bibi is as obsessed with Sunday as any Catholic and insists on gathering as many of the family in one room as is humanly possible. Harbinder thinks of the flat above the family shop and her heart twists, even though she knows that, after half an hour with her brothers, she'll be longing for the peace of her West London bedroom. She'll have an early night and tomorrow she'll go out and really explore London, go to some markets, eat exotic food, send some pictures to Neil. 'Arancini are what we Londoners call rice balls.' Thinking of food reminds her that she hasn't eaten yet. What's on her shelf of the larder? She thinks there's some pasta and a tin of tomatoes. Harbinder is nowhere near as good a cook as her mum and, besides, she can't face anything that reminds her of home.

After the rather tasteless pasta and several episodes of *Bones*, Harbinder judges that it's late enough to go to bed. She considers having a shower and decides against it. The bathroom is freezing and there's always the chance that she'll bump into Mette, who doesn't seem to feel the need to wear clothes much. Harbinder doesn't know if this is to do with Mette being Scandinavian but it's rather disconcerting and makes Harbinder feel like a prude in her cosy M&S dressing gown. She'll just brush her teeth and get into bed. Harbinder is turning off her laptop when her phone rings.

It's one of her sergeants, DS Jake Barker. Harbinder tries to call him to mind. Shortish, darkish, one of those accents characterised by Sussex-born Harbinder as 'northern'.

'Hi, Jake. What is it?'

'Hi, boss.' How Harbinder loves this form of address. She wishes she could use it as her ring tone. 'We've had something called in. Unexplained death. I think you'd better come.'

'Unexplained death?' Not as good as a suspicious death but her Saturday is definitely looking up.

'A man killed at a school reunion.'

'Interesting.'

'Wait till you hear who it is.'

'I really don't like waiting for this sort of thing, Jake.'

'Garfield Rice. Garfield Rice MP.'

Even Harbinder, who is allergic to politics, has heard of him.

Chapter 2

Harbinder

'It's Manor Park school,' says Jake. 'And you know what people who go there are like.'

Harbinder has no idea what they are like. She thinks of her old school in West Sussex, Talgarth High. It was often spoken of with horror by local residents, as if 'Talgarth kids' was shorthand for marauding Viking hoards. But it wasn't such a bad place even though it had once been the centre of a murder investigation. Honestly, thinks Harbinder, what is it with these educational establishments?

'I'm not from around here,' Harbinder says now. Jake is driving them through the London streets with the ease of a native, although his accent doesn't exactly scream 'cockney' to Harbinder. Cockneys are apparently people born within the sound of Bow bells. Whatever that is. Harbinder thinks it's got something to do with a nursery rhyme. 'Here comes a candle to light you to bed. Here comes a chopper to chop off your head'. Hardly the cosiest lullaby.

'It's one of those posh schools,' says Jake, taking a shortcut through one of the old Peabody Estates, all high walls and sad squares of grass.

'A public school?' Harbinder has always thought it strange that, in England, public school means the opposite. It means very private indeed, inaccessible to anyone but the super rich.

'No, it's a comprehensive,' says Jake. 'But it's where trendy lefties send their kids. Pop stars and actors. Labour politicians too. It's free but you have to live in Chelsea, which means you're probably rich enough to pay anyway. But you're too mean or too right-on.'

There's a lot going on here, thinks Harbinder. She knows that Jake is married with one child. Presumably, on a sergeant's wage, he isn't living anywhere near Chelsea. Maybe he's just bitter because his offspring won't be attending Manor Park and mixing with pop stars' children.

'What was Garfield Rice doing at this trendy school?' she asks.

'It was a reunion,' says Jake. 'I suppose he was a pupil there.'

'And he was found dead in the loos?' This much was on the call-out sheet.

'Suspected drug overdose,' says Jake. 'It'll be all over the papers.'

'Vultures,' says Harbinder, as she is expected to. But she is secretly hoping that her parents read about 'DI Harbinder Kaur, who is in charge of the case . . .'

Manor Park is a disappointment at first. Harbinder had expected either a Gothic pile or a shiny modern building with tinted glass and a roof garden. This school was probably built in the sixties and consists of concrete blocks connected by iron walkways. In the dark the buildings seem to loom in a rather threatening way and the security lights isolate areas of grey grass and exposed brickwork.

Two uniformed officers stand by the main entrance. *Manor Park School. Headteacher: Sonoma Davies.*

Harbinder shows her warrant card.

'Where's the deceased?'

'Still in situ, ma'am.' If there's one thing Harbinder likes more than 'boss', it's 'ma'am'.

'Have the paramedics been?'

'Yes, they pronounced life extinct.'

That's good news – it means Harbinder can get the scene of the crime team on the job at once.

'We've asked everyone to wait in the library,' says the PC. 'Some of them are a bit upset.'

Given that their old schoolfriend has dropped down dead, Harbinder thinks this is likely to prove a bit of an understatement. Also, it's nearly eleven o'clock at night and most of them are probably drunk. Grief-stricken as newts.

'Lead the way,' says Harbinder. She is texting SOCO as she walks.

Once again, the word 'library' is misleading. Harbinder is expecting a book-lined room, perhaps with oak panelling and window seats. The original library at Talgarth was actually very like this. The room Harbinder enters is simply another modern box with metal bookcases pushed against the walls. There are some fairy lights, though, and record decks, which indicate that the participants have been indulging in that most pathetic of activities – nostalgic disco dancing.

There's no dancing now. The ex-students are sitting around the edges of the room. Most are silent although someone is sobbing on an eerily continuous keening note. A voice says, 'Boss?'

Harbinder turns and sees her DS, Cassie Fitzherbert. She hardly recognises her at first. At work, Cassie wears her fair hair in a tight ponytail and favours dark, shapeless clothing. Now, with dishevelled blonde tendrils and a top that shows her shoulders and cleavage, she's an entirely different person. An extremely attractive one, Harbinder is annoyed to find herself thinking.

'Cassie. What are you doing here?'

'I was at the reunion,' says Cassie. 'I went to Manor Park.'

'Good,' says Harbinder. 'You can be useful. Unless you've had a lot to drink. You haven't, have you?'

'No,' says Cassie. 'I'm driving. My husband's here too. It's his turn to get drunk.' It's hard to know if she's joking. She gestures towards a thickset man sitting with his legs apart, staring at the floor. He certainly has that pale, intent look that people sometimes get just before they throw up. Harbinder hopes he doesn't do it here and contaminate the scene further.

'Do you know the deceased?' she asks Cassie.

'Yes, he was in my year.'

'Come with me. Jake, you stay and take names and addresses.'

Police tape criss-crosses the corridor outside. A body lies, half in and half out of a doorway. Harbinder can see dark hair falling over an incipient bald patch, an expensive-looking white shirt. She can't see the shoes, which is annoying. Harbinder always takes notice of shoes.

'Did anyone try to revive him?' she asks Cassie.

'Aisha. She's a doctor.'

'Can you ask her to join us, please.'

Aisha is a small woman wearing a hijab. At least she'll be sober, thinks Harbinder, but then mentally chides herself for stereotypical thinking. People often assume – wrongly – that she doesn't drink just because she has a Sikh name. It's a nightmare getting a glass of Champagne at weddings.

But Aisha certainly doesn't *seem* drunk.

'Someone shouted to me that Garfield had collapsed,' she says. 'I tried CPR, but I knew almost immediately that it was useless.'

'Did you move him at all?' asks Harbinder.

'I rolled him onto his back. That's all.'

Harbinder leans over the body. She can see white powder caked around his nostrils.

'Was he known to take drugs?' she asks.

It's Cassie who answers. 'No,' she says. 'I would have said Gary was the last person . . . I mean, he was a real fitness freak, wasn't he, Aish?'

'Yes,' says Aisha. 'Always running marathons for charity.' There's something in her tone that makes Harbinder think that Aisha wasn't the politician's biggest fan.

'Did anyone else touch the body?' she asks.

'No,' says Aisha. 'Apart from the ambulance crew. Cassie made everyone else wait in the library.'

'Good work,' says Harbinder. 'SOCO are on their way. We'll need to take your prints in order to eliminate them, Dr . . .?'

'Dr Mitri.'

'In the meantime, let's talk to the party-goers.'

Harbinder takes one last look into the room that contains the legs and feet. It's a male lavatory, she can tell immediately by the smell. Garfield Rice was wearing pink Converse.

It's a surprise.

★

As Harbinder turns to go back into the library, she hears sounds of an altercation outside. She catches the words 'Deputy head' and looks at Cassie.

'Archie Flowers,' says Cassie. 'I completely forgot about him.'

The uniformed officer is barring the path of a bespectacled man who, even at this distance, looks sure of his rights.

Harbinder approaches with Cassie in tow. The man addresses Cassie first, they are obviously on first-name terms. 'Cassie? What's going on? I heard sirens. Can you tell this chap to let me in?'

'This chap is a police officer,' says Harbinder. 'I'm DI Kaur. I'm in charge here. Who are you?'

'Archie Flowers. Deputy head.'

Archie Flowers is wearing jeans and a blue jumper but still looks like a man in a suit. Harbinder wonders where he's been for the rest of the evening.

'This is a crime scene, Mr Flowers,' she says. 'We're not letting anyone in this way. Come through the library and we'll talk there.'

'Do you know him?' she asks Cassie, as they wait at the door of the library.

'A little,' says Cassie. 'He's been to one of Pete's rugby weekends. I was surprised to see him tonight though. Sonoma, the head, was meant to be here. I don't know why she wasn't.'

Archie appears at the inner door, accompanied by Jake.

'Thanks, Jake,' says Harbinder. 'I just want a quick word with Mr Flowers. How's everyone holding up?'

'They're all very shocked,' says Jake. 'But not so shocked that they aren't demanding to be allowed to go home. Can't keep the au pair up too late.' This last is said in an approximation of a posh female voice. Don't take the one-man show to the Edinburgh fringe, Harbinder wants to tell him.

'We can let them go home when we've got all their details,' she says. 'Now, Mr Flowers . . .'

She ushers the deputy into a small landing off the main corridor. A staircase leads upwards. Signs in French, German and Italian warn against running, or so Harbinder assumes from the accompanying artwork showing disembodied legs falling down steps. She isn't much of a linguist.

'Did you organise the event tonight?' she asks.

'No, Sonoma – she's the headteacher – she organised it. She was a pupil here herself, you know. A very inspirational figure. But, at the last moment, she had to attend an event at her daughter's school. So I said I'd step in.'

'Did you actually attend the . . . er . . . party?' It seems the wrong word for disco dancing in a school library, but she can't think what else to call it.

'No. I thought I would be in the way. I stayed in my office.'

'Doing what?'

Archie blinks. 'Watching a film on my iPad.' He gives a Spanish title, overdoing the accent, in Harbinder's opinion.

'What do you know about Garfield Rice?'

'Garfield? He's one of our most prestigious alumni. Very generous too . . .' Archie stops, realising, at last, the implications of the question. 'Oh my God. Garfield isn't . . .'

'Garfield Rice has been pronounced dead at the scene,' says Harbinder. 'We're treating his death as unexplained. I'm sorry. This must be a shock.'

Archie certainly looks shocked. Under the overhead light, his face looks almost green.

'How did he die?'

'As I say, his death is unexplained, as yet. Did you know Mr Rice personally?'

'No. Just by reputation. I met him for the first time tonight.'

'Do you know any of the other guests?'

'Not personally. But there were some very famous names. It was quite a class, the class of 1998. Kris Foster, the pop star. The actress Isabelle Istar. Henry Steep, the Labour MP.'

These names mean nothing to Harbinder. She really must start reading the news instead of playing Panda Pop.

'Are they all here tonight?'

'Yes. They're all still involved with the school. Mr Foster recently paid for a new music room. Henry Steep regularly takes pupils on tours of the House of Commons.'

'How nice. Well, Mr Flowers, if you give me your details, you're free to leave. We'll be in touch in the next few days.'

As they walk back along the corridor, the scene of the crime team are arriving, massive in their white suits, like visitors from another planet.

Chapter 3

Harbinder

Sunday

'So, what do we know about Garfield Rice?'

Harbinder faces her new team in her new incident room. She's not nervous, she tells herself, just apprehensive. After securing the scene last night, she got back to the flat at two a.m. After a few hours' uneasy sleep, she went into the kitchen for toast and Marmite, her comfort food. To her surprise, Jeanne joined her at seven. 'It's a nightmare,' she said. 'I'm exhausted at the end of a week's teaching but I can't sleep in, even on a Sunday. What's your excuse?' Harbinder said that she had to be in work for a meeting. 'It's my first big case,' she said, without adding any details. 'What I tell my pupils,' said Jeanne, stirring yoghurt into muesli, 'is that nervous and excited are two sides of the same thing.' Well, Harbinder is not exactly excited that someone has died and she is in charge of the investigation. But it's not far off.

There's a skeleton staff at the station on Sundays but, even so, the room feels crowded. Jake Barker is leaning back in his chair and regarding Harbinder with what she considers to be a challenging stare. Harbinder has already decided to make Jake her deputy on the case. He has the seniority and he seems to be efficient. Plus, she thinks he's the type who would make a fuss if he wasn't given his due.

The other DS, Kim Manning, an older woman with dyed red hair, appears to be locating a bit of breakfast in her back teeth. There are also three DCs and two civilian analysts. Cassie Fitzherbert can't be involved in the investigation because she's a witness, but she has provided Harbinder with some useful inside knowledge.

'Conservative MP.' Harbinder writes this on the whiteboard, rejecting 'Tory' as biased. 'Aged thirty-nine. He was a back bencher but in the news a lot. Even I've heard of him.' There's a faint reaction to this although people are probably scared of laughing at the new DI. 'Climate change denier. Described himself as a petrol head. Married to Paula, two children. Yesterday he attended a school reunion at Manor Park school in Chelsea and was found dead in the men's lavatories. There were traces of cocaine around his nostrils but cause of death hasn't been confirmed.'

The post-mortem is scheduled for that morning. Harbinder is planning to ask Jake to attend. The previous DI, Dean Franks, used to attend every forensic post-mortem but Harbinder prefers to get her report from the pathologist and avoid getting blood on her shoes. Speaking of which . . .

She projects pictures of the corpse onto the screen. One shot shows jeans and almost shockingly pink trainers.

On cue, Jake says, 'Was he gay?'

'What makes you say that?' asks Harbinder.

Jake colours slightly. 'Pink shoes. Men's loos.'

'He was married,' says someone.

'So?' says Jake, rather pugnaciously.

'Even straight people go to the loo,' says Harbinder. The sight of the school urinals has actually sparked a memory from her own school days. Snogging with Gary Carter after a school disco. This reminds her of two things. Gay people don't always seem so. And Cassie had called Garfield 'Gary'.

'If he died of an overdose then it's not a case for us,' says Kim.

'That's true,' says Harbinder. 'But it's an unexplained death and we have to treat it as if it's suspicious until we know otherwise. It's much easier to scale back the investigation, if we have to, than to scale up. And there's a lot of media interest.' She'd had to use the back entrance to the station that morning because reporters were camped at the front. The superintendent has already been on the phone stressing the need to 'be seen as a twenty-first-century force'. Whatever that means.

'Other guests at the reunion,' says Harbinder, 'include Kris Foster, Isabelle Istar and Henry Steep.'

She helpfully projects their images too. 'Kris Foster' — 'Chris with a C at school,' Cassie had said drily — 'the lead singer of The Cubes. The actress, Isabelle Istar, currently starring in a Channel 4 series about a Venetian courtesan. Henry Steep, the Labour MP.'

There are some gasps in the room.

'So you see,' says Harbinder, 'the press will be interested.'

'All these people at a school reunion?' says Kim. 'What a bunch of saddoes.'

'It's that sort of school,' says Jake.

★

Jake heads off to the post-mortem.

'Good luck, Anton,' says someone.

'I'm not the squeamish type,' Jake swaggers.

Harbinder is pondering this exchange when Cassie walks past the glass wall of her office. On impulse, she calls her in. Time for some more background information.

'Did I just hear someone call Jake Anton?' she asks.

Cassie smiles. 'It's a nickname. This place is hot on nicknames. Jake's from Newcastle and he's quite short so his nickname used to be Ant 'n' Dec. Now it's been shortened to Anton.'

Harbinder is wondering if she can ask Cassie what her own nickname is but Cassie volunteers, 'I'm Smoothie because I had a phase of drinking smoothies. Kim's Blondie because she used to have blonde hair. It's very basic.'

Kim's hair is now the colour of a fire engine. Harbinder estimates that she is in her late forties or early fifties.

'Have you worked with Kim a long time?' she asks.

'Yes,' says Cassie. 'Kim's great. She was really kind to me when I first started. She's a good detective too. And she knows all the best places to get sandwiches. Kim's a Londoner born and bred.'

Cassie is too, as far as Harbinder knows, but she also understands that Cassie means something different by the phrase. If this was a Disney film Cassie would be Mary Poppins and Kim whatever the chimney sweep was called.

'Tell me about Garfield Rice,' says Harbinder, switching to the matter in hand. 'What was he like at school?'

Cassie looks up, as if remembering. She has very blue eyes. Harbinder has noticed this before. It makes her gaze disconcertingly direct.

'He was nice,' she says at last. 'Very clever. But then there were lots of clever kids in my year. Aisha, Gary, Chris, Sonoma, Henry. I wasn't one of them, but I was sort of in the group. Gary and Henry always argued about politics but, funnily enough, in those days Gary was more left-wing. He was good at sport too. Captain of the football team, in the rugby and cricket teams. That mattered a lot at our school. And he was good-looking. Lots of girls fancied him.'

'Did you?'

Cassie laughs, not seeming offended. 'I think I did, back in Year Ten or something. But he was going steady with Izzy by sixth form.'

'Isabelle Istar?'

'Yes, she was the girl everyone fancied. They were the perfect match really.'

'Did the relationship last after school?'

'No. Izzy went to RADA and Gary to Oxford. I think they drifted apart. Gary married Paula. She's lovely.'

Lovely Paula is next on Harbinder's list.

Chapter 4

Harbinder

Paula turns out to be 'Powla'. She's Italian and, even in the midst of her grief, takes time to correct their pronunciation.

'I'm sorry,' says Harbinder. She is too. She hates it when people mispronounce her name, which they do very often, despite it being completely phonetically regular.

'It's OK,' says Paula, dabbing her eyes with a tissue. She's a small woman, with short dark hair in a style that looks chic rather than purely practical. The room is stylish too, lots of bright colours and rather startling pieces of art, neon signs and spotlit pieces of drift-wood. At least Harbinder assumes they are art and not the work of a deranged hoarder. There are numerous photographs of Garfield and Paula with their children, Rocco and Mia, and a large one of Garfield in running gear brandishing a medal.

'I'm sorry,' says Harbinder again. 'Are you up to answering a few questions?'

Paula looks at Helen, the family liaison officer, who pats her hand and gives Harbinder a disappointed look. Harbinder knows that she shouldn't really be doing this home visit. She should leave such things to her sergeants and concentrate on strategy. But, she tells herself, this is such a high profile case that her presence is justified. And she has taken Kim with her and is letting her lead the interview. Harbinder wants to get to know the older woman better.

'This must be such a shock to you,' says Kim now. She has a nice, easy manner with people. Harbinder, who hasn't, watches to see how it's done. Kim doesn't say much but her body language, leaning forward slightly with her head on one side, is open and unthreatening. Harbinder uncrosses her legs and arms.

'I just can't believe it,' says Paula.

'How did Garfield seem when you last saw him?' asks Kim.

'Fine. Looking forward to the reunion. There were some people going who he hadn't seen for years.'

'You didn't want to go with him?' Kim's tone is deliberately casual.

'No,' says Paula. 'I never go. I don't want to hear people talk about school. It's very boring.'

Harbinder is in complete agreement. But 'never' implies that the reunions are regular events. How many times can you reminisce about school? She doesn't think Talgarth High has ever tried to gather its former students. To be fair, it would be hard with so many of them electronically tagged.

'Did Garfield go to lots of reunions?' she asks.

'You know what it's like in English schools,' says Paula. 'The rugby club get-together. The football club get-together. It's never-ending.'

'I bet the rugby club reunions were wild,' says Kim. 'Lots of drinking.'

'I suppose so.' Paula flashes her a suspicious look. 'As I said, I didn't go.'

'Did you ever hear any talk about drugs?' asks Harbinder.

Paula's eyes flash. 'Gary never took drugs. Never. He wouldn't even eat sugar. He was fanatical about fitness.'

A fitness freak, Cassie had said. Freak and fanatic are not exactly compliments.

Harbinder asks Paula if Garfield was still in touch with any of his old schoolfriends.

'Like I said, he saw some people at the rugby and football events. I don't think any of them were close friends.'

'What about people in his year at school?' asks Harbinder. 'Isabelle Istar, for example?' This time the glance is distinctly unfriendly.

'I suppose he saw her on TV like everyone else.'

'Henry Steep? He was an MP too.'

'You'll have to ask his agent,' says Paula. 'I never got involved in the politics. That wasn't important to me. All that climate change stuff. What was important was that he was my husband and my children's father.'

And she starts to cry in earnest.

Garfield's agent is called Deborah Green. Harbinder rings her on the drive back to the station. Kim is at the wheel, driving in an alarmingly casual fashion.

'It's just terrible,' says Deborah. And she does sound shocked. 'I couldn't believe it when I heard it on the news.'

So, Paula hadn't thought to inform Garfield's agent of his demise.

'They're saying that it's drugs,' Deborah went on. 'That's crazy. Gary wouldn't take drugs.'

'We can't confirm cause of death,' says Harbinder. 'But do you know of anyone who might have had a grudge against Garfield? A disgruntled constituent, for example.'

'Well, there were the bleeding heart letters, I suppose.'

'The *what*?' Harbinder's voice is so sharp that Kim turns to look at her. The car swerves, narrowly missing a bollard.

'Garfield was getting these anonymous notes saying "bleeding heart".'

'What?' says Harbinder again.

'Most of them just contained those two words. Bleeding heart. Some of them had a drawing of a heart with an arrow through it.'

'Did you keep any of them?'

'Garfield threw them away, but I kept one or two. I thought we should tell the police at the time.'

'Pity you didn't,' says Harbinder. 'Can you put the notes in a plastic freezer bag? I'll send someone to collect them.'

'You don't think they're connected to his death?'

'Anything unusual needs to be investigated,' says Harbinder. 'Do you know what the phrase "bleeding heart" could mean?'

'Politicians talk about bleeding heart liberals sometimes,' says Deborah, 'but no one could accuse Gary of being a liberal.'

When Harbinder gets back to her office she has a missed call from Alice Hunter, the pathologist. She rings back.

'Hot news,' says Alice. She has a sweet, almost childish voice and a vocabulary to match, which seems bizarrely unsuited to the more gruesome aspects of her job. Harbinder distrusted Alice at first, because of the voice and her school prefect appearance, but the pathologist isn't a bad sort.

'Tell me,' says Harbinder.

'It's not drugs,' says Alice.

Harbinder feels an almost narcotic rush of excitement. Not that she'd know. She has never even smoked weed.

'How do you know?'

'Cocaine residue around his nostrils but none in the nasal cavity. And none in his blood.'

'What's the cause of death then?'

'There was bruising on his head. Could be from the fall or maybe someone hit him. But I don't think that was the cause of death. We also found what look like two hypodermic injection sites.'

'Someone injected him with poison?'

'We'll know more when we get the bloods back, but my guess is insulin. His pupils were very dilated and there was an abnormal amount of sweat on the body.'

Harbinder thinks back to the photo of Garfield with a medal round his neck. Surely an evening's disco dancing would not be enough to make this athlete sweat?

'I've come across death by insulin poisoning before. It's quite hard to detect, isn't it?'

'It's difficult because insulin gets absorbed by the body but, with so recent a death, we can check glucose levels in the blood. We might also find traces of the preservatives used in commercial insulin preparation. Food for thought, eh?'

Harbinder agrees that it is. If Garfield had cocaine residue around his nostrils it means that someone put it there, hoping that his death would look like a drug overdose. Which means planning, malice aforethought and all sorts of other interesting things.

★

'We're now looking at a murder enquiry,' Harbinder tells the team. 'Garfield Rice had no cocaine in his bloodstream. Injection sites were found on the body. We're possibly looking at death by lethal injection.'

She writes 'Operation Wilson' on the board. It's a boring case name, apparently generated at random from a list. Harbinder momentarily misses Neil, who loves coming up with codenames. He'd call this one Old School Die, or something equally cringe-making.

'Someone injected him?' says Kim. 'With what?'

'Alice's guess is insulin,' says Harbinder. 'I've checked and Garfield wasn't diabetic so increased insulin levels in his bloodstream would be suspicious. Did anything else come from the post-mortem, Jake?'

'The injection sites were on the buttocks,' says Jake. 'Pretty impossible for Garfield to have done it himself.'

Harbinder is pleased to see that nobody laughs.

'We need to interview everyone who was at the party,' she says. 'Particularly Garfield's closest friends. Cassie says that, at school, he was close to Isabelle Istar, Chris Foster, Henry Steep and someone called Anna Vance.'

'Can I interview Chris Foster?' says a DC, inexplicably called Tory.

'He's too old for you,' says Kim. 'I'd better talk to Chris. I'm immune to handsome men. Take a look at Malcolm, if you don't believe me.'

You and me both, thinks Harbinder. Malcolm is Kim's husband. He came to collect her the other day and didn't look any uglier than most straight middle-aged men. Not that she's biased.

'The Cubes are a good band,' says Jake.

'If you want something to send you to sleep,' says Kim.

Harbinder remembers Neil playing The Cubes in his car. There was one song that seemed to be everywhere about seven years ago.

How did it go? 'You know everything but you don't know you're beautiful'. Neil used to sing along. It drove Harbinder mad.

'You can have Chris if I can have Isabelle,' says Jake, who is apparently on first-name terms with the actress.

'OK,' says Harbinder. 'Let's all calm down. These people might be well known but they're still witnesses, and potential suspects, in a murder case. We have to treat them as we would anyone else.'

'Do you really think that someone at the reunion killed Garfield?' says Jake.

'It seems that someone injected him with a drug and tried to make it look like a cocaine overdose. Everyone who was at Manor Park that evening has to be a suspect. We need to find out who had means and who had motive. Aisha Mitri will have had access to insulin, for example. So would anyone who was diabetic. We need to look at relationships, resentments, past conflicts. Cassie says that Garfield went out with Isabelle when they were at school. Let's check that out. Maybe they were in touch again. We'll also look at Garfield's political colleagues. He was outspoken. He must have had his enemies. His political agent said that he'd received anonymous notes calling him a "bleeding heart".'

'Bleeding heart?' says Jake. 'What does that mean?'

'There's a phrase, "bleeding heart liberal",' says Harbinder. 'I looked it up and it means people – usually on the left of politics – who are soft-hearted about things like immigration. That doesn't seem to apply to Garfield Rice.'

'No,' says Kim. 'He seemed one of the hang 'em and flog 'em brigade.'

Jake looks as if he might belong to that brigade too. He probably even has a badge. He mutters something about common sense.

'Henry Steep might know something,' says Harbinder. 'He's an MP too, though on the other side, of course.'

'Two MPs in the same year group,' says Jake. 'What a school.'

'We had an estate agent in our year,' says Kim, as if offering her trump card. She is looking at the list on the whiteboard. 'Anna Vance is the odd one out,' she says. 'She's not famous or well-known.'

'That's why she interests me the most,' says Harbinder.

Harbinder has asked Laura, one of the civilian data analysts, to look up any mentions of Manor Park school in the news. She finds Laura waiting for her outside her office.

'Find anything?' she says.

'Lots of stuff about record GCSE results, trips to China and fun-runs for charity,' says Laura. 'It's a really high-achieving school. But I went back to 1998 and I found something slightly less wholesome.'

'What?'

'A student called David Moore died after falling onto a railway track. He was apparently celebrating the end of A levels.'

'I think I remember reading about that in the paper,' says Kim, who is at Harbinder's shoulder. 'Poor sod. Made me almost glad that my three didn't have any A levels to celebrate.'

'That's not the significant bit,' says Laura. 'There was one witness. Another student. He was the one who called the police. He's not named in the article, but I double-checked with the police file.'

'Who was it?' asks Kim. Although Harbinder thinks she can probably guess.

'Garfield Rice.'

Chapter 5

Cassie

It was very hot, the year we took our A levels. By the time the schools broke up for the summer, the fine weather had gone. I think it rained all through August. I seemed to sit in my bedroom for weeks, just watching the rain. I didn't go inter-railing as I'd planned. I could've gone to Tenerife with Mum and Dad but I didn't. I couldn't even bring myself to go to the park with Anna. I just sat there.

But May and June were beautiful. London smelt of grass cuttings and petrol. I'd look up from my exam scripts and see the glass walkways shimmering as if they were portals to another world. Everything was hyper-real, hard-edged, diamond bright. I'd walk home, aware of every dust particle on my skin. I'd touch Gary and feel a pulse beating between my legs. The sky was so blue it broke your heart. I was taking English, Maths and Psychology. I'd revised hard but I knew that I'd never do as well as Gary or Sonoma, although neither of them ever seemed to do any work. Henry worked hard too. He'd sit opposite me in the library with his stack of index cards, working steadily through his books with a marker pen. Chris would sit beside him reading Terry Pratchett. Chris only cared about getting into art school, which was almost a certainty given the huge canvases on display in the entrance hall, but I knew that he'd probably beat me in English too. Izzy practised audition speeches in the drama studio. Anna wrote a murder mystery in the back of her science book.

It's hard to remember now when the real murder started. Was it when I said 'no' and David took no notice? Was it when Gary told me that he didn't really want a steady girlfriend? Or did it all converge on that final, fatal minute when David indicated that he found my appearance satisfactory? I do remember the first conversation about it though. We were in the Crow's Nest, the attic in Gary's house, which had been converted to create teenage heaven: sofa, bean bags, TV, CD player, speakers, even our own kettle and mini fridge. Gary treated it all so casually. His father was a famous MP, his mother had been a model. They had this huge house with a grand piano in what they called 'the drawing room'. Gary was an only child and, like the prince in the stories, his every wish was granted.

On this day, when school had ended but exams hadn't yet started, I was stretched out on the floor making notes in the Arden edition of *The Tempest*. Chris was strumming on Gary's guitar. Gary and Izzy were mock-fighting on the sofa and I was trying to ignore them. Henry was riffling through his cue cards. Sonoma said something about Caliban in *The Tempest*. Anna, who was staring out of one of the odd-shaped windows, suddenly said, 'You know David Moore?'

'Isn't he in the cricket team?' said Gary. He always knew all the teams.

'Maybe,' said Anna. 'All I know is he tried to rape me at Molly's party.'

'Molly's party,' said Henry. 'Was that when Cassie got off with that boy from Latymer Upper?'

I saw Gary look at me but couldn't read his expression. Shock? Jealousy? Disgust?

'That's so not the point,' said Anna. 'The point is he tried to force himself on me.'

'Force himself?' said Izzy. 'This isn't a Jilly Cooper novel.'

'Shows that you've never read a Jilly Cooper novel,' said Anna. 'They're about female empowerment. And horses. David and I were in the snooker room and he tried to kiss me. I tried to fight him off but he was too strong for me. I really think he would have raped me if someone hadn't come in.'

'He tried it on with me once,' said Izzy. 'But I wasn't having any of it. I kicked him in the balls.'

Someone laughed and Gary said, with such loving admiration that I wanted to cry, 'I bet you did.'

I sat up, pushed my hair back, and said, 'Well, he did rape me.'

What I remember was how completely I had Gary's attention.

'What?' he said. 'Was that when you were going out with him, Cass?'

I'd been on a couple of dates with David. I didn't think Gary had even noticed.

'Yes,' I said. 'It was at his house. His flat. He wanted to have sex. I said no but he took no notice.'

'Did he actually rape you?' asked Izzy. There was a note of scepticism in her voice which made me curl my hands into fists.

'Yes, Izzy,' I said. 'He actually raped me. Sorry to shock you.'

'Well it's shocked me,' said Gary. 'I'd like to kill him.'

'Shall we kill him?' said Anna. 'I'm sure I could think of a way to do it.' Anna read a lot of crime fiction.

'Death's too good for him,' said Izzy in her Lady Bracknell voice.

Everyone laughed, which made me angry again.

'You should tell the police,' said Sonoma. 'It's a crime. A serious crime.'

'They won't be interested,' said Gary. 'They never listen to women. They'll just say Cassie led him on.'

This, I thought, was true. The police would find out that I wasn't a virgin and say that I was an evil temptress who tempted a poor weak-willed male. After all, I had gone into his bedroom with him. What did I expect? What was I wearing? A miniskirt? Practically asking to be assaulted.

And Gary, of course, knew that I wasn't a virgin.

'We could poison him,' said Anna. 'My mum says you can get poison from flowers.' Anna's mother was an aromatherapist and a single parent, two circumstances that made her almost a white witch in our eyes.

'Digitalis,' said Chris. 'We could put it on a brownie and give it to him.'

'David would never eat anything we gave him,' said Henry. 'He hates us.'

'He doesn't hate us,' said Chris. 'He wants to be one of us.'

Was that right? Gary sometimes said that we were the elite of the school, the inner circle whose membership rules were known only to those already inside. The beautiful and the damned, Sonoma called us, not realising how prophetic this was. But Gary, Izzy, Sonoma and Chris were beautiful. Gary, the football and rugby star.

34

Izzy, with her dark ringlets and nymph-like slenderness. Sonoma, with her afro and cheekbones. Chris with his dirty-blonde hair and easy charm. I supposed I owed my place at the table to the fact that I was considered 'pretty' at school. Certainly, I didn't have much else to recommend me. I didn't have Chris's wit, Henry's sharpness or Anna's dreamy intelligence. I was just the girl with blonde hair who used to date Garfield Rice.

'We could push him downstairs,' said Izzy. Manor Park has many staircases, all accessorised with warning notices. *Don't run! Don't push! Single file only!* There was already an apocryphal story about a first year who'd fallen to her death from the music rooms. You could see her blood, people said, if you looked under the mat that said *Welcome* in thirty languages.

'We can't kill him,' said Chris. 'But we could beat him up a bit.'

I remember being almost more shocked by this than by the murder talk. Chris, dreamy guitar-playing Chris, talking about inflicting physical violence.

'We could scare him,' said Gary. 'We could scare him to death.'

There's a disused Tube station between South Kensington and Sloane Square. It's called Imperial and rumour has it that, in the war, it's where they stored explosives to be studied at nearby Imperial College. The track runs above ground and, as you go past, you can see the platform with posters advertising pre-war goods. *No, no, no to underarm O. Seven days make one week, Bovril makes one strong.* But trains haven't stopped there for decades. Blink and you miss it, a moment's time-slip before the District Line dives underground again.

Imperial was where students from Manor Park went to take

drugs. The school has always had a reputation for narcotics, probably because many of the students were both rich and from arty backgrounds. Neither of these things applied to me. My parents were a GP and an ex-nurse. Dad's father had also been a doctor and had left him the house on Chelsea Manor Street where he used to have his practice. Dad now worked in a modern surgery in Hammersmith and the house was in dire need of repair. But it was within the Manor Park school catchment area.

The plan was that we'd lure David to the station on the day of our last A level exam and pretend to push him under a train.

'Let him see what it's like to be terrified,' said Gary. 'To be in someone else's power.'

'How will we get him there?' said Sonoma. She was the least enthusiastic about the plan. I knew she wanted to mention the police again.

'Let's say we've got some coke to celebrate the end of exams,' said Henry. 'David will be there like a shot.'

'Let's *actually* get some coke to celebrate the end of exams,' said Chris, whose parents were both barristers.

'Cassie should tell him,' said Gary. 'He'll follow her.'

I still remember the pain this remark gave me. Gary knew that I was still in love with him. We'd gone out in Year 10 for a few months and we still had guilty snogs at parties when Izzy, Gary's official girlfriend, wasn't looking. Once, when she'd left Chris's New Year's Eve party early (who does that?) we had sex against the garage wall. Even now, a breeze block can make me feel faint with longing.

Gary knew all this but he also knew that David, supposedly, still had a crush on me. It's a violent word, isn't it? Crush. Smitten. Bowled over. Fallen like a ton of bricks. Love can be so dangerous.

So, when I said to David, on that Wednesday after our final exam, 'Let's go to Imperial. Chris has got some *merchandise*,' he agreed immediately. I remember imagining, as we walked through the innocent afternoon streets, that someone was following us, some angel figure who would rescue me and punish David. But all that happened was that David took my hand and held it tightly.

Crush.

Chapter 6

Anna

Saturday

I didn't want to go to the reunion. I've never understood why people get so fixated on their old schools. It's just a place you go, usually unwillingly, between the ages of four and eighteen. You don't choose your school. Well, maybe some children look through a catalogue of upper-class establishments and say 'I want that one, Daddy,' but, more often, you go to the school that's nearest or most in line with your religious and political beliefs. We lived about half a mile from Manor Park so didn't even have to fudge the application forms. I'm willing to bet, though, that not many of the pupils came from a tenth-floor council flat.

Mum always said she picked the school because Sophie and I could walk there. I think she might also have noticed the excellent exam results because she was ambitious for us, in her unconventional way. She wasn't immune to the fact that we were mixing with the children of politicians and actors. When I brought Chris home, I was embarrassed to realise that, not only did she know his parents were barristers, she'd actually followed some of their cases. Mum rarely bought a newspaper but, when she did, she read it from cover to cover: marriages, births, deaths, court reports, the lot.

I wasn't unhappy at school. I had some fun, made some friends, stored up a few memories. But, when I left in 1998, I never wanted to go back. I went to Edinburgh to study French and Italian. I spent my third year in Florence and, as soon as I graduated, I raced back there as fast as my 2.1 could take me. I remember walking across the Ponte Vecchio one autumn morning, as the mist rose from the Arno and the shopkeepers arranged their myriad postcards of Michelangelo's *David*, and thinking: I'm as far from Attlee Towers as I can possibly get.

I kept in touch with Cassie mostly because she kept in touch with me. At school, Cassie was one of the popular ones: blonde, pretty and safe. She was the girl boys fancied because they didn't dare to aspire to Izzy who, even then, had a kind of dangerous, operatic beauty. Izzy once said that boys didn't ask her out because they were scared of her and I think this might have been true. Maybe it explains why she said yes to Gary who, in those days, wore horn-rimmed glasses and a woolly hat with a Lenin badge on it. I liked Cassie. She was good-natured and fun, always ready for what we euphemistically called 'a laugh'. But if I had to say who was my best friend at school, I'd say Chris. And I hadn't seen him for twenty-one years.

Cassie wrote to me when I was in Florence, long letters in turquoise ink, chatty and surprisingly funny. I sent postcards back. Cellini's *Perseus With the Head of Medusa*. Masaccio's *Holy Trinity*. I was, no doubt, attempting to seem cultured. When Cassie married

Pete, who was two years above us at school, she sent me an invitation. I didn't intend to go but Sophie was graduating from King's College London, so I was there anyway. Cassie was beautiful in off-white satin. Pete, whom I remembered as a rather meat-headed rugby player, looked like he couldn't believe his luck. Izzy and Henry were at the wedding and that was the last time I saw Izzy. No Gary. No Chris.

Cassie wrote and told me of the birth of her children, Lucy and Sam. If I'd had similar announcements, I'm sure I would have made them. But I was resolutely child-free and I wasn't convinced that Cassie would have been interested in my job teaching English as a foreign language. Everyone else in The Group seemed to have yielded to the urge to reproduce. Gary had the regulation wife and two children, according to his Wikipedia page. Chris had two children with a woman called Siobhan, whom he'd met at art school, and was now dating an actress improbably called Stormy. Izzy was married to Oliver West, a bona-fide film star. At the time of counting they had one child. A daughter called Anna.

I'd stopped coming back to England. Mum and Sophie would visit me in Florence once a year. But then Mum got ill and, somehow, during the WhatsApp chat that had replaced the turquoise letters, Cassie knew I was in London and asked if I wanted to go to the reunion. 'Pete's nagging me to go. He's always meeting up with the rugby team and sobbing over memories of smelly changing rooms and training runs in the rain. They go clay pigeon shooting and paintballing. But this one is our year. Sonoma's organising it. A civilised catch-up. And it is our twenty-first anniversary. What do you think?'

Sonoma was in our year too. She stood out, partly because

she was so clever and partly because she was half-American. She was black too but that wasn't rare in our school, which was what was then known as 'racially diverse' and professed an 'equality of opportunity' which didn't always manifest itself in reality. What was unusual was Sonoma's focus, which probably came from her colonel father. She knew, from the first, that she was destined for great things. Sonoma and Gary both went to Oxford and had their names inscribed on a special board at Manor Park. I wasn't sure what I expected Sonoma to do next, but it wasn't go into teaching and eventually become head of our alma mater (as no one called it). She was married too with three children, one of whom was old enough to go to the Manor but didn't.

My first instinct was to refuse the invitation. I was tired and depressed. Mum's cancer was terminal and, while she was being resolutely upbeat, creating memory boxes and talking about 'death playlists', I was in pieces. I sat in my childhood bedroom with its view over the London rooftops and wept over old photographs. Even the skyline was different; the space-age skyscrapers with bizarrely homely names, like Gherkin and Cheese-grater, the new railway tracks that hovered in mid-air. I'd been away too long. I couldn't wait to leave.

Maybe it was depression that finally made me go. Maybe it was Cassie's soft but deadly pressure. 'Who knows when we'll get another chance?' Maybe it was just because she said, 'Chris will be there.'

I said I'd meet them at the school but, of course, Cassie knew where my mum's flat was and, at ten to seven, she was outside in her sensible-looking car. She said she'd come up, but I belted down all ten flights of stairs (the lift was broken as usual) to stop that happening. Mum would have liked to have seen Cassie – 'a sweet little thing' she always called her – but I couldn't face the awkward chatting or seeing Mum's emaciated appearance through Cassie's eyes, facing the sympathetic questions afterwards.

'How's your mum?' asked Cassie when I got into the back of the car.

'Great,' I said. 'Fine. In sparkling form.'

'I always liked her,' said Cassie. 'Did you ever meet Star, Pete?'

'I don't think so,' said Pete, twisting round in his seat. 'Hi, Anna. Good to see you again.'

At first sight, Pete had aged more than Cassie. His hair was greying and, from what I could see, he seemed to have spread out somewhat. It had been a shock to me that morning, looking in the mirror, to see a grey streak running alongside my parting. I had rather got out of the way of looking in mirrors. People say Italians are obsessed with appearance but that's not quite true. As a young woman I certainly got my share of wolf whistles, although never the rather sinister attention I often received in England, but, as I got older, I became comfortably invisible. Now, at nearly forty, I never wore make-up and lived in jeans and trainers. I made a bit of an effort for the reunion. Jeans and trainers, of course, but the good ones, and a green silk top. Mum, unsurprisingly, had a full make-up bag in her medicine cabinet but when I tried to put on eye liner, I stuck the applicator in my eye. Blusher made me look like a clown and Mum's old lipstick was too dark and made me look like a ghoul. I wiped it all off and settled for pale and interesting. Someone was sure to ask why I hadn't got a tan since I lived in sunny Italy.

The car moved away with a spectral smoothness. I can't get used to electric or hybrid cars. There aren't many in Italy. I find the silence disconcerting. Cassie drove fast and confidently. I supposed that came with the job.

Was I surprised when Cassie became a police officer? It wasn't what I would have imagined but – as with Sonoma – I didn't really imagine any of us grown up. I suppose I did think of the police force as a rather *active* job. More suited to Maggie Fanshaw, captain of both the hockey and netball team in our year, than to Cassie, who always claimed that she had period pains in PE lessons. 'I've had constant PMT for four years,' she boasted to me once. If I had picked a job for Cassie it would probably have been a nurse or a teacher, those two female staples of our career guidance. Cass was so small and slight. I couldn't really imagine her wrestling a criminal to the ground. But maybe that wasn't what a detective sergeant did.

'She could be a DI,' Pete told me with rather touching pride. 'But she won't do the exam.'

'I don't want to be a DI,' said Cassie, who was searching for a parking space. 'Too much pressure. Not enough real policing.'

'She's got a new boss who's younger than her,' said Pete. 'Indian girl.'

'British woman,' corrected Cassie, but without rancour.

I couldn't remember what Pete did. Something in computers, I thought.

When we got out of the car, I saw that Cassie really had made an effort. She was wearing jeans too, but they didn't sag in the wrong places like mine. Her black top had cut-outs over the shoulders that showed her gleaming, glittery skin. Had she sprayed something on? She was, if anything, even blonder than she'd been at eighteen.

As we walked towards the school, I had one of those weird

time-slip moments. Was I fifteen, carrying my art portfolio, worrying that my hair was too curly and my nose too big? Was I
eighteen, walking to my English exam and trying to remember
Tempest quotes? 'These are the pearls that were his eyes'.

As I dithered, lost in my own backstory, a black car with tinted
windows drew up alongside us.

'Chris is here,' said Cassie.

Chapter 7

Anna

The group didn't see much of each other in that strange disjointed time after what happened to David. For days afterwards we just stayed in our separate homes, which suddenly seemed very dear and safe. Gary, Sonoma and Chris eventually went inter-railing. Cassie was meant to go with them but didn't. I called on her a couple of times, but she didn't want to go out, even for a walk in a park, an activity so dull that it seemed to come from one of our set texts. It was a cold, wet summer. The rain fell almost continuously. 'There was no possibility of taking a walk that day.'

I last spoke to Chris when we went to collect our A level results. I remember his whoop of delight when he opened the envelope, immediately followed by a look of embarrassment, an expression so rare on his face that it made me want to hug him. Chris, Gary and Sonoma all achieved three top grades. Henry had two As and one B. I had an A and two Bs which was enough to send me to Edinburgh, the furthest university I could find. Cassie didn't do as well as she'd hoped but eventually got into Sussex through clearing. Even on that day, as we walked the familiar streets to Gary's house and the Crow's Nest, we were already separating. Izzy was away doing Youth Theatre but she'd got into RADA, one of the teachers told me. Chris, Gary and Henry walked ahead, occasionally pushing each other into the road in an excess of high spirits. Cassie and I followed more soberly. Sonoma had gone home to celebrate with her parents.

David's grades were ABB, like mine. I read about it in the paper. 'Tragic Teen's Top Grades'.

The car door opened, and a figure unfolded itself. Like Cassie, Chris had become blonder with age. His hair used to be the colour of wet sand, now it was beach boy brilliant. His smile, too, seemed blindingly bright as it flashed at me from the dark interior of the chauffeur-driven car. I backed away slightly.

'Anna!' Now he was standing in front of me, wearing jeans and a leather jacket, smile lines at the corners of his eyes.

'Hi, Kris with a K.'

He laughed. 'Hi, Anna. Hi, Cassie. Hi, Pete.' He waved at the car without turning round and it moved away. Another of those sinister soundless vehicles.

Cassie kissed him on both cheeks and Pete did one of those macho one-armed hugs. I didn't step closer although I imagined what it would be like to embrace Chris, to smell his aftershave – subtle and lemony – and feel his designer stubble against my face.

'Long time no see,' said Chris as we walked towards the main gate.

In fact, I had seen him last year, when The Cubes played Milan. Me and about three thousand other people at the Alcatraz. But I wasn't about to admit this.

'What have you been doing with yourself?' I said. 'Did that music career ever get off the ground?'

I was taking a risk, teasing him like that, because he could always come back with my own lack of career and failure to catch a husband or produce children. But Chris just said, 'I've missed you, Anna.'

'Shame there was no way of keeping in touch,' I said. 'No internet or anything like that.'

'"She Doesn't Know She's Beautiful",' said Chris, naming his first number one. 'That was about you.'

'Thanks,' I said. 'But I do know I'm beautiful.'

We had reached the gates. Cassie keyed in the code and they opened. A man was waiting in the area that we used to call the Bins.

'Are you here for the reunion? I'm Archie Flowers, deputy head.'

'Where's Sonoma?' asked Cassie. She sounded put-out.

'She's very sorry but she can't be here. Family commitments.'

Cassie had told me that Sonoma was the one who had organised the reunion. Why would she do that and not turn up herself? 'Family commitments' definitely sounded made up.

'Mr Foster.' Archie was almost licking Chris's designer trainers. 'We were so grateful for the money for the new music studio. It'll mean so much to the students.'

'No problem,' said Chris.

'This is Anna Vance.' Cassie was making brisk introductions.

'Hi, Anna.' A quick on-off smile, like a flashlight. 'We're in the library,' said Archie Flowers. 'I'm sure you can all remember the way. Mr Rice is already there.'

So, Gary had made it too. This really was a star-studded affair.

Now all it needed was for Archie to add, in a hushed voice, 'And Isabelle Istar.'

I recognised her immediately, of course I did. Only a day ago Mum and I had been watching her on the TV, having tasteful BBC 2 sex in a gondola.

'Who would have thought,' said Mum, licking her yoghurt spoon. It's almost the only thing she can eat because of the mouth ulcers brought on by her chemotherapy.

'I always thought she'd end up a Venetian prostitute,' I said.

Izzy was wearing a stripy dress, black tights and clumpy shoes. I'd forgotten the way she'd always wear something different to a party and make it the perfect outfit. My jeans felt more shapeless than ever and I was aware that the buttons of my silk shirt were straining.

'Anna!' she shrieked. 'Is it really you? I thought you were in Italy.'

'Luckily some international travel is still allowed,' I said. 'Even after Brexit.'

Izzy hugged me and I was almost asphyxiated by her scent. It was lovely to see her again.

'Chris! Did you bring Stormy?'

'No.'

'Quite right. It's never a good idea to bring partners to a school reunion. I've left Oliver at home. Even Paula hasn't come.'

She pronounced Paula the Italian way, so I didn't identify her as Gary's wife until the man himself came over with a bottle of wine and several glasses. After he'd kissed me and remarked on the incredible fact that I wasn't in Italy, he said that Paula was at home with the kids.

'Who'd have thought that childcare would be our biggest problem?' he said.

'It's not a big issue for me,' I said.

Gary didn't answer. He was too busy clapping Pete on the shoulder and being all manly about rugby. Gary was the one who'd aged most, I thought. His hair was still dark, but it was definitely thinning and he had the perma-tanned, overexercised look of someone keeping middle-age at bay. He was also wearing pink shoes.

'Well, if it isn't the Tory scum.' Henry had joined our group, which was becoming the centre of the room. I was aware that all the other attendees were looking at us and not, I imagined, with much affection.

'Hallo, you pinko bastard,' said Gary, and he and Henry hugged with what looked like genuine warmth. Then Henry turned to me, without even saying hallo, and whispered, 'I still hate him.'

Chapter 8

Anna

It's funny that Henry is the only one, besides Cassie, that I've kept in touch with. We weren't especially close at school. If you were to divide The Group it would have been Gary, Henry and Sonoma on one side and me, Chris and Izzy on the other. Cassie managed to float between the two. If you wanted to get all pretentious about it, Gary's group represented politics and our group the arts. Although Chris was actually quite passionate about issues like the environment. But, at that time, Chris planned to be an artist and I was sure that I'd be a writer. Izzy was clearly an actress from the day she was born.

But we were all interested in politics, back then. In 1997, when we were in the lower sixth, Labour came into power on the wave of a landslide win. None of us were old enough to vote but we were *obsessed*. I remember coming into school on the day after the election and finding everyone, pupils and teachers alike, in a trance of happiness. Mr Spencer, the economics teacher, was clearly still drunk, wearing his red rosette and telling anyone who would listen that things could only get better. Our English teacher, Miss Jones, brought in a life-size cut-out of Tony Blair. We sat on a patch of grass we called (without irony) the Grassy Knoll and talked about the promised land. Sometimes, even today, it makes me feel tearful to remember it.

But, although we all supported the new government, there were differences. Gary talked pompously about 'being on the left of the party'. Henry liked to think of himself as Machiavellian and cynical. It was not important to keep promises, he used to say, before quoting the old Florentine spin doctor: '"Experience shows us that those who do not keep their word get the better of those who do."' Sonoma called herself a Democrat, centrist and sensible. Strange to think that Gary became a Tory MP and Sonoma the head of a comprehensive school. Although, as noted earlier, she doesn't send her son to the Manor. He goes to the Oratory. Sonoma has clearly become a Catholic along the way too. Cassie's daughter goes to a Catholic school too. Cassie converted when she married Pete.

And Henry was a Labour MP, leftish enough to appeal to the Instagram generation, careful enough to be in the shadow cabinet. He embraced the battle against climate change just as Gary decided that it was all a hoax perpetuated by unscrupulous wind-farm owners. At school, the three of them used to be fearsome debaters. I wondered who would have the upper hand now.

'Good to see you too,' I said to Henry. He looked the same, I thought: sandy hair, freckles, disconcertingly wide smile. But, then, I'd seen him comparatively recently. The passing years weren't such a shock on his face. At school, Henry had seemed too slight compared to the other boys but now that slenderness made him look youthful. He wore glasses, unlike Gary who appeared to have swapped his spectacles for contacts, and there were a few grey hairs at his temples. Otherwise, he could be the boy reading *The Prince* in the school library.

Henry went to Durham University. I was in Edinburgh so it was fairly easy to meet. I liked having a link to home but a safe one, with none of the intensity of my feelings for Chris or Izzy. We never talked about school. Henry even came to see me in Italy and we slept together, a pleasant enough experience but also one that never features in our conversations. He's married to a man now.

'Let's get away from these people.' Henry steered me into a corner near to the place where the DJ was making ominous noises about getting the party started.

'You don't want to chat about the good old days?' I said.

'Christ, no. It's bad enough that I have to see him in the House.'

'"The House". Get you.'

'What do you want me to call it? It's where I work.'

'Who would have thought it?' I said. 'Back in the good old days.'

'Just about everyone, really. I always thought Gary would be PM and you'd write a best-selling book.'

'One out of two isn't bad, I suppose.'

'There's still time,' said Henry. But he didn't say for which one.

'What are you two whispering about?' It was Cassie, who could still just about get away with that kind of remark. 'Have you seen the pics?'

There were photos dotted around the room. Sports squads, school plays, previous reunions. Henry and I wandered around the perimeter and I noted, without surprise, that I didn't feature in any of the groups. I wasn't in any of the teams at school, I never had a part in a production. Like I say, I wasn't unhappy. I had my friends and I spent most of my time scribbling stories in the back of textbooks. I was an observer, I told myself; that was my role. Like Henry, I was convinced that I'd be a famous writer one day. Well, instead, I was a teacher at a language school with grey in my hair.

'Look, there's Pete,' said Cassie, pointing at a picture of a group of boys who could barely fit their oversized thighs onto the school chairs. 'He hasn't changed at all.'

I saw Gary holding a cup aloft, Izzy as Abigail in *The Crucible*, Sonoma with the debating team, Henry brandishing a violin. Did I even go to this school? I wondered. In a way, it would be easier to imagine that I didn't.

We stopped in front of the cricket team. There was Gary (of course) and Chris. Even Henry had been dragooned into a white shirt and pads. But I knew we were all looking at the tall boy at the end of the line. David.

The DJ started playing 'Tubthumping' by Chumbawamba. Cassie dragged Henry onto the dance floor while I was able to escape before I was called upon to demonstrate that I got knocked down but could get up again.

The corridor outside smelt of the past: shiny paint, strip lighting, notices about chess club and No Meat Mondays, inspirational sayings from Gandhi, GCSE artwork heavy on symbolism, eyes floating in oil-painted seas. I was getting my bearings back. The library was on the ground floor, in front of me was the staircase to the modern language department, a place where I'd spent a lot of my time at school. There had been only three people doing A level Italian and we'd commandeered the smallest classroom on the top floor with a view over the sports field. Being an inner London comprehensive we didn't have much green space but, from behind the pages of *Italiano Due*, with the smell of grass floating in through the open window, there had been an elegiac playing-fields-of-Eton atmosphere, only slightly ruined by the red buses and the dome of the Albert Hall. I started to climb the stairs but stopped when I heard voices coming from the direction of the boys' loos.

'No one knows.'

'Then what's the problem?'

'Think what it would mean for all of us. Izzy. Everyone.'

I shrank back into the corner of the stairwell, next to a poster exhorting me to 'be the change I wanted to see in the world'. I was grateful for my temporary invisibility. I had recognised the voices instantly. Gary was the one worrying about Izzy.

The other voice belonged to Sonoma. Who was supposedly busy with family commitments elsewhere.

Chapter 9

Anna

By ten o'clock, I was ready to go home. I knew there was no chance of persuading Cassie, who was dancing in an ironic kind of way to Abba. Izzy was holding court at the other end of the room. Chris and Gary had disappeared. I walked over to Henry, who was by the door talking to a woman in a hijab whom I recognised as Aisha, a girl from our year who'd become a doctor (not all the clever people were in our group).

'I'm off,' I said.

'So soon?' said Henry.

'There's only so much fun I can stand.'

'See you in another twenty years,' said Aisha.

I liked her tone and wished I'd spoken to her earlier – twenty-one years earlier, possibly – but before I could say more, the doors crashed open and someone yelled, 'Aisha! Come quickly!'

There's never a good reason why a doctor is needed urgently. There was a silence, broken only by the dancing queen, young and sweet, only seventeen. Then the DJ switched the music off. I heard the name 'Gary'. Henry and I looked at each other and moved towards the door. Cassie got there first.

'Everyone stay in this room,' she said.

I almost asked what the hell she was doing but then I remembered that, despite the cleavage and the glittery shoulders, Cassie was a police officer and, presumably, in charge in any given emergency. At any rate, we all did as we were told. Cassie went out and it seemed that no one spoke until she came back.

'I'm afraid I'll have to ask you all to stay here,' she said. 'The emergency services are on their way.'

Emergency services. Not just an ambulance, then, by the sound of it. The police too.

'Is it Gary?' Henry asked.

Cassie nodded, pressing her lips together.

'Is he dead?' Henry went on. I wouldn't have been able to produce the word. Cassie nodded again.

From the other side of the room, Izzy started to cry.

Time started to behave very oddly. I've noticed before that, in stressful situations, I start to dissociate, to go into myself. This time I was aware of sitting on a school chair, watching balloons (*21! Celebrate!*) float in the dusty industrial-chic rafters. Someone had turned on the overhead fluorescent lights, but the fairy lanterns were still twinkling. Izzy continued to cry and, rather to my surprise, Henry went over to comfort her. Several days seemed to pass. I shut my eyes and, when I opened them, a small woman in a leather jacket was striding into the room, followed by a man wearing a polo neck and a scowl. I saw Cassie approach the woman and say, 'Boss?' So this was the 'Indian girl' who was Cassie's superior at work, despite being younger than her.

The woman and Cassie conferred for a few minutes and left the room without speaking to us. The man cleared his throat and said, 'I'm DS Jake Barker. I'm going to need names and addresses and contact numbers.' He had a Geordie accent, possibly north of the Tyne. Cassie came back in and took Aisha back out with her. We all watched them go, swivelling our heads in unison.

Across the room, Chris caught my eye and winked. I hadn't seen him come back in and the wink made me feel awkward, almost complicit. Despite everything – the police presence, the approaching sirens, the seriousness of DS Barker's voice as he circled the room taking names – I still couldn't believe that Gary was dead. Gary, the star of the group, the one who might become Prime Minister one day. I remembered the voices I'd heard in the corridor. 'No one knows. Then what's the problem?' Should I tell someone?

But, when it was my turn, I just gave DS Barker Mum's address, explaining that I was staying there for a few weeks. 'My permanent address is in Italy.' He grunted, as if this confirmed his worst fears.

More sirens, running footsteps, voices and snatches of radioed communication. Then the woman came back into the library and introduced herself as DI Harbinder Kaur.

'We'll need to talk to you all in the next few days,' she said. 'You're free to go now. Please leave by the far door. I'm sorry. I know this is a very distressing situation.' Cassie stood watching her boss with what I thought must be her professional expression, respectful and composed. That's why I was surprised when she followed me out of the room, grabbed my arm and pushed me into one of the classrooms. Posters of the rain forest were on the walls. Save the world's lungs.

'Oh my God,' she said. 'What a nightmare.'

'It's awful,' I said. 'Poor Gary.'

'Yes,' she said, running a hand through her burnished hair. 'But what if they . . . what if they find out about the other thing?'

I stared at her. 'What other thing?'

Her eyes seemed wild, pupils huge. 'When we killed David.'

'But Cassie,' I said, 'we didn't kill David. He fell on the train tracks. It was an accident.'

Chapter 10

Cassie

It was past midnight when I got home. Pete had left earlier to relieve the babysitter. Chris offered him a lift in his richmobile but I think Pete walked. It wasn't far and he would have wanted to clear his head. I stayed to help DI Kaur secure the scene. It was the first time I'd seen her in action and I was impressed. She worked quickly but without any sense of panic. My previous boss, DI Franks, was always going on about the first twenty-four hours being the most important. 'You don't get those hours back!' he'd yell, veins standing out on his forehead, eyes popping. It was a surprise to me that he'd retired to Tenerife rather than dropping down dead of a heart attack. DI Kaur – Harbinder as I was supposed to call her – conferred with the SOCO team and worked out a list of priorities which she shared with me and Jake. 'You can't be part of the enquiry,' she told me, 'but you can help a lot with inside information.' 'Like telling us which of your old schoolmates did it,' added Jake, swigging pea protein from a flask.

The house was quiet. Kevin, our spaniel, must have recognised my key in the lock because he didn't bark but I could hear his nails clattering in a dance of delight. When I let myself in, he squirmed against me, plumy tail tickling my arms when I cuddled him. The sparkly top with its ridiculous cut-outs felt wrong now so I pulled on an old jumper of Pete's and went into the kitchen to make myself a herbal tea. I looked around the comfortable, untidy room, the kids' homework open on the table, clothes drying in front of the Aga, and tried a few calming breaths.

Gary is dead.

Was Gary murdered?

Did one of my friends do it?

Did anyone know about David?

I didn't know why I'd said that to Anna. She wasn't there that day. I don't know why because she was always with Chris at that time. But Chris had been at the station on his own. He'd seen me arrive with David. And he'd seen me leave.

We had laid our plans carefully. After our last exam – English set texts – I would lead (or lure) David to the station, where Gary, Henry and Chris would be waiting. We'd confront him with his crimes against me and Anna. 'Make it like a court,' said Chris, a true son of lawyer parents. 'Read out the charge sheet.'

'Henry can do that,' said Gary. 'And I'll do the intimidation. I'm the only one who can really scare him.' This was true. Gary, star of football and rugby, had a physical presence that Chris and Henry didn't possess. Plus, I remember thinking, Gary had more than mere strength. It sounds silly but Gary was the star of the school. He was the cleverest, the sportiest and the richest. When he marched David to the platform and threatened to throw him in front of the next train, I thought that David would be genuinely terrified.

'What shall I do?' said Chris.

'You guard the exit,' said Gary. From what? I thought.

David and I reached Imperial at four-thirty p.m. The entrances were boarded up, but everyone knew how you could get in. There was a door that led directly to a steep flight of stairs, down to the platform itself. It was probably a side exit in the old days and had been prised open years ago. All you had to do was turn the handle. David laughed at the detritus around the doorway: syringes, condoms, McDonald's cartons.

'All human life is here.'

Yes, he could be witty. That was one of the things I'd once liked about him. One of the reasons why I'd accompanied him to the cinema, why I'd gone home to meet his family, why I had followed him into his bedroom.

'The entrance to the underworld,' I said.

'Reminds me of *Paradise Lost*,' he said. 'No light but rather darkness visible.'

'Let's not talk about exams,' I said.

We walked down the urine-scented stairs.

'Where's Chris?' said David. His voice echoed against the sooty brick walls. 'Where are the drugs?'

'He should be here soon.'

Chris had been by the entrance. I had seen him but hadn't said anything. He'd been staring at the decades-old timetable like one of those ghosts said to haunt railway stations, trying to stop a fatal crash that has already happened. Like in *The Signalman*. 'Below there! Look out! For God's sake, clear the way'.

Henry and Gary were meant to be waiting for us on the platform but, when I looked around, there was nothing and nobody except a nest of blankets probably left by a homeless person. Opposite there was an empty warehouse, a cliff face of broken windows. It felt like David and I were the only people in the world.

'I've got you on my own.' David gave a wolfish smile.

Really? I thought. Are you really going to do this? After that time in your bedroom, when I said no, and you raped me anyway. And then, afterwards, you dared to ask, 'How was it for you?'

The ground began to vibrate. A train was coming.

'You're so pretty,' said David.

Then I pushed him.

Chapter 11

Harbinder

Monday

Anna Vance lives in a place called the Attlee Estate. 'It's not the best of addresses,' Kim had said. 'It's a dump,' said Jake. 'Even drug dealers don't go there at night.' Harbinder is surprised how quickly the landscape can change in London. One minute they are driving along the Fulham Road surrounded by expensive-looking shops and smooth stuccoed terraces, the next they are in a world that reminds Harbinder of the more depressing chapters in *The Lord of the Rings*: four concrete towers facing each other over a wasteland of abandoned supermarket trolleys and wind-blown rubbish.

'Bit of a change from Garfield Rice's house,' says Harbinder, feeling strangely reluctant to get out of the car.

'It's only temporary, according to Jake,' says Kim. 'Anna's staying with her mum. She normally lives in Italy. Probably a film star or something.' But the woman who opens the door to the tenth-floor flat doesn't look like a film star. She looks disconcertingly normal:

dark curly hair lightly touched with grey, no make-up, wearing jeans and a blue jumper. She actually has quite cool trainers though. Stan Smiths. Old-school.

Harbinder knows that she shouldn't really be doing this interview. But the superintendent, Simon Masters, has been on the phone again stressing the need for a quick result. The first forty-eight hours are the most important, Harbinder told the Operation Wilson team. They will get the initial legwork done quicker if everyone helps. Besides, as she said, she is fascinated by the non-famous member of the group.

'Anna Vance?' says Harbinder. She's out of breath from the climb but didn't fancy the tiny metal lift. Kim, who took this option, said cheerfully that it smelt of urine and death.

'Yes, come in.' Not friendly but not exactly unfriendly either.

A woman in a red dressing gown is hovering in the background. 'I'll go into my room, Annie, so you can have the sitting room.'

'No, you're OK, Mum. Your comfortable chair's there and all your stuff. We'll go into my room.'

Harbinder always warms to people who treat their parents with respect and are obviously fond of them. There is genuine warmth in this exchange. It's also clear that Anna's mother is ill, probably suffering from the effects of chemotherapy. She has a scarf tied around her head and looks, despite the fluffy robe, worryingly thin.

'Shall I make us all a cup of tea?' says Kim, probably thinking the same thing.

Both of them decline. The mother ('call me Star, dear, it's not my name but everyone does') says she can only drink water at the moment; Anna says that she's just had a cup.

'Anna prefers espresso,' says Star. 'It comes from living in Italy.'

'I like a good English cuppa,' says Anna. It's obviously an in-joke because they both laugh. Harbinder is annoyed to find herself feeling slightly choked. Just for a second, she wants to be with her mum, teasing her about her fondness for Jaffa cakes.

Anna's room is small and has traces of the teenage bedroom it once was. The walls have been painted a neutral beige, but the wardrobe still has stickers on it. One says, 'Enjoy cocaine: it's the real thing'. Anna's suitcase is in the middle of the room and her laptop is open on the bed. Harbinder takes the only chair and Anna fetches another for Kim. Then she sits on the single bed, shutting the computer.

Anna answers their questions easily but without much emotion. She hadn't really kept in touch with most of her old schoolfriends. She only went to the reunion because she happened to be in London anyway, visiting her mum. Cassie invited her. She didn't talk much to Gary . . . Garfield . . . that evening, only to say hallo at the beginning. She'd talked mostly to Henry Steep. Yes, she'd kept in touch with him, but they weren't close exactly.

'Did you take any pictures of the evening?' asks Kim. They are trying to put together a pictorial order of events.

'No,' says Anna. 'I don't have the kind of phone that takes pictures.' She gestures at the ancient Nokia lying next to her computer.

Even though her mother still talks about 'the interweb', Harbinder slightly distrusts people, especially people her own age, who don't own a smartphone. Why would anyone make their life more difficult just for the pleasure of looking superior?

'Can you remember when you last saw Gary in the room?' says Kim. Harbinder notes that she's using the name his schoolfriends still use.

'I couldn't really say,' says Anna. 'I know that, when I was about to leave, he wasn't there. I went over to talk to Henry and Aisha and then someone shouted for Aisha and . . . well, you know the rest.'

'Did you notice anything about Gary's behaviour that evening?' asks Kim. 'Anything unusual.'

Anna's replies so far have been so anodyne that Harbinder is surprised when she says, pleating the flower-patterned duvet, 'There was something . . .'

'Yes?' says Kim encouragingly.

'I was halfway up the staircase outside the library. I was going to look at the modern languages classrooms. Just for old times' sake. And I heard Gary talking to someone. The voices were coming from the end of the corridor, by the loos.'

'Who was he talking to?' asks Harbinder.

'Well, that's just it, I thought it was Sonoma.'

'Sonoma?' says Harbinder. The name rings a faint bell.

'Sonoma Davies,' says Anna. 'She was in our year. And she's the headteacher at Manor Park now. She organised the reunion, but she wasn't supposed to be there. The deputy head told us that she had family commitments.'

'And you're sure it was her?' says Kim.

'I can't be a hundred per cent sure,' says Anna. 'I didn't see her face and I haven't seen – or heard – Sonoma for years. But she has a rather distinctive voice. Still very American around the vowels.' She smiles slightly. 'I'm good at accents. It comes from being a language teacher.'

'What were they saying?' asks Kim.

'Gary was saying no one knew and Sonoma asked what was the problem. Then Gary said, "Think what it would mean for all of us. Izzy. Everyone." Then they moved away and I couldn't hear any more.'

Anna isn't only good at accents, thinks Harbinder. Her recall of speech is obviously excellent too. Unless she's lying.

'Have you any idea what they were talking about?' she asks.

More duvet pleating. 'No.'

'What happened next?'

'I went into the library.'

'When was this?' asked Kim.

'Earlyish. About eight-thirty.'

Garfield's death had been called in at ten-thirty. The first responders were there ten minutes later. Harbinder arrived at the school at eleven.

'Did anyone else see Sonoma?' she asks.

'I don't think so. I asked Cassie and a few others, but nobody had.'

Kim takes Anna through her movements for the rest of the evening. After giving her details to the police, Anna had been given a lift home by Chris Foster ('he has a driver'). She didn't speak to any of her other friends ('I think we were all in shock'). Harbinder waits until they are standing up to go before asking her last question, like that shabby detective in the American programme her dad likes. 'Anna, do you remember the death of David Moore?'

Anna blinks at them. Her face, which had been relaxing, seems to tighten.

'Yes. It happened on the day of our last A level exam. So awful.'

'What do you remember about it?'

'It happened in the old Tube station. Imperial. It was boarded up but we used to go there sometimes to . . . to hang out. He fell on the lines and was run over by a train.'

'Were you there when it happened?'

'No. I only heard about it afterwards. Gary actually saw it happen.'

'Was Gary at the station?'

'No, he was on the footbridge. It was Izzy who told me about it that evening. She was really upset. We all were.'

'Was David a friend of yours?'

'No, but I knew him. We all knew him. So awful for his parents.'

Harbinder has researched the case. David was an only child. She remembers an article showing the couple opening their dead son's exam results. Did Anna and her high-flying friends remember him when they opened theirs?

'Did you discuss David at the reunion?' asks Harbinder. They are at the front door now. *Bargain Hunt* is on in the sitting room. She recognises the music.

'No,' says Anna. 'We never talk about him.'

Which is interesting in itself, thinks Harbinder, as she descends the ten flights of stairs. Kim is waiting for her by the main doors.

'Anna Vance seems a nice woman,' she says.

'She's hiding something,' says Harbinder.

'Oh, she's definitely hiding something. Who shall we see next?'

'Let's go to Manor Park and talk to Sonoma Davies,' says Harbinder. 'Find out whether she really was Anna's mystery voice.'

'Good idea,' says Kim. 'We can stop off for a sandwich on the way. I know a good place under the arches.'

Harbinder thinks she's going to enjoy working with Kim.

Chapter 12

Harbinder

Manor Park is still shut but Sonoma tells them that she will be in her office. Harbinder imagines hundreds of children – student roll: 1,526 – rejoicing at their unexpected holiday, rolling over for another hour or four in bed. However much you like school, a day off always feels like a gift from heaven.

There's police tape across the main gate and a uniformed officer is standing on guard. The scene-of-the-crime outer cordon surrounds the whole school. The inner cordon consists of the library, boys' lavatory and the corridor outside. The SOCO team will still be working there. As Harbinder and Kim cross the road, Harbinder thinks that she spots reporters waiting in two parked cars. She hopes they don't recognise her. Her media training has so far consisted of one email telling her to reply 'no comment' to any question.

But Harbinder and Kim reach the gate in safety. The officer lets them in with a sketchy attempt at a salute. They then follow signs to 'The Headteacher's Office' thoughtfully provided in three languages.

Sonoma Davies rises to greet them. She's a tall woman with a poise that probably comes from bossing 1,526 people about every day. Although she's off-duty she is formally dressed in a red dress and a black jacket. Harbinder can't see her shoes because they are hidden by the desk, but she bets they are medium-heeled black courts.

'Thank you for seeing us,' she says. Although the interview would have been hard to refuse.

Sonoma inclines her head graciously.

'This must be a terrible shock for you,' says Kim, starting off with the empathy.

'It was,' says Sonoma. 'It is. I mean, that it should happen at all, but I knew Garfield well. He was in my year at school.'

'And you went to Oxford together, didn't you?' says Harbinder, to show she's done her research.

'Different colleges,' says Sonoma, 'but yes.'

'Did you keep in touch afterwards?'

'A little. Just Christmas cards. That sort of thing.'

'When did you last see him?' asks Kim.

'I think it was about a year ago. He invited me for lunch with some of his colleagues.' A faint ring of pride accompanies these words. Sonoma likes status, thinks Harbinder, looking at the myriad cups and certificates displayed in the room. But, then, that's part of her job. And, to be fair, Harbinder would be chuffed to be invited to lunch with a bunch of MPs, especially if it was at the House of Commons. Her mum would never get over it.

'Were you at the reunion last night?' asks Harbinder, trying for the idle shabby detective voice.

Sonoma straightens the papers on her desk. 'No. I had originally planned to attend but my daughter was performing in a ballet show so, of course, I had to be there.'

'What time did that end?' asks Harbinder.

Sonoma's eyebrows go up. 'About eight. Why?'

Harbinder decides to come out with it. 'It's just that someone said they saw you at the reunion.' Although Anna hadn't seen Sonoma, she just thought she'd heard her voice.

'That's impossible,' says Sonoma. 'After the concert I went for a meal at Pizza Express with my husband and children.'

My husband and children. The perfect straight package, thinks Harbinder. It also sounds weirdly like something a politician would say. Although 'my wife and children' would be more likely, usually when asking the press to respect the husband and father's privacy when he's caught in some sleazy affair.

Harbinder asks which Pizza Express. She is definitely going to check it out.

All this means that Sonoma is slightly chilly for the rest of the interview. She organised the reunion because it was twenty-one years since they'd left the school. She hadn't really kept in touch with anyone. She exchanges cards with Garfield and Cassie, she once went to see Kris Foster and The Cubes in concert but hadn't visited him backstage. She watches Isabelle's show on BBC2. Yes, she's done really well. They all have. No, she isn't surprised. It was that kind of school.

'Must be quite something,' says Kim. 'To be headteacher of the school you used to go to.'

'It is a little surreal,' says Sonoma, unbending slightly. 'I couldn't have imagined it when I was here. But then I didn't think I would go into teaching.'

'What did you imagine yourself doing?' asks Kim.

'Oh, I don't know. Business or politics. Something like that. I studied PPE at Oxford.'

Harbinder isn't sure what this stands for. Politics, economics and something else beginning with P? But she isn't about to ask.

'But representation is so important,' Sonoma continues, looking at Harbinder. 'There still aren't enough teachers of colour in the profession. Let alone headteachers.'

Harbinder wonders if it would have made a difference to her if she'd had even one non-white teacher. She supposes it would, but she slightly resents Sonoma's assumption of a bond between them.

'Will your children go to Manor Park?' she asks.

'My eldest goes to the London Oratory,' says Sonoma, with a rather defiant look. 'But then he's musically gifted.'

They do music at Manor Park, thinks Harbinder; she saw notices for orchestra practice in the corridor. But this was obviously not good enough for Sonoma's precious son. She bets the ballet dancer daughter won't darken the doors of her mother's old school either. They make their farewells and leave.

Back at the station, Harbinder calls a progress meeting. Jake and Tory are both rather starry-eyed from their encounter with Isabelle Istar.

'She was so lovely,' says Tory. 'Just like a normal person.'

'We had great craic, as my Irish grandmother used to say,' enthuses Jake. 'And Isabelle's even more gorgeous in the flesh. Seriously hot.'

'Even I fancied her,' says Tory, with a giggle. 'And I'm not that way inclined.'

'Fascinating,' says Harbinder. 'More importantly, did she have a motive for killing Garfield Rice?'

'I'm sure she didn't,' says Tory. 'She seemed really upset. She actually said that she and Garfield went out together at school.'

Harbinder wonders if she can get Tory transferred to another team. Every detective should know that romantic involvement is a motive for murder not evidence against it.

'Was she in touch with Garfield?' she asks.

'We asked that,' says Jake. 'She said not but I wondered if there was a slight hesitation.'

'His wife said the same,' says Harbinder. 'I didn't get the impression that she was much of a fan.'

'Isabelle's married,' says Tory. As if that proves anything. 'And she's got a lovely little girl called Anna.'

'Called Anna?' says Harbinder. 'After Anna Vance?'

'I don't know.' Tory and Jake exchange looks.

Harbinder turns back to the board. 'There are a few things that need checking out. Anna Vance says she heard Sonoma Davies talking to Garfield Rice at the reunion. Sonoma says she wasn't there. We need to check her alibi. Then there's David Moore's death. I still think there could be a link.'

'It was twenty-one years ago,' says Jake.

'Yes, and it was their twenty-first reunion.' Harbinder remembers the balloons. 'Memories might have been triggered. Garfield Rice witnessed the incident and, twenty-one years later, he's murdered. Did you ask Isabelle about it?'

'Yes,' says Tory. 'She said Garfield saw it happen and was really affected by it. Isabelle said she was too. She had to have therapy afterwards.'

Before going to RADA a few weeks later and embarking on her stellar career, thinks Harbinder. 'Isabelle wasn't with Garfield Rice that day, was she?'

She addresses Tory but it's Jake who answers. 'No, but she said they were meeting at Garfield's house later to celebrate. To have a bonk, more likely.'

'Isabelle did say that students sometimes went to the old Tube station to take drugs,' says Tory.

Harbinder had guessed as much from Anna's assertion that they went there 'to hang out'. She remembered the faded sticker on Anna's wardrobe. *Enjoy cocaine, it's the real thing.*

'Talking of drugs,' she says. 'We've had the toxicology results. Garfield's blood shows high levels of insulin combined with low c-peptide which, according to Alice Hunter, indicates that he was killed by insulin poisoning. Two people who were present at the reunion are diabetics – Cassie and Chris Foster. We need to find out if they had insulin on them and, if so, who had access to it.'

'Can me and Jake interview Chris Foster?' asks Tory.

'No,' says Harbinder. 'You two go to see Henry Steep. Kim and I will take the pop star.'

She's not going to risk another fan-girl moment.

Chapter 13

Harbinder

Chris Foster has given an address with the postcode EC1V.

'Clerkenwell,' says Kim, as they get into the squad car. 'Very trendy.'

Harbinder can't get used to being taxied. In Shoreham, she and Neil shared the driving, although his cautious 'mirror, signal, manoeuvre' approach made her want to scream. In London, most of CID don't have their own cars but rely on police drivers. 'It's usually quicker by public transport,' says Kim, 'though that's not much use if you're chasing a mugger.'

'Is Clerkenwell the East End?' asks Harbinder, as they settle back in their seats.

'Not really,' says Kim, 'though it is east London. It used to be the Italian quarter and it's still got lots of restaurants and delis. There's the Italian church too. St Peter's. My nephew was christened there. His mum's Italian. But now the place is full of city types living in converted warehouses. That's where we'll find Chris Foster, I bet.'

'Were you born in London?' asks Harbinder.

Kim laughs. 'Yeah. Born east of Aldgate Pump.'

'What does that mean?'

'It means you're a proper East-Ender. Like being born within the sound of Bow bells.'

'I've heard that one,' says Harbinder. 'Is it something to do with a nursery rhyme?'

'"Oranges and Lemons",' says Kim. 'The great bell of Bow. There's a church on Cheapside called St Mary-le-Bow. If you're born within a sound of its bells, then you're a true cockney. My dad used to say that, in the old days, the land around it was so flat, you could hear the bells as far away as Stepney. It's all built up now though. My mum and dad were from Shoreditch. Proper East End. Though that's quite trendy too now.'

'Are your parents still alive?'

'My dad died five years ago. My mum's in a home out Surrey way. What about you?'

'They're both alive and living in Sussex,' says Harbinder. 'They emigrated there from India.'

'So, you're from the east too.'

Harbinder wonders whether to be offended but decides that the remark was kindly meant. It's a point of similarity, not difference, after all.

'I was born in Chichester,' she says. 'I don't think you can hear the Bow bells from there. Even on a good day.'

Kim's hunch is correct. The car stops outside a tall brick building which still has winches and iron railings on the outside. Inside, the industrial chic theme is carried on by brushed concrete and metal rafters. A lift opens its doors noiselessly.

Kim looks at Harbinder. 'Taking the stairs again?'

'If I could find them.' After looking at the featureless walls for a few seconds, Harbinder steps into the glass box. In a thankfully short space of time, the doors are opening again, straight into a cavernous sitting room.

However uninviting the ground floor, the top of the building is luxurious in the extreme. A wall of glass looks out over rooftops and chimneys with the Thames a glittering snake in the foreground. Harbinder is aware of low sofas, wooden floors, bizarre lighting fixtures and splashes of modern art on white walls. It's very smart but it's not exactly cosy. Harbinder remembers seeing the same panorama from Attlee Towers and wonders whether, death-scented lift aside, she wouldn't rather live in Anna Vance's flat. A tall blonde man in jeans and a Ramones T-shirt is standing framed by the view. Funnily enough, he's wearing the same trainers as Anna Vance.

'Hi. You found it then? People often think the building is uninhabited.'

'Chris Foster?' says Harbinder, more for form's sake than anything.

'That's right.'

He's very friendly, waving them to the sofas, offering tea or cold drinks. They both ask for water. Harbinder is pretty sure that this is just so that they can say that Chris Foster waited on them. Fame is an awfully infantilising thing, she thinks. Chris Foster is just an ordinary man, fortyish, a witness to a crime. Yet just because he's an average guitar player with an above-average voice, two adult police professionals are slightly breathless after two minutes in his company. Harbinder is only relieved that she didn't let Tory do the interview.

Kim opens with a few admiring comments about the decor. It turns out that the art is Chris Foster's own. Harbinder remembers Cassie saying he went to art school.

'What's this one called?' says Kim, staring at a canvas that seems to be just a square of blue. A nice shade, true, but still . . .

'Death of a Planet,' says Chris cheerfully. His voice is rather posh accessorised with touches of cockney and American. Harbinder wonders what Anna Vance, with her ear for accents, would make of it. Her own voice had been flat and classless, maybe the result of living abroad or perhaps an effort to distance herself from her upbringing on the tenth floor of a tower block.

'Tell us about the reunion,' says Kim, trying for the cosy tone she usually establishes in interviews. 'I can't imagine meeting up with anyone I was at school with.'

'It was strange,' says Chris. 'I hadn't seen most of them since leaving the place. Manor Park is always having reunions, but I've always managed to resist before.'

'Then why go to this one?' asks Kim.

Chris gives them a rueful smirk which is clearly meant to charm them. Kim smiles back. Harbinder stares at him stonily.

'I suppose it was because of Anna,' says Chris.

'Anna Vance?' asks Harbinder, although there's no one else it could really be.

'Yes. I was really good friends with Anna at school but we drifted apart. She went to Italy and I was busy with the band and . . . and things. I heard she was in England and I really wanted to see her again.'

Anna Vance might be the only one who's not wildly successful, thinks Harbinder, but she has certainly had an effect on her class-mates. Isabelle possibly even named her baby after her. Chris obviously still has feelings for her.

'Did you chat to Anna at the reunion?' asks Kim. 'Catch up a bit?'

'Yes, I did,' says Chris. 'As much as anyone can chat at those things.'

'And you gave her a lift home afterwards?'

'We were all so shaken,' says Chris. 'I didn't like to think of her going home on the bus. Or walking. And I had a driver. It's a bit grotesque, I know, but I wanted to drink and I don't like taking taxis.'

'Did you see Sonoma Davies that evening?' asks Harbinder.

'Sonoma? No, she wasn't there. Shame. I would have liked to have seen Sonoma in her fiefdom.'

Fiefdom. It's an odd choice of word. Harbinder isn't even com-pletely sure what it means. But she gets the implication; Manor Park belongs to Sonoma Davies now.

'Were you friends with Sonoma at school?' she asks.

'Yes. We even went inter-railing together after A levels. With Gary, as a matter of fact. But Sonoma and Gary were closer than I was to either of them.'

'What about Henry Steep and Isabelle Istar?' asks Kim. 'Have you kept in touch with them?'

'I hadn't seen Henry since school. I sometimes run into Izzy at events,' says Chris. 'But we're not close exactly.'

'And Garfield Rice?' asks Harbinder. She can only imagine what sort of events attracted both Chris Foster and Isabelle Istar.

Chris Foster looks out of the window before replying. Really, thinks Harbinder, *view* is too small a word for what is revealed by the vast panes. It's a display, a happening, a *performance*.

'It's a bit strange,' he says.

The two women wait.

'What's a bit strange?' asks Kim, eventually.

'I hadn't heard from Gary for years,' says Chris. 'Not since school really. But then, last summer, he invited me to lunch.'

'To lunch?' says Harbinder. 'At his house?'

'No,' says Chris. 'At his club. Well, a sort of dining club. In Bleeding Heart Yard.'

Harbinder and Kim exchange glances. 'Where?' says Harbinder.

Chris obviously thinks they are querying the unusual name.

'It's a courtyard in Holborn,' he says. 'Not far from here. I think it gets its name from a pub. Anyway, there's a nice restaurant there. Garfield invited me to meet some of his friends. Apparently, there's a bit of competition to invite guests who are . . . you know . . . well-known. I can only assume that's why he thought of me. As I say, we hadn't kept in touch. And he's a Tory. I'm still an old leftie.'

He laughs. Looking for approval, Harbinder thinks.

'Why did you go then?' she asks.

'Curiosity, I suppose,' says Chris. 'I mean, Gary's made a bit of a name for himself. He's always in the papers going on about climate change being a hoax. That's why I was surprised . . .'

'Surprised by what?' prompts Harbinder because the singer seems to have dried again.

'All the diners, the members of this club, were men,' says Chris. 'And they were all really rich and successful. A couple of MPs, several businessmen. There was lots of banter, lots of in-jokes. Bullingdon Club humour. Well, that's what I imagine anyway. I didn't go to that sort of university. Anyway, there were drinks and then we had lunch, which was really good. Then, after dinner, there was a speaker. She talked about climate change and – my God – she laid it on thick. Rising sea levels, shrinking glaciers, thawing permafrost, temperatures only likely to rise, it's a hundred seconds to midnight on the doomsday clock. I know a lot of this stuff and I was still depressed. But I expected Gary to argue, to shout her down. I mean, that's been his schtick for the last few years, right? Global warming is cyclical, it's all a ruse by lefties to shut down the coal business. That sort of thing. But he agreed with every word. They all did. Then I realised. They believed in climate change. They knew it was happening. They knew better than anyone, with all their directorships of oil companies and the like. They knew but they wanted to stop anyone else understanding the full extent of it. Because it was bad for business.'

'Who were these people?' says Harbinder. 'Do you remember their names?'

'I think so,' says Chris. 'I'll write them down for you. They called themselves the Bleeding Hearts. Ironic, eh?'

'Very,' says Harbinder.

'Anna Vance, Chris Foster, Isabelle Istar, Henry Steep, Sonoma Davies,' says Harbinder, turning back to her list. 'What have we found out about them?'

'They called themselves The Group at school,' says Jake. 'They used to meet up in the attic at Garfield Rice's house. They called it the Crow's Nest.'

Harbinder thinks of Archie Flowers saying, 'It was quite a class, the class of 1998.' In more ways than one, she thinks. Henry Steep has also been the only person of interest to produce any pictures of the night. Cassie had left her phone in her bag. Isabelle had said, unconvincingly, that she hated photos of herself. Anna's ancient phone was, of course, useless.

Henry's photos show Cassie arm-in-arm with Garfield Rice. Cassie's smile is wide, but the MP looks slightly distracted, as if someone off-camera has just asked him a question. Anna Vance and Chris Foster stand side by side, neither of them smiling, holding their drinks in front of them like shields. Isabelle is dancing, her hair flying out around her. Garfield stands pointing at a picture, which is stuck onto the library wall. Chris watches him, his face inscrutable.

'What else did Henry say about Garfield?' asks Harbinder.

'He seemed quite angry about him,' says Jake. 'Quite resentful about how he'd turned out. He said that Garfield was really Labour at school, but he'd turned into a capitalist pig. His words.'

'Cassie said something similar,' says Harbinder. 'Without the insult.'

'Garfield's father was a Labour MP,' says Jake. 'Must have been a rich one if he had a big house in Chelsea.'

'Sir Fulton Rice,' says Kim. 'He was before your time, but I remember him. Think he made his money in coal mining. One of your champagne socialists.'

'Fulton. Garfield,' says Tory. 'Why do they have such weird names?'

Someone has to say it. 'Coming from a woman called Tory,' says Jake.

'It's short for Victoria,' says Tory, with a slight pout.

'Well, a Tory is what Garfield became,' says Harbinder. 'And it seems that he was still interested in coal and oil, all the fossil fuels. Did Henry say anything else interesting?'

'He said that Izzy used to go out with Garfield and Chris fancied Anna. It was all very incestuous in The Group, he said.'

'Chris Foster as good as admitted that he had a thing for Anna,' says Harbinder. 'What about Henry?'

'He's gay,' says Tory, before adding, 'but he seemed very nice.'

Harbinder really must look into a transfer. 'Did you ask Henry about David Moore?' she says.

'Yes. He remembers it well. He says he was actually going down the steps into the station when it happened.'

'Why was he there?' asks Harbinder.

'He said he was going to buy drugs,' says Jake. 'He was quite open about it. But everyone at Manor Park seemed to be a druggie. Famous for it.'

'What happened to keeping an open mind?' says Harbinder. But Chris Foster had said something similar. 'I'd heard someone was at Imperial selling drugs. Sorry, detectives, but that's where dealers used to go in those days. I was outside the station when I heard someone screaming. Later I found out it was Gary. It was shocking to think of him making a sound like that.'

'We asked Chris about being a diabetic,' said Kim. 'He said that he uses an EpiPen to inject himself with insulin but didn't take it to the reunion.'

'I asked Cassie too,' says Harbinder. 'She did take a syringe with her, maybe two. I've asked her to check that they are still in her bag.' Along with her phone, she thinks.

'Do you really think Cassie could have killed Garfield?' says Tory, wide-eyed.

'We have to investigate every possibility,' says Harbinder. 'And, talking of leads, we heard something interesting from Chris Foster.' She tells the rest of the team about Bleeding Heart Yard. 'There may be some motive there. Kim, do you remember what Sonoma Davies said?'

'She went to lunch with Garfield and some of his colleagues. Do you think it was at Bleeding Heart Yard?'

'I think we need to ask,' says Harbinder. 'And we need to check all the names on Chris Foster's list of attendees.'

'But they weren't at the reunion,' says Tory.

'They're powerful people. If they wanted to kill someone, they could. They might even have employed a hit man,' says Harbinder, wondering if these words were actually coming out of her mouth. She wishes Neil were there to hear them. 'And someone sent Garfield Rice messages, notes mentioning bleeding hearts. His agent found a couple of them. They're with forensics now.'

'It could have been any of them,' says Jake happily. 'Just like that game.'

'Cluedo?' says Kim.

'No. Murder in the Dark.'

Chapter 14

Harbinder

That evening Harbinder travels home on the bus, thinking that no one would imagine that the Indian girl, gazing out of the window with her headphones on, was actually lost in a world of hit men, drug overdoses and a pop star who got a strange look in his eyes when describing his old schoolfriends.

Back at the flat, Jeanne is eating cereal in the kitchen.

'I can't face real food,' she says. 'My Year Eights were a nightmare today.'

'How old is Year Eight?' asks Harbinder, putting her Tesco Metro bag down on the table.

'Twelve to thirteen,' says Jeanne.

'The worst,' says Harbinder. 'Too old to be scared of the teacher, too young to care about exams.'

'Exactly. Have you ever been a teacher?'

'No, but a good friend of mine is. She's a deputy head now.' Harbinder thinks of Clare with her elegance and her floaty clothes. For all Clare's serenity, she can't imagine any pupils giving her a hard time. 'I haven't got the guts to be a teacher,' she adds. 'That's why I became a police officer.'

Jeanne looks up, milk dripping from her spoon. 'You're in charge of the Garfield Rice case, aren't you? I saw you on TV. I know you can't talk about it,' she says hastily, 'but I think that's pretty cool.'

Harbinder hasn't quite steeled herself to watch the clip. All she can remember is her voice, sounding unusually high-pitched, saying 'no comment'.

'It's my first case with the Met,' says Harbinder, 'and it's all over the news. I'm terrified.'

A clatter announces Mette's arrival. She's forced to carry her bicycle up three flights of stairs after a previous version was stolen from the hall. Mette loves her bike, a tall silver steed she calls Sven.

'Hallo, flatmates.' The Danish girl appears in the doorway, a vision in Lycra. 'I've had the shittiest day.'

Mette is fond of this word, which she uses as both adjective and noun. It sounds rather exotic the way she pronounces it.

'Join the club,' says Jeanne.

'What about Detective Harbinder? Did you catch the shits?'

'Not yet,' says Harbinder.

'Let's go to the pub,' says Mette. 'We can have gin and feel better.'

'No thanks,' says Jeanne, standing up. 'I'm going to have a bath then watch *Buffy* for two hours.'

Harbinder wonders whether *Buffy*, which is about vampires in an American high school, is suitable viewing for someone traumatised by Year Eight. But she doesn't say this. Instead, rather to her own surprise, she finds herself agreeing to accompany Mette to the pub.

★

The Bird in Hand is one of those old-fashioned corner pubs that still populate London, hanging baskets outside, brass and mahogany within. Harbinder doesn't go into pubs much. She and Neil occasionally had a drink after work, and once she met her Ukrainian friend Natalka in her local. But mostly they just seem like places where straight white men go to drink beer. Mette has no such inhibitions. She pushes open the swing doors and beams at the clientele who stare at her as if they have never seen a six foot tall blonde dressed in a denim boiler suit. At least she has changed out of her cycling gear. Harbinder thinks that the sight of Mette in Lycra might have finished off a few of the older drinkers.

'Gin?' says Mette.

Harbinder had been going to drink red wine but she feels suddenly reckless and asks for a gin and tonic. The barman then reels off a seemingly endless list of varieties before Mette settles on a pink one because she likes the colour. Harbinder chooses the same. They both order food too, beef and ale pie for Mette, lasagne for Harbinder.

'I love English pub food,' says Mette, as they take their seats on a high-backed sofa. 'Not that lasagne is exactly English.'

'I know what you mean,' says Harbinder. 'My parents never go out to eat because my mum says she cooks better food at home. It's true too but I used to long to be able to eat fish and chips like my friends.'

'We lived miles from any restaurant when I was growing up,' says Mette. 'I used to dream about chips.'

'Where did you grow up?' asks Harbinder.

'A little place on the west coast of Jutland,' says Mette. 'Very flat, very windy, always cut off by snow or floods. But beautiful in its own way. Then I went to Aarhus to study architecture and did a masters in the US. In New York. Columbia.'

Harbinder feels inadequate, as she always does when faced with someone better travelled than she is. To be fair, that applies to almost everyone. After all, it took her thirty-eight years to make the move to London, only sixty miles from where she was born.

'I've lived almost all my life in the same place,' she says now. 'I was brought up in Shoreham, on the south coast, where my parents have a shop. Went to university nearby in Chichester, then joined the police. I still lived at home until a few months ago. God, it sounds dull when I say it out loud.'

'Joining the police isn't dull,' says Mette. 'What made you do that?'

'I studied criminology at university,' says Harbinder, 'so the force was the obvious next step. But, really, I suppose it's because I like justice. Even as a child, it drove me mad when people got away with things. The same kids used to shoplift from the shop again and again. I used to say to my dad "call the police" but he just shrugged and said they'd only break our windows if we did that. We were one of the only non-white families in the area. There was quite a bit of racism, name-calling, intimidation, that sort of thing. I thought it was wrong that people weren't punished for it. I still do.'

Harbinder takes a gulp of her drink. She can't remember when she's given such a truthful answer to this question. She wonders if she sounds a complete nutter. The word 'punished' seems to hover in the air.

'You must be good at it,' says Mette. 'You're a detective inspector.'

'I am good at it,' says Harbinder. She isn't going to be falsely modest for anyone. 'But it's hard when your first case is in the public eye.'

Mette doesn't ask any questions about the case. Harbinder doesn't know whether to be relieved or slightly disappointed. Their food arrives and Harbinder gets them more drinks. Another gin for Mette, sparkling water for her. Mette tells her about the building she is working on, an apartment block in Chelsea.

'Have you heard of a place called Bleeding Heart Yard?' asks Harbinder.

Mette plunges a knife into her pie. 'Yes, I worked on a development near there. It's one of those secret little courtyards that you seem to find in London. Leads to Ely Place, which was a palace once, I believe. A bishops' palace. Do bishops live in palaces?'

'I bet they do,' says Harbinder. 'Nothing would surprise me about the Christian hierarchy. Do you know how Bleeding Heart Yard got its name?' She seems to remember Chris Foster saying something about a pub.

'One of the other architects told me that it was because a woman was murdered there and her heart was found on the cobbles,' says Mette. 'Still pumping out blood. Enjoy your meal.' She grins, showing very white teeth with a slight gap between the middle two. Harbinder is surprised to feel her own heart beating slightly faster.

'My parents buy hearts from the butchers to feed to their stupid dog,' she says.

'I love these strange London place names,' says Mette. 'Crutched Friars. Shoulder of Mutton Alley. Savage Gardens. I'm making a list of them. There's a good restaurant in Bleeding Heart Yard. We should go there one day.'

This leaves Harbinder with several questions. Would this be the same restaurant where Garfield Rice met his climate-change-denying friends? Did Garfield know about the courtyard's grisly history? And, would the meal with Mette be a *date*?

They walk back to the flat in companionable silence. Barlby Road looks suburban and friendly, lights in most of the windows, fallen leaves on the pavement. Mette kicks her way through them in her DMs. It will be October soon, thinks Harbinder. Then Hallowe'en, then Bonfire Night, then Christmas. All the Christian festivals. She hopes she'll have found Garfield Rice's killer by Christmas. Her mother will never forgive her if she doesn't come home.

Outside number 45, Mette stops. A woman in a dark coat and knitted hat is standing by their gate.

'DI Kaur?' she says.

'Who's asking?' Mette steps in front of Harbinder.

But Harbinder has recognised the voice.

'Isabelle Istar?'

'Yes. I must speak to you.'

'What are you doing here?'

'I saw you on the bus,' is the surprising answer. 'And I followed you home earlier. I live nearby. I need to talk to you in private.'

'Give me your address and I'll call on you tomorrow. You can't go around following people and loitering outside their houses. It's a criminal offence, for one thing.'

Isabelle hands over a card. 'Can you come after nine? I'll be alone then.'

Harbinder doesn't ask why Isabelle needs to be on her own. She takes the card and watches with Mette as the dark figure zigzags across the road like an extra in a spy movie.

Chapter 15

Harbinder

Tuesday

Isabelle lives just off Ladbroke Grove. Harbinder has researched local property prices and knows that the brick-fronted terraced house, with its wrought-iron balconies and sash windows, must be worth at least five million pounds. Who on earth could afford that? As Harbinder waits for Kim by the steps to the green front door, she watches the other inhabitants of the street. Several elegant mothers ushering blazered children into vast four-by-fours, a man in a pin-striped suit, a woman with a pug on a lead. They all look wealthy enough, but multimillionaires?

'Bloody hell,' Kim emerges from the squad car. 'Nice gaff.'

'We're certainly seeing the high life,' says Harbinder. 'This is just around the corner from me but it could be another world.' She remembers how disconcerting it was when affluent Fulham Road turned into Mordor and the Attlee Estate.

'Where do you live?' asks Kim.

'Barlby Road.'

'Very nice too. Rented?'

Somehow Harbinder doesn't mind Kim asking these questions, possibly because she's so forthcoming with her own personal details. From yesterday Harbinder knows that Kim lives in Hammersmith with her husband Malcolm, an electrician, and two adult children who 'look like they're never moving out'. Another daughter, Amy, is married with a child of her own and lives nearby.

'Yes,' says Harbinder, 'and I share it with two other women. But it's a good place to live.' She hadn't seen Mette that morning but heard her manoeuvring her bike down the stairs at seven-thirty. Did Mette always leave for work so early? Harbinder can't shake the thought that her flatmate was avoiding an awkward breakfast encounter. But why would it be awkward? They'd had a drink and a meal and, on the way home, met a crazed actress. Normal London life, surely?

Isabelle looks surprised to see two of them. Harbinder knows that she was hoping for a one-to-one interview, but she is determined to play this case by the book. She doesn't want the CPS throwing out any of their evidence.

'This is DS Kim Manning,' she says briskly. 'You said you had something to tell us.'

Isabelle leads them upstairs to a room on the balcony floor. It's exactly like the property ads: wooden floors, white sofas, bookcases, mirrors reflecting yellowing plane trees. Isabelle, in leggings and a soft grey jumper, fits the setting exactly. She offers tea or coffee. 'Oliver's taking Anna to school but Maria's in the kitchen.'

Harbinder has no idea who Maria is but she gets the picture.

Someone, whose function is nameless, is downstairs doing the domestic tasks. Harbinder is quite sorry to miss Oliver West though. She watched him in a police drama a few years ago and would have liked the chance to tell him that he got almost everything wrong.

Both Harbinder and Kim decline to bother Maria.

'OK,' says Harbinder. 'Are you going to tell me why you were lurking outside my house last night?' Kim looks up. Harbinder hasn't shared this detail before.

'I'm sorry,' says Isabelle, lower lip quivering.

'Just don't do it again,' says Harbinder. 'What was so important that you had to stalk me?'

Isabelle flinches slightly at the word. Harbinder thinks, perhaps uncharitably, that 'fragile' is the look the actress is going for today. Her face is pale, with just a hint of grey eye shadow, and her long, dark hair is tousled. She certainly looks younger than her thirty-nine years. That's the useful thing about this case; all the suspects are the same age.

'It's complicated,' says Isabelle.

The two police officers wait.

'You know that Gary – Garfield – and I were friends?'

'I know you were friends at school,' says Harbinder.

'We were very good friends at school,' says Isabelle. 'Childhood sweethearts really. Romeo and Juliet. Well, you never forget that sort of thing, do you?'

In Harbinder's experience, you not only forget it, you lock it up in a box marked 'never to be opened'. She wonders what Gary Carter is doing these days.

'We drifted apart when we went to university,' said Isabelle. 'And then, of course, we both married other people. But then we got back in touch through a Facebook chat group. There's a reunion page for Manor Park. Someone shared a picture of a play that I was in and Gary commented. We messaged each other. Then we met up. And, I suppose, that was that.'

There's another pause. Kim says, 'You started seeing each other again?'

'Yes. At first it was just as friends. But then it got more serious.'

'Did his wife know?' asks Harbinder. She remembers Paula saying that Garfield saw Isabelle on TV 'like everyone else'.

Isabelle shudders. 'No. But we had got to the stage of thinking we would have to tell our partners. And then . . .'

And then Gary got murdered, thinks Harbinder. She wonders why Isabelle is telling them this. She must know that a mistress has more motive than a friend. Is she just confessing to the affair before they find out from someone else?

'I just keep thinking about something Gary said,' says Isabelle, the words now coming out in a rush. 'Just a few days before . . . before it happened. It was about David. You know, the boy who died.'

The Boy Who Died. It's like the title of a film – a psychological thriller or something weepy. In either case, Harbinder wouldn't watch it.

'What about David?' she says.

'Gary saw it happen,' says Isabelle. 'He was walking over the bridge and saw David fall in front of the train. It was horrible. Traumatic. I think he suffered from PTSD actually. But doctors didn't know as much about it then. When I had therapy years later, it all came out. But, at the time, it happened just before we all left school, and we didn't even have a chance to talk about

94

it. To get closure. Anyway, a week before the reunion, Gary did mention it. He said that David was murdered and he knew who did it.'

She leans back, as if to observe their reactions. Harbinder keeps her face still.

'Did he say who it was?'

'Not exactly. Gary went to another reunion a few days before our one. One for the rugby team. They do all these ghastly activities. Paintballing, go-karting, that kind of thing. This one was clay pigeon shooting. Anyway, Gary rang me afterwards. That was unusual. We normally had to be careful.'

Because you were both having affairs, thinks Harbinder.

'What did Gary say?' asks Kim. 'Can you remember the exact words?'

'I kept the message,' says Isabelle unexpectedly. 'I've got another phone for . . . for Gary.' She reaches into the sofa cushions. She has prepared the scene.

Isabelle touches the screen. A voice rings out, slurred but possessing the kind of patrician certainty that Harbinder associates with politicians. Especially Conservative ones.

'Babes. I love you. I'm a bit drunk but I love you. So much, babes. Look, there's something I want to tell you. It's about David. Sounds crazy but I think he was murdered and I know who did it. Bloody hell. I love you. Did I say that? I still do.'

'Did you call him back?' says Harbinder.

'Of course I did. I rang him the next day but he was at work and he couldn't talk. I said I'd see him at the reunion. Well, I did, but I didn't get to speak to him alone. We'd arranged to meet in the language lab on the first floor at ten but, when I went up there, it was empty. I went back to the library and, the next thing I knew, people were calling for doctors and saying Gary was . . .'

She covers her face with her hands. Harbinder remembers a woman sobbing when she arrived in the library. That was Isabelle, she realises now.

Kim says, 'Izzy. Can I ask you something?'

Isabelle looks up, possibly startled by the urgency in Kim's voice. Or by the fact that she's now 'Izzy'.

'Why didn't you tell this to DS Barker and DC Hamilton-Fletcher?'

Harbinder had forgotten Tory had a double-barrelled surname. It doesn't necessarily mean you are posh these days. She is, though.

'I wanted to tell DI Kaur. She's the one in charge.'

Harbinder believes this. Isabelle is the sort of person who always asks to speak to whoever's in authority. She'd do it with charm but she wouldn't waste her time on underlings. Jake and Tory, both in awe of Isabelle's glamour, would have had 'middle management' written all over them. Thinking of her team makes Harbinder ask, 'Did you tell Cassie?'

'Cassie?'

'Yes, wouldn't she be the person to talk to? She was there that night. She knew Gary. And she's a police officer.'

'I couldn't tell Cassie,' says Isabelle, opening her eyes very wide. 'Because she was in love with Gary too.'

'Do you think that's true?' asks Harbinder. They are on their way back to the station. The squad car makes its way through back streets Harbinder would never recognise again: kebab shops, boarded-up houses, signs saying 'God is Near'.

'I can't imagine it,' says Kim. 'Cassie and Pete always seem such a happy couple.'

'How long have you known Cassie?'

'Since she transferred to CID. About five years. She's a good officer. Everyone likes her.'

'I'll have to interview her again,' says Harbinder. She knows she hasn't treated Cassie like a suspect though she has – thank God – kept her away from the investigation.

'Everything seems to come back to this David, doesn't it?' says Kim.

'Anna said they never spoke about him,' says Harbinder. 'That's significant in itself.'

'Anna wasn't there that day,' says Kim, 'but Chris Foster was, by his own admission.'

'Henry Steep was there too,' says Harbinder. 'He told Jake and Tory that he was on his way down the steps when the train went by.'

'And then there's all the Bleeding Heart stuff,' says Kim. 'Could they be linked? Could someone have been blackmailing Garfield Rice?'

'I don't know,' says Harbinder. 'But I'll be interested to see if forensics has found anything on the notes. And I want to talk to Sonoma Davies.'

She has trouble getting through at first. The school is open again but 'Mrs Davies' seems perpetually busy. Eventually Harbinder says, 'It's DI Kaur from the Criminal Investigation Department of the Metropolitan Police. Can she ring me back immediately?' Sonoma is on the phone within five minutes.

'What is it? I was taking an assembly.'

'Good morning,' says Harbinder. 'I was interested in something you said when DS Manning and I spoke to you yesterday.'

'Yes?' Sonoma is giving nothing away. Harbinder imagines her in her office surrounded by trophies, probably wearing a red power suit.

'You said that you'd had lunch with Garfield Rice and some of his colleagues. Where was that?'

'Where was it?'

'Yes,' says Harbinder patiently, 'where was the lunch?'

'In a restaurant near London Bridge. One of those little court-yards.'

'Bleeding Heart Yard?'

'Yes, that's right.'

'Who was there and what did you talk about?'

'I can't remember all the guests. There were a few of Gary's fellow MPs, some businessmen.'

'Business*men*?'

Sonoma gets the emphasis. 'Yes, all men, I'm afraid. We've got a long way to go, DI Kaur.'

Once again, Harbinder slightly resents the first-person plural and the invitation to identify.

'Was there a guest speaker?' she asks.

'Yes. Someone spoke about rewilding. It was fascinating.'

Another environmental topic, thinks Harbinder. She can't imagine that Garfield Rice was into rewilding. The garden of his Hampstead home seemed to be full of concrete and strange statues.

A message flashes up on Harbinder's computer. It's from the data team. She scans through it while Sonoma tells her about reintroducing beavers to Cornwall.

'Mrs Davies,' she says. 'Sonoma. Did you talk to Garfield Rice on the night of the reunion?'

'I told you,' says Sonoma. 'I wasn't there.'

'That wasn't what I asked.'

A pause.

'I'm just looking at Garfield's phone records,' says Harbinder, 'and they show that, on the night of the twenty-first of September, the reunion night, he spoke to you for twenty minutes between eight-fifteen and eight-thirty-five.'

Anna must have heard Sonoma's voice on speakerphone, thinks Harbinder. Garfield, like half the nutters on the bus, had forgotten to switch this function off. There are no calls to Isabelle. Maybe Garfield, too, had a second phone for his extra-marital conversations.

'He did ring me,' says Sonoma at last. 'Just to ask why I wasn't at the reunion. Like I said, I had intended to be there.'

'Twenty minutes is a long time for that sort of call,' says Harbinder.

'Gary was a bit worried,' says Sonoma. 'He'd been thinking about David Moore, you know, the boy who died.'

There it is again. 'What was Gary worried about?' asks Harbinder.

'Maybe worried was the wrong word,' says Sonoma, too quickly. 'Something had occurred to him about it. You know Gary actually saw it happen. I often think that it might have had its effect. Even at Oxford, he seemed to throw himself into everything, partying, politics, almost as if he wanted to forget. But obviously something had resurfaced. The subconscious is a funny thing.'

Isn't it just, thinks Harbinder. 'Did you talk about Isabelle Istar?' she says.

'No,' says Sonoma. 'I don't think so.'

'Our witness thought they heard the name "Izzy".'

'Gary might have said that Izzy was at the reunion,' says Sonoma.

But Anna had heard the words, 'Think what it would mean for all of us. Izzy. Everyone.' Harbinder would like to know the exact nature of the relationship between the actress, the headteacher and the politician, even if it does sound like the beginning of a joke.

'Did Gary tell you what had occurred to him about David Moore?' says Harbinder.

'No. Just that he was bothered by something.'

'And you didn't think this was worth mentioning yesterday?'

'I didn't want to bring it all up again. David's death was a terrible time for the school.'

And a worse one for his parents, thinks Harbinder. She brings the conversation to an end, partly because the chief forensics officer is standing in the doorway.

'Hi, Mac. Have you got something for me?'

His name isn't really Mac, it's James Macintosh, but the station nickname culture is getting to her.

'Something potentially interesting.'

She can tell by his tone that it's very interesting indeed.

'We found an empty syringe at the crime scene.'

'Where was it?'

'In a rubbish bin about forty metres outside the inner cordon.'

Going through the rubbish is an occupational crime-scene hazard, thinks Harbinder. Mac has sent the syringe for fingerprint analysis and, by the afternoon, they have the results back. There are finger-prints on the plastic casing and, luckily, they belong to someone already on the database.

Cassie Fitzherbert.

Chapter 16

Cassie

It felt very strange, knowing that a major investigation was going on but not being part of it. The team all had that absorbed, slightly self-important expression that I remembered from previous cases, not that I had ever been involved with anything as high profile as the murder of Garfield Rice MP. I saw the words 'Operation Wilson' on the whiteboard every time I walked past the incident room. There were names underneath: Henry Steep, Chris Foster, Isabelle Istar, Anna Vance. It seemed wrong not to see my name there and, for a second, I felt the same stab of loneliness I experienced at school every time The Group met without me or talked about something I didn't understand.

Did I tell The Group about David to make them feel sorry for me, to make them like me more? I've often asked myself that question. I still remember the glow of happiness I felt when Gary said, 'I'd like to kill him.' Maybe I thought of that when I put my hand on the cracked leather of David's baseball jacket and pushed.

I still don't know why Gary was walking over the footbridge.

He was meant to be in the station, ready to march David over to the tracks and say, 'Now you're going to pay.' We had discussed the words one night in the Crow's Nest after drinking Anna's mum's home-made cider and ended up getting quite hysterical. 'It's your round, now you're going to pay', that sort of thing. 'David's notoriously stingy,' said Chris and it's true that, even when we went to the cinema together, David didn't offer to get my ticket. Is it terrible that I think of those evenings in Gary's teenage penthouse suite with real affection and nostalgia?

But Gary wasn't at the station. Henry was, as it turned out, but he too kept this from the authorities. Gary was the one who told the police that he'd seen David walking along the edge of the platform, stumble and fall. 'I called out to him,' he said, 'but I was too far away to help.' The police seem to have accepted his account completely. David's death was treated as misadventure from the start and no one even interviewed his friends. Now I think that was rather remiss. There were other students in the vicinity. At the very least the police should have considered a teenage prank gone wrong. I think it was Chris who swung it. Chris came forward and said that he'd seen David going down the steps to the station and assumed that he was going there to take drugs. 'I'm afraid lots of us do it,' he said. And I can imagine the look of slightly shamefaced candour that accompanied this confession. The police swallowed it like drugs mules and assumed that David had fallen onto the rails whilst under the influence of cocaine. They didn't examine his body for drugs. But, then, there wasn't much of it left.

I didn't see Henry when I emerged onto the platform with David. I know he was there because, minutes after it happened, he grabbed my arm and dragged me away. For weeks afterwards I worried that someone had seen me, some homeless person squatting in the derelict warehouse opposite, some passing carrier pigeon. Thank God they didn't have drones then. All summer I sat in my bedroom waiting for the knock on the door. My parents thought I was traumatised about David. They knew that we had been out on a couple of dates. 'You mustn't blame yourself,' Mum said, 'it wasn't your fault.'

Gary's name wasn't even mentioned in the papers. I think his father had something to do with that. 'An eyewitness saw the deceased standing on the edge of the platform, looking slightly unsteady. As the train approached, he toppled and fell.' Chris didn't get into trouble either. His parents were barristers and must have seen to it that he didn't face any repercussions. The only consequence was that counsellors visited Manor Park for a week-long 'drugs education' course although the older students, arguably the ones most likely to be involved, had already left. But the idea stuck. I think the police didn't pursue the matter for fear of upsetting David's family – or Gary's.

'Now you're going to pay.' I remember the push, the rush of air from the train and then, nothing. Sometimes, in dreams, I see David on his knees in front of me, begging for his life. And then – bang – he disappears. Sometimes I see the 'bang' like in cartoons, held out on the end of a stick. Crash, bang, you're dead. In a cartoon, he'd climb back up onto the platform squashed flat, amusingly 2-D.

But what really happened was that Henry pulled me into the dark of the smelly stairs. 'Go home,' he said. 'Go home now.' I ran all the way. I wasn't much of an athlete then but I'm sure I clocked a personal best time. I hoped the house would be empty, but Mum was in the kitchen.

'How was it?' she said. 'Traumatic?'

For a moment, I thought she knew. I imagined flinging myself into her arms and sobbing on her shoulder, 'I've just killed a man.' But, of course, she was talking about the exam.

'It was OK,' I said. 'The Milton question was hard.'

'No light but rather darkness visible.'

'I don't know why they put those gloomy old authors on the list,' said Mum who, as an ex-nurse, prided herself on being 'practical not intellectual'. 'Shall I make you a nice cup of tea?'

What would have happened if I'd told her? She would have been shocked, would have called Dad, cried a lot. But I'm pretty sure she would have insisted that we go to the police. I might have got off with manslaughter. Dad would have paid for a good lawyer. Chris's mum, perhaps, who specialised in under-age offenders. But, from that day onwards, I would have been a murderer. Instead, I refused the tea and went upstairs to my bedroom. Later, we had supper and watched *EastEnders*. When Izzy rang to tell me the news, I was able to say, 'Oh my God!' so convincingly that both my parents looked up from the television in concern.

Chapter 17

Anna

Monday

I felt oddly unsettled after the police officers left. They had been friendly enough. I thought that DI Kaur looked at Mum with real compassion though she was sensible enough not to ask about her or her condition. She's an impressive woman, Cassie's boss. All I knew about her was that she was younger than Cassie – and therefore younger than me – and her slight build and enviably unlined skin certainly gave her a youthful appearance. But her eyes, which were brown with darker shadows underneath, were shrewd and watchful. The other officer, Kim, was older, with dyed red hair and a husky, London-accented voice. Kim was the friendly one, commenting on the view and the fact that the lift was still working. DI Kaur just watched. She looked around my room, a car crash of my previous and present lives, as if making an inventory. What would she have seen? The desk, with its view over the rooftops, where I had done my homework, now housing Mum's sewing machine and a cage belonging to a long-dead canary. The marks on the walls where my posters had been: Leonardo DiCaprio and Claire Danes in *Romeo and Juliet*, a reproduction of *Tropical Storm with a Tiger*, the album cover of Oasis's 'Don't Look Back in Anger'. The bed with its flowery duvet from the Laura Ashley sale (I had been so proud of this, the only vaguely expensive thing in the room). The embarrassingly druggy sticker on the wardrobe.

I told the police about overhearing Sonoma's voice but not about Cassie's strange behaviour, when she had talked about us killing David. DI Kaur did ask about David though. She did it as an afterthought, like Columbo. I'd watched the programme with Mum quite recently. At the door, he would say, 'Just one more thing . . .' but that was always the most important bit. Did DI Kaur think that David was somehow important to this case?

After they had left (Kaur taking the stairs and Kim the lift), I went into the sitting room. Mum was asleep in front of *Bargain Hunt*. She was so still that I thought, for one heart-stopping minute, that she was dead. But I touched her hand, bruised from many cannulas and still boasting a swab of cotton wool attached by a plaster, and it twitched. Her skin felt paper thin. I thought, as I had done many times since arriving, about what would happen when I went back to Italy. Mum had already booked herself into a hospice, which she described like someone full of excitement about their upcoming holiday ('spa treatments, plunge pool, view of the lake'). But I knew that, when I left, there was a real chance that I would never see her again. How could I return to Italy, knowing that? But how could I stay? I had a job and an apartment in Florence and, besides, Mum had already said, 'I don't want you and Sophie hanging around waiting for me to die. You've got your own lives to live.'

My phone was on silent, but the vibration made me jump. Unknown number. Was it the police again?

I went into the hall so as not to disturb Mum. 'Hallo?'

'Anna? This is Chris.'

I felt so many different emotions that it was hard to speak. In the end, I settled on grumpiness, 'How did you get my number?'

'Cassie gave it to me.'

Of course. Cassie, the keeper of the records.

'Anna, can I see you?'

Why? I wanted to say. But instead I said, 'When?'

'Now? I could send a car over.'

'Of *course* you could.'

'Well, what's the use of being ridiculously rich if you can't give your friends lifts?'

He'd said something like that when his chauffeur brought me home after the reunion. He obviously thought he was being charmingly honest. I just thought he sounded like a bit of a dick.

'I can't come now,' I said. 'I've got things to do.' *Bargain Hunt* wouldn't watch itself, after all.

'Later then?'

'I don't want to leave Mum.'

But I'd forgotten about her bat-like hearing and ability to move from fast-asleep to wide-awake in seconds.

'Don't mind me,' she shouted. 'Anita is coming in ten minutes. And Roxy will be in later.'

Anita was her Macmillan nurse and Roxy her carer. Both much loved.

'And Sophie will be round after work.'

My younger sister is an accountant, married to an accountant, with two children. Despite this, I still like her.

'Give your mum my love,' said Chris.

I pretended not to hear. 'Haven't you got some showbiz thing to go to?' I said. Then thought: who says *showbiz*?

'Not tonight,' said Chris. 'Can you come around later? I'll cook for you.'

'Don't you have a chef?'

'No, I like cooking.'

The prospect of a meal cooked by Chris was too much. I graciously agreed that the car could collect me at eight.

Sophie was irritatingly excited.

'I can't believe you're going out on a date with Chris Foster.'

'It's not a date,' I said. 'We're probably just going to talk about what happened at the reunion.'

'I always liked Chris,' said Sophie. 'I remember when he used to come here all the time. You know that when he did that concert at the O2 I emailed him and he sent me tickets?'

I did know. I was horrified when Soph told me. What was the point of severing all ties when my sister emailed asking for a freebie? I was also jealous.

'You'll have to dress up,' said Sophie. 'Put on something pretty.'

'There's some of my old warpaint in the bathroom,' said Mum. One of Mum's many jobs was as a model in the seventies. Sophie and I used to laugh hysterically at the photographs: flares, stripy jumpers, heavy fringe, Cleopatra eyes. But now I can see that she was gorgeous. That was where she met our dad, Tony, a photographer. He moved out when Sophie was two and I don't really remember living with him, though I used to pretend I did to annoy her. We're in touch now, in a distant kind of way. He lives in Somerset with his wife, Anne-Marie, and has a second family.

'Wear a skirt for a change,' said Sophie.

After that, I had to stay in my jeans and old jumper. But I did surreptitiously apply some mascara and arrange my hair to hide the grey as much as possible.

'Give Chris my love,' said Mum, as I made for the door. I didn't want to keep the driver waiting although it was apparently his life's purpose to serve Chris.

'He sent you his,' I said.

'Give him mine too,' squeaked Sophie.

I didn't answer that one.

Chris had told me that he had a flat in Clerkenwell and a house on the south coast. I knew, from my intensive internet stalking, that his ex-partner, Siobhan, and children, Connor and Harriet, lived in Lewes. I wondered, as the car left the Attlee Estate behind it and purred through leafier streets, just how 'ridiculously rich' Chris was. The Cubes were now the sort of band who filled the O2 arena and 'She Doesn't Know She's Beautiful' had been followed by several other number ones.

The flat confirmed my worst fears. It was a penthouse, no less, with vast windows that showed the lights of London spread out like Christmas decorations.

The first thing Chris said was, 'We're wearing the same shoes.'

We were too. White Stan Smiths.

'Do you remember when we used to do that at school?' said Chris. 'Accidentally turn up wearing T-shirts the same colour?'

Of course I did. Gary called us 'the terrible twins'.

'If you're going to start the *do you remember?* stuff,' I said, 'I'm leaving.'

'I promise I won't.' Chris pulled me deeper into the flat. It was so artfully lit that I could hardly see where I was going. Were those actual candles burning on the coffee table? Vanilla and jasmine mingled with a delicious smell of cooking.

'I didn't know men bought scented candles,' I said.

'You have to watch these sexist attitudes,' said Chris, steering me towards a low sofa. 'Drink?'

He made us both huge g and t's with ice and lemon and little sprigs of rosemary. I nearly asked whether he had a mixologist in the other room but it was so nice to be drinking delicious alcohol in this scented eyrie that I allowed myself to relax. We talked about Italy and Clerkenwell and whether gin tasted better in balloon glasses. I'd almost allowed myself to forget the morning's visit, even the events of the reunion, Gary's death and the strange conversation with Cassie. It was a shock when Chris said, 'The police were here this afternoon.'

'They came to see me too,' I said. 'This morning.' Was I first on DI Kaur's list? The thought was an alarming one.

'What did you make of them?' he asked. 'Harbinder and Kim.'

'Are you on first name terms?' I said. 'She was DI Kaur to me.' But Kim was Kim, I realised.

'She asked me about David,' said Chris. 'Did she ask you?'

'Yes, just as she was leaving. I thought it was a tactic.'

'What did you say?'

'Just that it was a terrible shock to us all. I suppose they asked because of the link with Gary. Because he saw it happen.'

'I suppose so,' said Chris.

'It's weird,' I said. 'Cassie mentioned it too. At the reunion. After it . . . after it happened . . . and we were all filing out, she pulled me into an empty classroom and said, "What if they find out that we killed David."'

'What did you say?'

'That it was an accident.' I looked up and saw Chris looking at me very intently. The candles made it look as if we were in church. I took a gulp of my drink. 'Gary saw him fall on the line. It was an accident.'

'But we did talk about killing him,' said Chris. 'Don't you remember?'

Chapter 18

Anna

What I chiefly remember about the day David died is this: it was the day Chris finished with me.

Chris and I were always meant to be together. Everyone said so and, for once, everyone was right. We didn't really know each other until sixth form. It was a big school and we were in different classes. I was aware of him as he changed from gawky schoolboy to blonde pin-up. I remember him playing the guitar in assembly, his hair falling over his face as he mastered the chords but, along with everyone else, I was too busy mocking the terrible lyrics the RE teacher had projected onto the walls. 'Like a bridge over troubled waters I will be your pal.' Secular schools always have trouble with that sort of stuff. I imagine it's easier at a convent where you just pray to God to make you a better person. And the music is better.

In sixth form we had two classes together. I was doing English, French and Italian. Chris was taking English, French and Art. It was clear that he was one of the best in the class at French. People whispered that his parents had a house in France and that their au pair did his homework. But Chris just enjoyed the language and, unlike the rest of us, didn't seem to mind if he got it wrong. He was always the first to volunteer in class, not in an insufferable 'I know the answer' way, but in a comradely attempt to get the party started. This made him very popular.

In English, Chris had a massive hate against A.E. Housman, one of our set poets. When I told him about the spoof poem, 'What, still alive at twenty-two . . .' he started to write his own parodies and leave them in my locker. I still have some of them.

The cherry is where the bird has its nest. I love lasses but lads are best. I'm just a cheerful Shropshire bunny. Murder is nice and suicide funny.

Despite the guitar-playing in assembly, Chris was really known in school as an artist. His huge abstract canvases were always hung in the entry hall where prospective parents could see them. But he also did lightning sketches on the back of exercise books or photocopied handouts: Gary yawning, Izzy playing with her hair, Henry frowning at the *Telegraph*. They were brilliant likenesses. When I wrote a murder mystery for the school magazine (edited by Gary), Chris illustrated it with dark alleyways and sleuths in trench coats and trilby hats.

With our in-jokes and our matching clothes, I suppose Chris and I looked like a couple long before we were one. But it wasn't until a month before A levels that we finally got it together. School was over for students taking exams. We were meant to be studying at home, but The Group gravitated to Gary's house where we had the run of an attic we called the Crow's Nest. We'd lie on the floor with our books and with the best intentions of working but, before long, we were playing Snog, Marry, Avoid with Busta Rhymes blaring out of the CD player.

Sometimes we'd explore London. It was a beautiful late spring although the summer would later turn cold and rainy. It was as if we had the capital to ourselves, while less fortunate souls were at work or school. One day we went to Hyde Park. Gary had been reading *Three Men and a Boat* and wanted to go boating on the Serpentine. In the end, only Gary, Henry and Cassie ventured onto the water. Izzy and Sonoma wandered off to get drinks and Chris and I lay on the grass. I can still remember the smell of it and the sounds of a London summer, a rounders game, radios playing, the siren call of the ice cream van. I was lying propped up on one elbow, talking to Chris who was flat on his back. I can't remember what we were talking about, only that Chris's eyes suddenly opened, and it was as if he was seeing me for the first time. The moment seemed to last for ever until I leant forward and Chris raised himself up so that our lips met.

I'd kissed boys before, of course. I'd almost had sex with my Year 11 boyfriend, saved only by his mother coming home from the shops early. But this was different. It was a perfect, movie-star kiss. I wouldn't have been surprised to see hearts and flowers surrounding us, like a cartoon. Instead what we got was Izzy spraying a newly opened can of Coke over us and Gary, still wearing his life jacket, saying, 'And about time too.'

That was it. We walked home holding hands and, two days later, I lost my virginity to Chris in the spare room of his smart house in Chelsea, the only room that had a key. I honestly thought it was for ever. I cringe now when I remember writing 'Mrs Anna Foster' in my diary, practising what I thought would be my adult signature.

We were inseparable until, moments after our final English exam, Chris said, 'I think we should stop seeing each other.'

'I don't remember talking about killing him,' I said.

'You must remember. We were in the Crow's Nest. You said that David had tried it on with you and Cassie suddenly blurted out that David had raped her. We were all really shocked. Sonoma said she should tell the police. Gary said that the police never listened to women and we should kill him.'

I did remember saying that about David but not what prompted it. I had been looking out of the window, not thinking of anything much. I can still see the view over the rooftops, the satellite dishes that were starting to sprout up, the lights in all those converted attic bedrooms.

'He didn't "try it on with me",' I said, putting tetchy quotation marks around the words. 'He forced himself on me. I remember Izzy mocking me for saying that.'

'So you do remember the conversation?'

'It was a joke,' I said, feeling a panicky sensation like the one I got whenever I entered the lift at Attlee Towers. 'Nobody took it seriously. We were treating it like a game, like one of those murder mysteries I used to write. I think I said you could get poison from flowers. Digitalis.'

'It wasn't a joke,' said Chris. 'I honestly think Gary would have murdered him. I was the one who said we couldn't do that. I said we should just beat him up a bit.'

'*You* were going to beat him up?'

Chris looks slightly offended and flexes an arm that looks more muscle-toned than it did when it used to wrap itself round me.

'I wanted to defuse things,' he said. 'Gary was scaring me. He could be so intense. And Cassie was really upset. Understandably, of course. Gary said that we should scare David. Scare him to death, was what he said. That's when we decided on the Imperial plan. Cassie would lure David there and Gary would pretend to push him onto the tracks.'

'I don't remember that,' I said.

'You might not have been there for all the conversations,' said Chris. 'But I knew something bad was going to happen that day. That's why I . . . why I didn't want you there.'

'Is that why you finished with me?' I said. 'I've often wondered.' I tried to keep my voice light but I could hear twenty-one years of hurt in my tone.

'I'm sorry,' said Chris.

'Don't give it another thought,' I said. 'Shall we eat now? I'm starving.'

At the table, which was by the window with its view over the unreal city, we ate Thai green curry, drank white wine, and talked about the day a group of sixth-formers planned to scare one of their classmates to death.

'Gary was going to tell him "now you're going to pay",' said Chris. 'It was all very melodramatic.'

'Why don't I remember any of this?' I said, less worried, perhaps, than I should have been. This was probably down to the alcohol. I'd rather got out of the way of drinking in recent years. Italians rarely fill up your glass if you're a woman.

'You weren't there for a lot of the discussions,' said Chris.

'Where was I?'

'Probably at work.'

That figured. I was the only one of the group without rich parents and, consequently, I had a job at the local Co-op. I worked there two evenings a week and all day Saturday.

'What actually happened that day?' I said.

Chris refilled our glasses and took a deep swig before replying. 'I got there first,' he said. 'After we . . . after you and I talked . . . I went straight to the station. That was the plan. That I'd be at the exit to stop David escaping. Although, what with me being such a wimp, I don't know what I could have done about it.'

'Stop sulking,' I said, 'and get on with the story.' Because it did seem like a story at that point.

'Cassie and David arrived together. David didn't notice me – he only had eyes for Cassie – but I think she did. They went down the steps and I heard them talking. David was laughing, I remember that. Then the train went past – it was like an explosion – and I heard this terrible scream. Jesus. I've never heard anything like it. I found out later that it was Gary, yelling from the bridge. I just couldn't believe that he could have made a sound like that. Anyway, seconds later, Cassie came running up the stairs with Henry.'

'Henry? What was he doing there?'

'The idea was that Henry and Gary would put David's crimes to him. Like a court. That was my idea. I was used to my parents talking about people breaking down when they were cross-examined or when they heard the jury's verdict. I thought David should know that he'd committed a crime.'

'Do you think he didn't know?'

'I think he must have known, at some level,' said Chris, 'but I'm not sure that he thought it was rape. Cassie said that he seemed quite surprised when she dumped him afterwards.'

I remembered David laughing as he pushed me against the pool table, the casual way he left me afterwards. I don't think either of us had a word for what happened.

'Henry and Gary were the eloquent ones,' said Chris. 'The debaters. They were going to tell David that he'd committed a serious crime, that he could go to prison, or juvenile detention, for years. Then Gary was going to say that, because of the well-known misogyny of the police, we'd decided to take matters into our own hands.'

'Jesus.'

'I really do think that David would have been terrified,' said Chris. 'But Gary wasn't there. For some reason he was late and only just crossing the footbridge. And he saw it happen.'

'What did happen?' I said. 'I only know what I read in the papers. I'm not sure that I even took it in at the time.' Because I was so upset about you, I added in my head.

'Gary said that David stumbled and fell,' said Chris. 'He always stuck to that story and I always believed him. Henry said the same. But, on the day, Henry was mainly worried about getting Cassie out of there.'

'Why?'

'He said afterwards that, if the police interviewed Cassie, they'd find out about the rape. She didn't want that. Plus, it would have given her a motive. That's why I told them that David had been on his own when I saw him arrive.'

'You lied,' I said.

Chris was silent for a moment, the candlelight playing on his face.

'Yes, I did,' he said. 'It seemed the right thing to do at the time.

That was the narrative. Exams were over. David went to Imperial to take drugs. He fell under a train. Tragic accident. Case closed.'

'Cassie was inconsolable all summer,' I said. 'She just sat in her room. Wouldn't even go to the park with me. Her parents were really worried.'

'I think she blamed herself for not saving him,' said Chris. 'Perhaps for telling us about the rape and setting the whole thing in motion. I remember her coming out of the station with Henry. She looked wild. Like a stranger. Henry told her to go home and she just ran without looking back. She didn't go inter-railing with us after A levels. It was as if she was punishing herself.'

'Unless,' I said. 'Unless she did push him.'

'If she did,' said Chris. 'Only one person knows for sure. And he's dead.'

But Henry was there too, I thought. I would give my old friend a call tomorrow.

Chapter 19

Anna

Tuesday

I rang Henry the next day and he invited me for tea 'at the house'. It was a few seconds before I realised that he meant the Houses of Parliament. It struck me as an endearingly immodest choice of meeting place. I was surprised, and rather pleased, that Henry would want to show off to me. I accepted, partly because I knew my friend Simonetta would be impressed. Since Brexit, British politics have become a popular spectator sport in Italy. You can't get in a cab without the driver doing an impression of the Speaker saying 'Order, Order'.

Mum was impressed too. She was very tired that morning, partly because I'd woken her up getting in at two a.m., so I brought her breakfast in bed. I knew she wouldn't eat much but I took care to make it look nice, flowers on the tray, paper towel folded like a napkin, the G2 bit of the *Guardian*. Mum always did this. We didn't have much money growing up – I know I'm a touch repetitive on this point – but, on our birthdays, she'd make laurel wreath crowns with branches nicked from the park and deck the room with fairy lights. We'd have breakfast in bed with flowers and the latest comic. I hoped she'd remember that now, but she just smiled faintly and made space on her bed.

She sipped some orange juice but didn't touch the toast although I'd cut it into triangles specially. She perked up a bit, though, when I told her about Henry.

'I'm so glad you're seeing all your old schoolfriends. Fancy Henry becoming an MP. Gary too. Poor thing.'

Mum was almost the only person who remembered to add the sorrowful sub-clause. And even she seemed to put Gary's death aside when she asked, with an expression on her thin face that was so transparent it was almost heartbreaking, 'How was Chris last night?'

'Fine,' I said. 'He cooked me a delicious curry and we talked about the old days.'

'You didn't stay the night then?'

'Mum!' I said, aiming for jocularity. 'Are you asking if I slept with him?'

'Yes,' said Mum.

She was always annoyingly straightforward about sex. I used to wish she was like other parents who assumed their teenage children didn't have sex lives. Izzy's parents even let Gary sleep in her bedroom because they were 'just friends'.

'Well, I didn't,' I said. 'It was good to see him again though.'

'I always liked Chris.'

'I know you did. He liked you too.' I hadn't told Chris about Mum's illness. I thought his sympathy would be the thing that finished me off completely.

'I like his songs too. "She Doesn't Know She's Beautiful" always reminds me of you.'

'He said it was about me,' I couldn't resist telling her. 'But I said I did know I was beautiful.'

'That's my girl,' said Mum.

But I would never be as beautiful as her.

I arranged to meet Henry the next day, but I actually had another encounter with an old schoolfriend that afternoon. I was in the chemist's looking for Bonjela for Mum's ulcers when a figure wearing sunglasses and swathed in a stripy scarf pushed past me to collect a prescription. I'd recognised the hair and even the perfume before I heard her identify herself as 'Mrs West'.

'Izzy?'

'Anna! What are you doing here?'

'I'm staying with Mum. She just lives around the corner.'

'Oh yes,' said Izzy vaguely. Unlike Chris, Cassie and Henry, she had never visited Attlee Towers. I knew that Izzy's parents had lived in a smart part of Chelsea and it didn't surprise me that she had drifted back to the same area. She didn't ask what I was buying, and I didn't enquire about her prescription. We walked a few hundred yards to where a Porsche was parked at an entitled angle.

'Wasn't it awful about Gary?' I said. I remembered that Izzy and Gary had always been close, but I didn't expect her eyes to fill with tears.

'Awful,' she said. 'I don't know how I'll cope. I've just been collecting some sleeping pills.' She rattled the chemist's bag at me.

'Terrible for his wife and children,' I said.

Izzy waved a hand as if dismissing Italian Paula and her progeny. 'Did the police come to see you?' she asked.

'Yes,' I said. 'They asked about David's death.'

'What did you tell them?' Izzy grasped my arm, rather painfully.

'Nothing,' I said. 'I wasn't there.'

'Nor was I,' said Izzy quickly. 'But Gary was and . . . oh, Anna . . . I've got an awful feeling that was why he was killed.'

'What do you mean?' I said. I thought of Chris saying: 'Only one person knows for sure. And he's dead.'

'I can't talk here,' said Izzy, taking a look along the parade of shops, almost empty at three o'clock in the afternoon. 'Come over later. About six. Oliver will be out then.'

I did wonder why that was so important.

I expected Izzy to live somewhere grand and I was right. It was in one of those millionaires' rows where the houses seem to be made of icing sugar, white with identical crenellations and porticos, demonstrating their individuality only by the colour of their front doors. Izzy's was emerald green.

What I hadn't expected was that she'd have her daughter with her. Or that the daughter would be so much of a *person*. Izzy introduced the girl as Annie. She was about seven, I suppose, with long dark hair in plaits. Izzy's eyes are meltingly brown but her daughter's are bright blue. This was from Oliver West, whose azure gaze was meant to drive middle-aged women to madness.

'We're making brownies,' Annie informed me.

'Only from a packet,' said Izzy with a shrug. 'It's Maria's day off.'

I had no idea who Maria was but it was fascinating to watch Izzy moving about her beautiful kitchen. It was bigger than Mum's entire flat with one of those island things and doors leading out into the garden. Izzy and Annie spooned the mixture into a baking tray and argued about who got to lick the spoon. Then Izzy approached a matt-black oven, pressed a hidden button and illuminated the interior. It was a like a *son et lumière* display.

'I'll set the timer,' Izzy told Annie. 'You can watch TV in the snug if you like.'

This was obviously a treat because Annie skipped off, plaits bouncing. As soon as she had gone Izzy headed for the giant Smeg fridge.

'Wine?'

'Yes, please.' I had a feeling I would need it. I remembered drinking gin and tonic in Chris's palatial apartment. Alcohol certainly seemed to take the edge off social inequality.

Izzy poured us both huge glasses and sat at the other side of the gleaming marble island.

'It's good to see you again, Anna. We didn't get much time to talk at the reunion.'

'Well, it was rather eventful,' I said. I remembered how pleased I'd been to see Izzy that night and, to my slight surprise, those feelings came rushing back.

Izzy's eyes filled with tears. 'It was awful. I still can't believe that Gary's gone. I have to stop myself crying in front of Oliver. I've had a continual headache since Saturday.'

I didn't ask why she couldn't cry in front of her husband, but she told me anyway. How she and Gary had got talking on a Facebook group (another good reason not to have a smartphone) and had 'fallen back in love'. 'There's nothing like first love,' she said. 'I don't have to tell you that.'

'What do you mean?'

'Well, you and Chris. We were the lovebirds of The Group, weren't we? Me and Gary, you and Chris.'

'I haven't seen Chris for twenty-one years,' I said. 'Until last Saturday.'

'Oh, I sometimes see him at events,' said Izzy carelessly. 'And I always think he looks a bit sad beneath it all. You know "She Doesn't Know She's Beautiful" always reminds me of you.'

Why did everyone keep saying this? It wasn't that much of a compliment, when you came to think of it. The song contains the words, 'I'm the only one who sees your imperfect perfection.' Well, thanks very much, Kris Foster.

'Was it serious, then,' I asked, 'you and Gary?' I tried to remember if I'd seen them together at the reunion, but my only memory was an aural one, Izzy wailing when the police announced Gary's death. Then I remembered Henry going over to comfort her.

'It became serious very quickly,' said Izzy. 'We were always meant to be together. It was just that we found each other too early and, when Gary went to Oxford and I went to RADA, it was too hard to keep the relationship going. But, deep down, I think we always loved each other. Gary married Paula right after I married Oliver, you know. He said he cried when he found out. He met Paula on a work trip to Italy.'

'Surprised he went on any work trips in Europe,' I said. Gary was, of course, a passionate Brexiteer.

'Oh, he's always been a Europhile,' said Izzy. 'Deep down.' It struck me that a lot of things, with Gary, were happening 'deep down'. 'I felt so guilty about Ollie,' she added. 'And, especially,

Annie. I love her so much. I didn't want her to come from a broken home. It's so damaging for children.'

'I was from a broken home,' I said. 'And I survived.'

'But you're so strong, Anna.' Izzy gave me one of those brimming looks again. 'I didn't want to break up my marriage, but I had to be with Gary. We were going to tell our partners after the reunion.'

After the reunion. The time when all would be revealed.

'You said earlier that you knew why Gary was killed.' The wine was making me brave. I couldn't quite believe that I'd said the words out loud.

Izzy looks quite shocked. 'Did I say that? I suppose I must have done.' She slopped more wine into our glasses. I was going to have to get a cab back to Mum's.

'Gary rang me,' Izzy continued. 'He'd been to a rugby club reunion. He rang me at midnight, rather the worse for wear, saying that David was murdered and he knew who'd done it. A few days later, Gary's dead. There has to be a link, don't you think?'

'The police asked me about David's death,' I said. I thought of Chris saying: 'We did talk about killing him. Don't you remember?'

'I spoke to DI Kaur this morning,' said Izzy. 'I thought the police should know.'

'You told DI Kaur what Gary said to you? About knowing who killed David?'

'Yes,' said Izzy, slightly impatiently. 'It meant telling them about me and Gary, which I didn't really want to do. DI Kaur seems like the judgemental type. But it was obviously important. And I want them to find Gary's killer.'

It struck me that this was the first time anyone had said this aloud. And I wondered if I really *did* want them to find Gary's killer.

'Who do you think Gary was referring to?' I said. 'When he said that he knew who'd killed David.'

'I don't know,' said Izzy. 'But I keep thinking about Cassie. She was there that day and she had a motive. Remember what David did to her?'

'He tried to do it to me too,' I said. 'And you. As I remember.'

'Oh, that was nothing,' said Izzy, with a flick of hair. 'David tried to kiss me at a party once and I kneed him in the balls. He didn't try again.'

I wondered if the encounter had really been so straightforward, so 'girl power', in the phrase we used, unironically, in the nineties. I had a memory of it sounding much more serious. But then, my memory was hardly to be trusted.

'Cassie said something to me after the reunion,' I said. 'She talked about when "we" – plural – killed David.'

'We?' says Izzy. 'I wasn't even there. Nor were you.'

'No. But we talked about it, didn't we? Killing him? That's what Chris said. I think I had managed to block a lot of it out. Or I wasn't there.'

'You might have been at your shop job,' said Izzy, which was probably how the others referred to it too. 'But I certainly don't remember planning to kill David. Not seriously. I mean, he wasn't very nice but we would never have murdered him. Think how obsessed Gary was with going to Oxford and becoming a politician. He would never have jeopardised that.'

'David was more than not nice,' I said. 'He was a rapist.'

'Do you think he really was?' said Izzy, examining her fingernails. Once again, I remembered Izzy in the Crow's Nest. 'This isn't a Jilly Cooper novel.'

'Yes, I do,' I said. 'I believed Cassie at the time. And I think he would have raped me too if we hadn't been interrupted. He was a predator.'

'Wow,' said Izzy. 'You sound as if you think we *should* have murdered him.'

'As I understand it,' I said, trying to keep my temper, 'the plan was to make David realise what he'd done and then to scare him. Gary was going to pretend to push him on the tracks. Except Gary didn't turn up on time.'

'I think that may have been my fault,' said Izzy, with slightly too casual a hair toss.

'What do you mean?'

'Well, it was our last exam. I was in a good mood. Gary and I went for a snog by the bins.'

'A snog by the bins.' I couldn't decide if this was the funniest line I had ever heard or the most tragic. Isabelle Istar, star of stage and screen, groping Garfield Rice in the noisome nook by the recycling. Not far, I realised, from the loos where Gary had breathed his last.

'We'd never, you know, have gone the whole way,' said Izzy. 'Well, we nearly did that day.'

'By the bins?'

'I know.' Izzy gave a giggle that suddenly made me like her again. 'I think that's what made me stop. Imagine telling people that's where you lost your virginity. Anyway, that was why Gary was late to the station. He wasn't going to miss the chance of a quickie. You know Gary.'

'I'm beginning to realise I didn't.'

'Well, you had Chris. Cassie was the one who still liked Gary.'

'Really?'

'Yes,' said Izzy, laughing rather harshly. 'She was still in love with him. She had sex with him at one new year party. Gary confessed it to me. He said she did all the running.'

'And you believed that?'

More hair flicking. 'Not entirely. I think Gary was frustrated because I wouldn't sleep with him. But I do think Cassie was in love with him. I told the police that.'

'You told them a lot,' I said. I was beginning to feel rather dizzy, unsure of my ground. It was partly the wine, partly the glamour of the house, with its shiny surfaces and flashing lights, and partly Izzy herself. I had forgotten how dazzling she could be, how she could change moods in the middle of a sentence, how she could make you believe in whichever part she was playing.

'I want them to find his murderer,' said Izzy. 'Before they kill again.'

This sounded so melodramatic that I almost laughed. But then the timer went off and Annie rushed back in to try the brownies. I had one too. They weren't very nice – they had a strange oily texture – but I enjoyed seeing Izzy and her daughter together. Izzy might delegate a lot to the absent Maria but it was clear that she was a devoted mother. On the way out, I asked if Annie had been named after me.

'Her real name's Anna, isn't it?'

'Oh yes. But it's not after you. I played Anna Magnani in a biopic once.'

Chapter 20

Anna

Wednesday

I enjoyed the trip to the House of Commons. I caught the bus to Parliament Square and walked across the grass, past the statues of prime minsters and genuine heroes like Mandela and Gandhi. I made a special detour to see Millicent Garrett Fawcett, whose statue had been added last year. Even the Italian papers had covered it. *Suffragetta onorata*. Millicent stood, looking rather long-suffering, holding up a banner with the words, 'Courage calls to courage everywhere'. I felt slightly guilty to find myself thinking that it looked a bit like a tea-towel. I must have been doing too much housework at Mum's. 'Thanks for the right to vote, Milli,' I said, aloud. I'd voted in every general election since 2000, mostly by postal ballot. I'd always voted Labour too, something I planned to mention to Henry.

Henry met me outside the vast oak doors. He kissed me on both cheeks, the only English person I know who manages this with Italian aplomb. We whisked through airport-like security and a half-finished bottle of mineral water was confiscated from my bag. Inside the building there was a general impression of vaulted ceilings, panelling and echoing stone floors. Architecture guaranteed to make you feel small. It was rather like a church, graven images everywhere, hands outstretched. In Italy, they would be saints with offerings left at their feet, like St Antonino in Sorrento where silver plaster casts of body parts are placed before the saint who had, supposedly, cured them.

We walked up a red-carpeted staircase and I have to admit to a slight thrill when Henry pushed open double doors marked 'Closed to Visitors'. The terrace restaurant was very full. I wondered if all the tables were full of MPs showing off to their old schoolfriends. Henry nodded to a couple of people and once exchanged a mock-serious half-hug that reminded me of Gary and Pete at the reunion. Henry and Gary had embraced that day too, just before Henry said, 'I still hate him.'

'Happy to sit outside?' said Henry.

It was a beautiful September day, so I said yes. The view was spectacular: the river, the skyscrapers, the domes and towers of the city. I thought of *The Tempest*.

> *The cloud-capped towers, the gorgeous palaces,*
> *The solemn temples, the great globe itself,*
> *Yea, all which it inherit, shall dissolve;*
> *And, like this insubstantial pageant faded,*
> *Leave not a rack behind . . .*

I thought of Chris's apartment and of the Crow's Nest. Being so high engenders feelings of superiority, which I suppose is why plutocrats live in penthouses. But, then again, you could see the same view from Attlee Towers. A waiter approached and we both asked for tea.

'Any cakes?' The man was twinkling at me with practised charm. 'Scones with clotted cream?'

'No, thank you.'

Even with no food, our table seemed full of paraphernalia: tea strainers, sugar tongs, jugs of milk. The cups had the House of Commons portcullis on them.

'Did you ever meet Gary here?' I said.

'No,' said Henry. 'We were on different sides. Gary wasn't just a Tory; he was involved with some seriously unpleasant people. Climate-change deniers. Corrupt businessmen.'

'Didn't Machiavelli say keep your friends close and your enemies closer?'

'I think you'll find that was Michael Corleone in *The Godfather*.' Henry was smiling. He loved old films, I remembered.

'You and Gary were friends at school,' I said. 'And you were both socialists then.'

'We were all socialists at school,' said Henry. 'That was the nineties for you. But I never liked Gary, even then. He thought he could manipulate us all. Maybe that's why I started reading Machiavelli. To get the measure of him.'

'What do you mean "manipulate us"?'

'Remember how he called us the elite? That was seriously messed up. We were nothing special, but he made us think we were.'

'"The beautiful and the damned" Sonoma used to say.' I have since read the F. Scott Fitzgerald book of this name. I found it extremely depressing. Rich people making each other unhappy.

'Gary knew how to get around Sonoma too. He was always telling me that he and I were the brains of the group. I know for a fact he said that to Sonoma as well.'

'He didn't say it to me.'

'No, because he was in awe of you. We all were. You were so cool.'

'Me?' I said, in genuine amazement. Of all the things I had thought about my teenage self, cool wasn't one of them. I never had fashionable clothes, like Izzy. I wasn't blonde and petite like Cassie. My hair was too curly and my nose was too big. I wore dungarees before they were cute. Ditto a butcher-boy cap. I carried my books in Mum's old satchel and not in a Hollister bag.

'So cool,' said Henry. 'You just didn't care. You dressed differently. You read different books. You even liked different music, you and Chris.'

It was true that Chris and I had different musical tastes from the rest of The Group. We used to go to gigs in deserted warehouses and support bands with names like The Sick Babies.

'I wish I'd known I was cool at the time,' I said, with a laugh that sounded unconvincing even to me.

'Of course you were cool,' said Henry. 'You went out with Chris, didn't you?'

This was said in a different tone, almost accusatory.

'For a few weeks,' I said.

'He's still got a thing for you,' said Henry. 'I saw that at the reunion.'

I thought of Izzy saying: 'We were the lovebirds of The Group, weren't we? Me and Gary, you and Chris.' I said, 'I saw Izzy yesterday.'

'Did you? I've been meaning to get in touch with her. She was so upset that night.'

'Did you know that she and Gary were seeing each other again?'

'I guessed. At the reunion I saw her sneaking out and I thought it looked like an assignation. Then, when she broke down like that . . .'

'Izzy said something very strange to me.' I told Henry about Gary's message to Izzy, saying he knew who had killed David. It felt very odd to be having this conversation in this place but, on the other hand, there was a sort of anonymity about it: the tables full of excited constituents, the bustling waiters, the attention-stealing view.

'Izzy even told the police about it,' I said. 'Have the police been to see you?'

'Yes. A good-looking DS called Jake and a Sloane called Tory.'

'Did they ask you about David?'

'Yes.'

'What did you say?'

Henry viewed me almost with amusement. 'I told them it was an awful accident. David slipped and fell on the tracks.'

'Is that what really happened?'

Henry actually laughed out loud. A group of women, who looked as if they were on a guided tour, glanced over curiously. 'No, of course not. Cassie killed him.'

'What do you mean?' I said.

Henry just leant back with a half-smile on his face. He didn't even seem to care that the terrace was full of MPs and gawping constituents.

'I was there,' said Henry. 'We'd all arranged to meet at the station. Gary and I were meant to confront David with his crimes. Then Gary was going to pretend to push him under a train.'

'That's what Chris said. But Gary wasn't at the station, was he?'

'No. I think he was too busy bonking Izzy.'

The word sounded wrong, too frivolous and *Carry On Matron*. What had Izzy called it? A snog by the bins. That wasn't much better.

'Izzy said something similar,' I said.

'Really? I've often wondered if she didn't hold him up deliberately, to stop him getting involved.' Like Chris supposedly had with me. The thought made me strangely happy.

'But you weren't really going to hurt him, were you?'

Henry shook his head. 'No. We just meant to scare him. That was the plan. But it was a dangerous combination. The end of exams, everyone a bit mad, Cassie wanting revenge, Gary in full messiah mode. We should never have been anywhere near a speeding train. A tragedy was always bound to happen. And it did.'

'I can't believe Cassie killed him deliberately. Maybe it was just a tussle. David lost his balance. A tragedy, like you said. Not a murder.'

'I was there,' repeated Henry, more soberly this time. 'And I saw her push him. He was laughing and he reached over to her – he always had a thing for her, well that's what all this was about – and she pushed him. He fell to his knees and then he just toppled into the track. The train came by. I'll never forget it. The speed, the sound, the smell of it. I pulled Cassie away. That was all that mattered then. Getting her away.'

'Why?' I said, slightly surprised that my voice was still working. 'Wouldn't it have been better to say that you'd both seen it happen? That it was an accident?'

'Cassie couldn't be there. It might have come out that she had a history with David. Even that he'd raped her. I believed her a hundred per cent about that. She couldn't be at the scene. I told her to run home and she did. Like the wind. Gary told the police that David had fallen from the platform. No one else in sight. Chris added that bit about drugs and the police just assumed that David was high. I was never even questioned. Nor was Cassie.'

'How has she hidden this all these years?'

'I've been doing a lot of reading about trauma,' said Henry, sounding every inch the conscientious public servant. 'Cassie could well have blanked the whole thing out. Of course, she should have gone to the police when David assaulted her but my guess is she wasn't even sure, at first, that it was an assault. Maybe she even blamed herself. That happens a lot. You know how Cassie was always sleeping with people because she felt sorry for them or wanted them to like her.'

'I didn't know that,' I said.

'It was quite well known amongst the male population of the school,' said Henry.

'Poor Cassie,' I said. At that moment I felt only pity for my old classmate. I should have been a better friend to her, I thought. We only really became intimate after Cassie told us all about David. After *that* conversation in the Crow's Nest, when I told The Group that David had tried to rape me.

'Poor David too,' said Henry. 'He didn't deserve to die.' He must have seen my face. 'He didn't. Maybe he didn't even quite realise what he'd done.'

'Oh, he knew all right,' I said, remembering the weight of David's body against mine, his strength, the pool table pressing into my back.

'I know,' said Henry. 'He wasn't a nice guy. But his parents didn't deserve to lose their son. He was an only child.'

I couldn't argue with that. 'Why don't I remember any of this?' I said, mindlessly fiddling with my embossed teaspoon. 'I suppose it was because I wasn't there. You know, sometimes I even wonder if I went to Manor Park at all.'

'But you were there, Anna,' said Henry. 'I saw you.'

'You were there'. It was all I could think about. All the way home on the Tube, climbing the stairs to the flat, preparing Mum's supper, listening to her talking to Roxy about *Strictly Come Dancing*. 'You were there'. Could that possibly be true?

Because the truth was that, for me, there are worrying blanks in the day David died. I remember sitting the exam. The questions about Shakespeare, Chaucer and Milton. The tricky one about Housman. I remember going up to Chris, grinning. 'I never want to read another book again.' And him saying, 'I think we should stop seeing each other.'

After that? Nothing. I must have gone home because I remember climbing the stairs. The lift was broken again. Mum was at work. She had a part-time job in Boots spraying perfume at people and offering them make-overs. Sophie was still at school. I was able to lie on my bed and cry. It felt like my life was over. Was it remotely possible that, in the intervening time, I had walked to the abandoned Tube station and watched a man die?

'I wasn't there,' I'd said to Henry, hearing my voice becoming high and panicky. People were looking over. What's Henry Steep saying to that poor woman?

'You were, Anna.' Henry was looking concerned. Or pretending

138

to look concerned. I remembered what a good actor he was at school. Proctor to Izzy's Abigail in *The Crucible*. Benedict to her Beatrice. 'I saw you. In the building opposite. I was looking directly at you.'

In those days, there was an empty warehouse overlooking Imperial. It was boarded up but, like the station, it was fairly easy to get inside. Students used it for drugs deals and homeless people slept there. I never went inside but Izzy, who loved a good ghost story, told me that it was haunted by a caretaker who fell into some unspecified mangling equipment. It's probably luxury flats now.

At least, I *thought* I'd never been inside.

'I saw you,' said Henry again.

'Why didn't you ever say this before?'

'We never talked about David. Remember, we said that we wouldn't. Gary said, "If you never talk about something, it never happened."'

I don't remember that either. It went some way to explaining Gary's attitude towards climate change though.

'Why are you saying all this now?' I'd asked him.

'Because Gary's dead,' said Henry.

'And you think it's linked to David's death?'

'Yes. Don't you? Isn't that why you're here?'

'I don't know why I'm here.' I'd stood up to go, dropping my bag and upending one of the Houses of Parliament cups.

'Don't go,' Henry had said. But he didn't do anything to prevent me.

That evening, Mum and I watched Michael Portillo travelling to a country we had never seen and would never see. In the 1997 general election, we had stayed up until the early hours to see Portillo lose his seat. Then, he had exemplified everything we hated about the government but now, as Mum said, 'He's even become rather attractive.' He'd become a snappier dresser too. As I watched Portillo's orange blazer moving through a street market, I thought about the day David died. The day of our last A level. The day Chris finished with me. It had been hot, sultry, the sky a strange yellowy blue. The teachers reminded us to drink water during the exam. Chasing Housman quotes round my head, I looked at the back of Chris's head and imagined myself touching his neck. Later, I remember thinking: I've lost the only man I will ever love. Ridiculous, I know, except that I have never met anyone I liked more.

'Have you heard from Chris today?' asked Mum. Her psychic powers were now no surprise to me.

'Just a couple of texts.'

'Are you going to see him again?'

'He's asked me to go to Brighton tomorrow.'

'Oh, I love Brighton,' said Mum. 'There's something very wicked about it.' She grinned and, despite her gaunt face, there was still a glint in her eye.

But I was still thinking about that day, twenty-one years ago.

Something very wicked.

Chapter 21

Cassie

It was easier at university. Because I applied through clearing, I'd never visited Sussex University, or even looked at the prospectus. I remember being vaguely surprised that the campus wasn't by the sea. Instead it was next to the motorway, a collection of low-lying buildings and landscaped grounds. Something about it seemed unreal, like a stage-set, the perspective always slightly wrong. This added to my sense of living in another realm, a ghost walking amongst the living. At night I'd dream about the murder and wake up thinking that David was still alive. Those moments were the worst, waking in my study bedroom with its exposed brick walls and fire regulations on the back of the door. I'd count the bricks to slow my breathing. I'd whisper to myself, 'This too shall pass', a favourite saying of my grandma's. Although I knew it wouldn't.

When I brought a boy back to the room at the end of Freshers' Week, I slept without nightmares. That was the answer, I thought. Never to be alone. As a result, I kissed a lot of frogs that first term.

In my second term, I met Freddie, who was studying history. By the second year, we were going steady and rented a flat in Hove with the regulation sea view. It was a staid existence for nineteen-year-olds: shopping at Waitrose on Saturday mornings, watching TV in the evenings. We commuted into lectures and rarely attended student events. When I went to the careers fair in my final year, the *trompe l'oeil* campus seemed like a foreign land. But that was the day I saw a pamphlet asking, 'Ever considered joining the police force?' There were three officers on the cover: two white women and a black man. They were all smiling cheerfully in their high-viz jackets. They seemed a world away from death, judgement, heaven and hell.

I'd thought about the police a lot over the last three years. Mostly about them coming to arrest me. 'You do not have to say anything but it may harm your defence if you do not mention when questioned something which you later rely on in court.' I kept thinking that I must have left something at the scene. A clue, which a Holmes-like detective would discover and ponder over until, years later, he would knock on my door and, by means of subtle questioning and superior intelligence, extract a confession. Wouldn't I be safer as a member of the jolly high-viz team, hidden in plain sight?

There were other, less histrionic, reasons. I'd become rather sporty in my university years, after years of feigning PMT in PE lessons. I used to run along the seafront every morning, from the peace statue to the pier and back again. I liked the idea of a physically active job. Freddie was going to teach but the thought terrified me. I thought I'd rather face Sherlock Holmes telling me that killers always make a fatal mistake than a class of eleven-year-olds. So I applied to the Sussex Police and, at the end of my two-year training programme, I met Pete at the gym.

'Hi,' he said. 'Didn't you used to go to Manor Park school?'

Pete was already home when I got back from work. After a long time working for a big tech company, he has recently set up on his own and I still can't get used to him being in the house so much. He has converted Sam's old room into an office and seems very happy in there, playing Planet Rock and emerging occasionally for crisp sandwiches. If I sometimes missed my sewing and watching Netflix room, I kept quiet about it.

'I'm home, love,' I shouted, although Kevin's yelping had probably given the game away. Kevin is named after Father Kevin McManus, the priest who received me into the Catholic church when Pete and I got married. It was Father Kevin himself who suggested it. I'd started to say that I'd name my first son after him but had stopped because . . . well . . . Kevin. Father K had laughed and said, in his lovely County Cork accent, 'Just name your first dog after me and I'll be happy.' Kevin arrived two years after Sam and, although I don't love him as much as Pete and the kids, it's a very near thing.

It was only three-thirty. Lucy would be getting the bus back from school. I looked on my 'Mummy Pig Calendar' (a supposedly jokey reference to Peppa Pig and decorated with pictures of a pink animal with a face like a hairdryer) and saw that Sam was at football. Poor Sam. He didn't really enjoy the game but it was part of our elaborately constructed timetable, ensuring that he never came home to an empty house. With Pete around more, possibly Sam could drop football, and tag rugby too, but, although he would never say so, Pete wants his son to enjoy the games he loves so much. The fact that Lucy is the star of the girls' football team doesn't seem to compensate.

Oh no. Peering at today's picture of Mummy Pig reading to Peppa, I saw the words: *Sasha and Rosie here.* Lucy was bringing friends home. I remember making the arrangement and feeling pleased about it. At the start of her second year at St Bede's, Lucy seemed to have settled into a nice, stable group of friends. I had been worried that the families would be too posh, too pressured, too busy racking up piano grades to befriend my clever but slightly unusual daughter. Unlike me at her age, Lucy never seemed to worry if she was carrying the right bag or wearing the right shoes. In this way, she reminded me slightly of Anna. My schooldays had been an agony of such tiny, but seemingly vital, details. But, also unlike me, Lucy seemed to have acquired a set of friends who liked her for herself.

It was Pete who wanted the children to go to Catholic schools. Despite my admiration for Father Kevin, religious indoctrination did not come high on my list of educational requirements. I only knew that I didn't want the kids to go to Manor Park. But, given that, our only choices were going private or fishing out the baptism certificates. And at least St Bede's was co-educational, unlike many London secondary schools, which meant that Sam could go there too. But it was a high-flying, competitive environment. When I thought of Sam entering through those gates (school motto: *Veritas*) my heart constricted in terror.

I was searching in the freezer for child-friendly food when Kevin gave the high-pitched bark he reserves for Pete. Kneeling on the floor I saw his feet first, giant furry slippers like sleeping animals.

'Hallo, love.' I stood up, though I still only came to Pete's chest. When you marry someone who is six foot four, it gives you delusions of petiteness. Bad for your neck though.

Pete kissed me. 'You're home early.'

I took a deep breath. 'I'm on leave,' I said.

'How come?' Pete turned to the calendar as if it would provide the answers. *Tuesday 24 September: Mummy Pig accused of murder.*

'It's a long story,' I said.

Chapter 22

Harbinder

Tuesday

Harbinder calls Cassie into her office. She asks Kim to join her and Cassie looks curiously at the two of them as she enters the glass-walled room.

'This isn't a formal interview,' says Harbinder. 'But a few things have come up.'

There's a conference table by the window. Cassie sits at the opposite end to her colleagues and fixes them with that disconcerting blue stare.

'We've had forensics back from the scene,' says Harbinder. 'And they found this.' She turns her laptop to show a photo of a syringe.

Cassie says nothing.

'Is it yours?' says Harbinder.

'I don't know,' says Cassie. 'I took a couple of syringes to the reunion. I told you yesterday.'

Cassie had told Harbinder that she took two insulin-loaded

syringes to the reunion in her clutch bag. She explained that syringes are single use only and she thought that the room might be hot which would speed up absorption of insulin.

'How long have you been diabetic?' asks Kim. 'Must make life difficult sometimes.'

'I've got Type One diabetes,' says Cassie. 'It's in my files. It came on while I was pregnant with Sam, my youngest.'

Harbinder knows that Cassie has two children. Lucy, who is twelve, and Sam, ten. She often complains about them in a way that fails to mask her adoration.

'Don't most people use a pen these days?' asks Kim.

'I tried a pen,' says Cassie, 'but I prefer a syringe.'

'This syringe was found in the grounds of Manor Park school,' says Harbinder. 'Your fingerprints are on it.'

'Where was it found?' asks Cassie. An odd question, Harbinder thinks.

'In one of the dustbins,' says Harbinder. 'Could it be yours?'

'I don't think so,' said Cassie. 'I checked my bag last night. The syringes were both still there.'

'Could there possibly have been a third syringe?'

'It's possible, I suppose,' said Cassie, still with that direct blue stare. 'I thought there were two but it's possible there were three.'

'Your fingerprints are on this,' says Harbinder.

Cassie's hyacinth eyes open even wider. 'I don't understand how that can be.'

'Could someone have taken a syringe from your bag?' asks Kim.

'Very easily,' says Cassie. 'I just left it on the chair when I was dancing.'

Harbinder remembers Cassie in the library with the tragic disco lights, her shoulders glittering through her black top. She can imagine Cassie boogying the night away. Although she obviously didn't dance round her handbag.

'I've got to ask you again,' says Harbinder. 'Have you any idea who could have killed Garfield Rice?'

Does Cassie relax slightly? 'I've been thinking and thinking,' she says, 'but I can't imagine that anyone – especially one of his friends – would do something like that.'

'You were close to Garfield at school, weren't you?' says Harbinder.

'Who told you that?'

'You did. You said that you went out together in Year Ten.'

'Oh yes.' Another exhalation of breath. 'But that was just childish stuff. He went out with Izzy later. That was much more serious.'

'Isabelle says that you were still in love with him,' says Harbinder.

'Izzy said that? It's rubbish. I've hardly seen him since school.'

Harbinder wonders how much to tell Cassie. The news that Isabelle and Garfield were having an affair might shock her into further revelations, but maybe that trump card could be saved for later.

'I'm putting you on paid leave, Cassie,' says Harbinder. Go home now. We'll be in touch soon.'

'Am I a suspect?' says Cassie, not moving.

'You're a person of interest because of the prints on the syringe,' says Harbinder, 'but I don't suspect you. Should I?'

'Of course not,' says Cassie, with what passes for a laugh.

'That's OK then,' says Harbinder.

'What do you think?' Harbinder asks Kim as the door shuts behind their colleague.

'She seemed a bit furtive,' says Kim, who is looking rather troubled. 'I just can't believe she had anything to do with Garfield Rice's death though.'

'Her prints are on the likely murder weapon.'

'But, if she left her bag on a chair, anyone could have picked it up.'

'That's true. I wonder how many of her friends knew that she was diabetic.'

'Do you really think one of them did it?' asks Kim.

'Garfield said that he knew who killed David. That must have been one of his old schoolfriends, surely? A week later Garfield himself was killed.'

'Do you think it was because of that? Because he knew something?'

Harbinder paces her office. She still can't stop herself thinking, Look at me with an office big enough to pace in.

'I think everything comes back to David's death. Remember what Anna overheard Garfield saying to Sonoma? "Think what it would mean for all of us. Izzy. Everyone". He could have been talking about what would happen if he went public with what he knew.'

'Think what it would mean to Izzy,' repeats Kim. She is leaning back in her chair watching Harbinder stride around. There's not enough room for two to pace and, besides, it's definitely a boss thing. 'But Isabelle wasn't even there when David died.'

'There are a lot of people who weren't there,' says Harbinder, coming to a halt by the window. Sadly, the view does not compare to the glittering skyscrapers of Chris Foster's penthouse. It shows a brick wall and part of the car park.

'Garfield just happened to be passing,' Harbinder goes on. 'Chris

Foster was by the door, Henry Steep was going down the stairs. Anna wasn't there. Cassie wasn't there. Sonoma wasn't there. It's a bit like that rhyme about meeting a man who wasn't there.'

'"Yesterday, upon the stair,"' quotes Kim, rather unexpectedly. '"I met a man who wasn't there. He wasn't there again today. I wish, I wish, he'd go away."'

'Can you remember what Garfield said in the voice message Isabelle saved?'

'I love you, babes.' Kim puts on a voice that sounds like a constipated Australian but is presumably meant to be posh English. Her impressions are as bad as Jake's.

Harbinder rifles through her notebook.

'"Babes. I love you. I'm a bit drunk but I love you. So much, babes. Look, there's something I want to tell you. It's about David. Sounds crazy but I think he was murdered and I know who did it. Bloody hell. I love you. Did I say that? I still do."'

Kim laughs, presumably because Harbinder reads in the flat voice of someone who doesn't want to get picked on in class. But Harbinder says, 'I *still* love you. Why "still"?'

'Because it's been twenty-four hours since he last said it?'

'Or, because whatever he heard at the rugby reunion implicated Isabelle. But he still loves her.'

'Bloody hell, boss, do you think Isabelle Istar killed Garfield Rice? Why would she tell us about that conversation if she killed him?'

'Maybe she's playing a clever game,' says Harbinder. 'Maybe she knew we'd find out about it eventually. We've got Garfield's phone, after all, though it looks as if he had a second one too.'

'But she seemed so upset,' says Kim.

'She's an actress, remember,' says Harbinder. She sighs. 'I still think it's one of them: Anna, Chris, Isabelle or Henry. Looks as if Sonoma has an alibi.' The pizza restaurant has confirmed that Sonoma and her family ate there on the night of the reunion, also that Mrs Davies went out to take a telephone call.

'I think we should talk to David Moore's parents,' says Harbinder.

Chapter 23

Harbinder

Tuesday

David's mother is dead but his father is alive and still living in London. Barbara Moore died on 31 December 1999. Cause of death is recorded as suicide. Harbinder thinks back to the start of the new millennium. She had been eighteen, the same age as the Manor Park students when their classmate died. Harbinder had wanted to go out with her friends on New Year's Eve but her parents insisted that it was 'a time for family'. Harbinder remembers the last day of the twentieth century as an unending buffet of Indian food interspersed with intrusive questions from various aunties. The first of January had dawned in thick fog, landmarks vanishing, sky and the sea merging together. Harbinder walked on the beach with her brothers and their dog Jack (predecessor to the family's current German shepherd, Starsky) and seriously considered the possibility that she had been transported to another planet. She was into science fiction at the time, which was probably why this thought occurred. She can only imagine what

David's mother must have felt, just over a year after her son's death, hearing talk of the glittering future. It must have been unbearable. And she hadn't been able to bear it.

Arthur Moore lives off Fulham Palace Road. None of them, thinks Harbinder, following the squad car's progress on her phone, have moved far from West London. Arthur's flat overlooks Margravine Cemetery where, he tells Harbinder and Kim, both Barbara and David are buried.

'It's convenient,' he tells them, as he makes tea in the tiny kitchen. 'And I can visit them whenever I want.'

It's said without self-pity but Harbinder finds the words rather chilling. Visit implies tea and biscuits, not standing by a headstone in the cold.

'I'm so sorry if this brings back painful memories,' says Kim as they take their seats. Behind her colleague's head Harbinder can see the gravestones stretching into the distance.

'It's with me every day, love,' says Arthur. 'And it's nice to talk about them sometimes. Is this to do with Garfield Rice's death?'

'It's part of the enquiry,' says Harbinder carefully. 'Was David friends with Garfield at school?'

'They knew each other,' says Arthur. 'Davy was on the cricket team with Garfield. He was the cock of the walk, Garfield. On every team. He would have been head boy if the school hadn't been too leftie to have prefects. His dad was famous. That was why. Didn't surprise me that Garfield went the same way. Doesn't surprise me that he died of a drug overdose either.'

Interesting, thinks Harbinder. The police have not revealed Garfield's cause of death but most of the papers have assumed that drugs were involved.

'What do you mean by that, Mr Moore?' asks Kim.

'They all took drugs,' says Arthur. 'All the rich kids at Manor Park. Garfield Rice. Chris Foster. Henry whathisname. He's an MP now too. Chris Foster told the police that David went to the Tube station that day to take drugs. That was a bloody lie. Davy never took drugs. He was a good boy.'

All parents think this, Harbinder knows, but there does seem a particular vehemence in Arthur's voice, even after all this time.

'Was Chris Foster a friend of David's?' she asks.

'No.' A drawn-out contemptuous syllable. 'David wouldn't have been friends with someone like that.'

'Do you know why David was there that day?' asks Kim.

'We always assumed he'd gone to meet Cassie,' says Arthur. 'Nice little thing, Cassie.'

The police officers exchange glances.

'Cassie Fitzherbert?' says Harbinder.

'Cassie Armstrong,' says Arthur. 'But I think Fitzherbert's her married name. She still sends me cards at Christmas and sometimes there's an address sticker on the back.'

'Was David close to Cassie at school?' asks Kim.

'They were childhood sweethearts,' says Arthur. 'David adored her. I often think about what might have been.'

Instead of calling for the squad car Harbinder suggests that they walk through the cemetery. It's another bright day and, despite the overwhelming presence of death, there's a pleasant, autumnal feel to the graveyard.

'My dad says there used to be orchards here,' says Kim. 'It was called Fulham Fields.'

'Now it's a field of graves,' says Harbinder. 'Rows and rows of them. It still seems strange to me. Sikhs don't have gravestones.'

'Really?' says Kim. 'Why not?'

'I think it's because the soul has already been reincarnated into another body,' says Harbinder. 'My uncle's ashes were scattered over the River Ouse.'

'I like the idea of reincarnation,' says Kim.

'The Sikh god is gender-neutral too,' says Harbinder. 'That's rather cool. Aren't you a Christian though?' She remembers a comment about St Peter's Italian church.

'Not really,' says Kim. 'I just pick the bits I like from every religion. Is there a word for that?'

'Heretic,' says Harbinder.

They pass a grave in the shape of a cushion and another of an empty chair raised on a plinth. But they are looking for the coordinates given to them by Arthur and, by the chapel, they find them. Two identical white stones.

David Nathaniel Moore 1980–1998
Beloved Son
Barbara Moore 1948–1999
Reunited

So few words, thinks Harbinder, but, really, they say everything. Barbara is now reunited with her beloved son. She can feel tears pricking behind her eyes.

'Bloody hell,' says Kim. 'That's bleak. My biggest fear is anything happening to my kids.'

'Do you really think they killed him?' says Harbinder. 'The Group?'

At this moment, she feels full of antipathy towards them all. Garfield Rice, the son of a Labour MP, who became a right-wing Tory. Chris Foster, who told the police that David took drugs, and now probably brushes his teeth with cocaine. Sonoma Davies, attending ballet recitals with her perfect family. Henry Steep, so earnest with his little round glasses and progressive views. Isabelle Istar, lounging on the sofa in her millionaire's house while Maria toils away in the kitchen. And what about Cassie? Like David, she was outside the gilded group. Anna Vance too. Did this create a bond between them?

'They never forgot David's death,' says Kim. 'That's for sure.'

'But Anna said they never talked about him,' says Harbinder.

'Garfield Rice talked about him,' says Kim. 'And then he was killed.'

A sudden breeze sends the leaves eddying around their feet. A crow calls from a nearby crucifix. In a horror film, thinks Harbinder, there would be someone watching us. But the field of death is deserted.

Jake and Tory have been following up on the other diners present at the Bleeding Heart lunch. Jake briefs them. Harbinder has to admit that he's quite efficient, although his habit of standing with his legs wide apart makes her want to throw things at him.

'James Fermoy MP. Simon Mallow MP. Sir Harry Giles, Chairman of Oilcorp. Sir Frederick Gallows, Chairman of Home Counties Insurance Group. Alastair Taylor QC.'

'All men, all white,' says Harbinder. Jake has helpfully provided pictures and the well-fed faces do look remarkably alike. Harbinder thinks of the end of *Animal Farm* (which she studied for GCSE) when the pigs and the humans end up looking identical.

'We've contacted them all by telephone,' says Jake, 'and interviewed James Fermoy and Simon Mallow. All of them have alibis for the night of Garfield's death. Sir Harry Giles was out of the country.'

'Did they say anything about the Bleeding Heart meetings?' asks Harbinder. 'Sonoma Davies said that they talked about rewilding the day she was Garfield's guest. There seems to have been a focus on environmental issues. I must say, I didn't have Garfield down as a friend of the animals. He studied Philosophy, Politics and Economics at Oxford, not Zoology.' Since talking to Sonoma Davies, she has checked what PPE stands for, to be sure.

'Everyone I spoke to said that they were a regular dining club interested in the issues of the day,' said Jake. 'I honestly can't imagine any of them murdering Garfield or sending him threatening messages.'

'It's not about what you can imagine,' says Harbinder. 'It's about evidence.'

'There's no evidence,' says Jake, widening his stance even more. With any luck, he'll rupture himself.

'Let's keep digging,' says Harbinder. 'We need to talk to all these upstanding citizens.'

'Sir Harry's in the Cayman Islands.'

Of course he is.

'Well, talk to him via video conference. Did you go to the seminar on Zoom?'

'I went,' says Tory. 'But I didn't understand any of it.'

'Read the notes,' says Harbinder, through gritted teeth. She could do with another DS but, due to the sensitive nature of the case, she wants to keep the inner team as small as possible. She briefs them on the news concerning Cassie, about her fingerprints on the syringe.

'You can't think Cassie's got anything to do with it?' says Jake.

'As I said, it's about evidence,' says Harbinder, 'and there is evidence pointing to Cassie. She's on paid leave at the moment and the best thing we can do for her is to investigate every lead thoroughly.'

'I feel so sorry for Cassie,' says Tory. 'She's such a lovely person.'

'I'm going to visit her this evening,' says Harbinder, trying not to grit her teeth. 'I'll pass on your regards.'

Chapter 24

Harbinder

Tuesday evening

True to form, Cassie hasn't moved far from Manor Park school. She lives in Fulham, in a terraced house that's probably worth more than Shoreham. Cassie opens the door in grey tracksuit trousers and pink hoodie. She looks flabbergasted to see her boss on the doorstep.

'Hi, Cassie,' says Harbinder. 'Just came to see how you're doing.'

'You only saw me a few hours ago,' says Cassie. She pulls the door behind her as if trying to keep Harbinder out.

'Things are moving fast,' says Harbinder. 'Can I come in?'

Reluctantly, Cassie pushes the door open. They are in a narrow hallway, silted up with school bags and discarded coats. A roar of sound is coming from somewhere in the house. There's a dog barking too. How many children does Cassie have again? Twenty-five?

'My daughter's got some friends round,' says Cassie, probably in answer to Harbinder's expression.

'Is there anywhere we can talk?'

'Pete!' Cassie hardly raises her voice but a man appears almost at once. Harbinder remembers Pete Fitzherbert from the reunion, staring at the floor and trying not to be sick. Now he's vertical and smiling, a big man but still chunky rather than fat. He's holding an overexcited spaniel by the collar.

'I'm going to talk to Harbinder upstairs,' says Cassie. 'Can you watch the kids?'

'Sure.' Pete smiles at Harbinder. 'You must be DI Kaur. I'm Pete, Cassie's husband. This is Kevin.'

Is the dog really called Kevin? Harbinder thought her parents' choice of Starsky was eccentric enough, although there is actually a weird resemblance between the German shepherd and Paul Michael Glaser. Who is Kevin named after?

'Hi,' says Harbinder. 'I'm sorry to intrude. I just need a quick word with Cassie.'

'It's good to meet you,' says Pete. He turns to Cassie, trying to keep the dog's scrabbling paws away from her. 'What are the kids doing now?'

'Playing Super Mario.'

'Great,' says Pete. 'I love that game.'

'He does too,' says Cassie. 'But Lucy will never let him have a turn.'

She leads the way up a steep staircase and into a tiny office. 'This used to be Sam's bedroom,' says Cassie, 'but then we did a loft conversion. It's bliss to have an en-suite.'

'Must be,' says Harbinder, thinking of the bathroom in Barlby Road.

There's barely room for the two of them in the space. There's a desk under the window with one of those ergonomic chairs pushed into it. Harbinder can't imagine how a bed could have fitted in.

There are still super-hero curtains at the window. The walls are bare apart from a calendar with a palm in the shape of a cross tucked behind it. Is that a Catholic thing?

Cassie fetches a chair from another room for Harbinder. They are close enough for their knees almost to touch.

'We went to see Arthur Moore today,' says Harbinder. 'He says that you still send him Christmas cards.'

Cassie looks at Harbinder with innocent blue eyes. 'I feel sorry for him. You know his wife died, not long after David?'

'Yes,' says Harbinder. 'A real tragedy. Arthur says that you were close to David once.'

'I wouldn't say we were that close.' Cassie starts to fiddle with a paperweight on the desk.

'Arthur says you were childhood sweethearts.'

'Hardly,' says Cassie. 'We went out together once or twice.'

'In Year Ten?' Harbinder can't resist asking.

'What?'

'You said you went out with Garfield in Year Ten.'

The blue gaze flickers. 'I think I went out with David in the sixth form.'

'Your husband was at Manor Park too, wasn't he?'

'Yes, but he was two years above. I hardly saw him at school. We didn't get together until after I'd left university and joined the police.'

'I joined the force straight after uni too,' says Harbinder. 'My family thought I was mad.'

Cassie seems to relax slightly. 'Mine too. My dad kept insisting I wasn't tall enough.'

'You're about my height, aren't you? Five three?'

'I'm five five,' says Cassie. 'But I feel a titch in this house. Pete's six four and Lucy's as tall as me at twelve.'

'My flatmate's six foot,' says Harbinder. 'I'd love to be that tall.'

'It's useful being small sometimes,' says Cassie. 'People don't notice you.'

Which is interesting in lots of ways, thinks Harbinder. Cassie *is* the sort of person you don't notice at first glance. Harbinder hadn't even registered her colleague's good looks until she saw her at the reunion. Maybe this is a deliberate ploy? Harbinder would like to tell Cassie that, as a woman of colour, it's still not that easy to blend into the background, however short you are. But, instead, she takes advantage of the improved atmosphere to say, 'Cassie, is there something you're not telling us?'

Flicker. 'What do you mean?'

'I feel there's something you're not telling us, and I think it's about David Moore. Was he deliberately killed? Do you know who was involved?'

'David fell on the tracks.' Cassie's voice is raised now. 'He was run over by a train. It was a horrible accident. I still have nightmares about it.'

'Were you there?' says Harbinder. 'Were you there when he fell?'

'No,' says Cassie. 'I can't . . .' She covers her face with her hands.

'Everything OK, Cass?' Pete Fitzherbert, all six foot four of him, is standing in the doorway.

'I'm fine,' says Cassie. 'Harbinder was just talking about David. That's all.'

'David?'

'David Moore. The boy in our year who died.'

Pete turns to Harbinder. 'Why do you want to know about

that?' His tone is mild but Harbinder can hear the protectiveness in his voice.

'It's all part of an ongoing investigation,' she says.

Pete holds out an iPhone. The case is sparkly but the screen is cracked. 'You've had a few missed calls,' he says to Cassie.

'Thanks.' Cassie puts the phone down face-up on the desk. Harbinder peers surreptitiously to see the name displayed there. *Henry Steep*.

'Thank you for your time,' she says. 'I'll let you get on with your evening now.'

The sounds from downstairs suggest that it will be a lively one.

Harbinder prefers buses to the Tube so she walks to Bayswater to catch the number 70. It's raining but she enjoys London at this time of the evening: the hurrying crowds, the lighted buses with their promise of adventure, the red and green figures gleaming on the pedestrian crossings. Stop, go. Stop, go. A bit like this case, muses Harbinder. As soon as she thinks she has something, it disappears. She'd thought that Bleeding Heart Yard was the clue but all the members of the luncheon club seem to have alibis. Now, she wonders whether Garfield's murder might be linked to the death he witnessed twenty-one years ago. 'I know who killed him,' he'd said to Isabelle. Did that person also kill Garfield? And is it remotely possible that the murderer is a member of Harbinder's own team?

It's seven o'clock by the time she gets back to the flat. Jeanne is cooking fajitas in the kitchen.

'Do you want some?' she says. 'I've made loads.'

The spicy smell is intoxicating and reminds Harbinder of home.

'That would be great,' she says. 'Thanks. How were Year Eight today?'

'Terrible. One boy pretended to faint so he could look up my skirt.'

'You should wear pants,' says Mette from the doorway. She is in her cycling gear, her face flushed from exercise.

'Of course I was wearing pants,' says Jeanne, affronted.

'Sorry. Language problem,' grins Mette. 'Trousers.'

It's a cosy evening. They eat fajitas in the kitchen and then, at Jeanne's suggestion, go to her room to watch *Buffy the Vampire Slayer*. Harbinder has never really got into the series and finds it rather confusing, especially as Jeanne is on season six, but she enjoys sitting on Jeanne's bed watching the teens battle with the undead. Mette lies on the floor with her feet on a chair. Her legs are so long that they seem to stretch the length of the room.

'This reminds me of my high school,' says Mette.

'Was that a portal to hell too?' asks Harbinder.

'Sometimes.'

'Finsbury Park High definitely is,' says Jeanne.

Harbinder thinks of Manor Park school twenty-one years ago, ruled over by The Group, as they called themselves. Had that made it hell for other pupils? Working class students like Anna and David? Cassie is not exactly working class – her father was a GP – but she wasn't raised in luxury like Garfield Rice. What was the exact relationship between Garfield and Cassie?

She realises Mette is talking to her.

'I like Willow, don't you, Harbinder?'

'Which one is Willow?'

'The one trying to kill Warren and his friends,' says Jeanne.

'She seems a delightful person,' says Harbinder.

When Harbinder finally goes to bed, she finds it hard to sleep. It's still raining hard outside. Vampires and werewolves chase around her head accompanied by Mette in Lycra. She's almost relieved when her phone buzzes at three a.m. It's the duty officer at the station.

'DI Kaur? A body has been found in Holborn.'

'Where in Holborn?' Harbinder is already reaching for her clothes.

'Place called Bleeding Heart Yard.'

Chapter 25

Harbinder

Wednesday morning

Harbinder dresses quickly. She puts on her heaviest coat and slips her phone and notebook in the pocket. Then, just in case, her vest with body cam over the lot. Carrying her boots, she tiptoes past her flatmates' rooms. Jeanne's light is on. Harbinder hopes she isn't having nightmares about Year Eight. Mette's room is in darkness.

The squad car is waiting for her outside. The drive through the empty streets takes very little time. The rain has stopped but the traffic lights reflect on wet pavements. Red, amber, green. Stop, go. Apart from a large urban fox near Portobello Road Market, the only living creature they see is a barefoot man in a pin-striped suit wandering along the Westway.

'Did you see that?' Harbinder asks the driver.

'Lots of nutters about,' is the answer.

Should she alert social services? But what can they do? Maybe he's just a tired businessman coming home from a corporate dinner.

Flashing lights illuminate the entrance to Bleeding Heart Yard.
Harbinder's first thought is that the space is not as evocative as its
name. The buildings look square and corporate. She marches up to
the police tape and shows her badge to the scene log officer.

'DI Kaur.'

The SLO steps back and calls, 'Guv!'

A large square shape looms. 'DI Kaur. I'm DI Akinyemi. I've got
a notification to inform you of anything that happens in this area.'

'Yes. It's part of an ongoing investigation.'

'Come in then and watch your step.'

DI Akinyemi accompanies his words with a sweep of his torch.

'Shit,' says Harbinder. 'What's that?'

'Looks like a heart,' says Akinyemi laconically. 'The body's over
here.'

Harbinder walks carefully across the cobbles, no longer attrib-
uting their slipperiness just to rain. Slumped against a doorway is
a human-looking shape. Akinyemi's torch shows a man in a suit
and coat, open to show a white shirt with a red mark in the centre.
The ace of hearts. Brown lace-up shoes. His face is pale but oddly
peaceful.

'That's Henry Steep,' says Harbinder.

'The MP?'

'Yes. I'm sure of it.' She leans closer. 'The heart. It's not . . .'

'No. Looks to me as if the victim was killed by a single knife
wound. There's not much blood. And no sign of dissection. My
guess is that the heart on the ground isn't human.'

His voice is calm. Harbinder thinks that her colleague could have
shared this presumption with her sooner. After the three a.m. phone

167

call, she had been expecting a bloodbath, a shambles. She is proud that her voice, too, is quite steady.

'Who found him?'

'A night watchman on his rounds. He called it in about an hour ago. Forensics are on their way. Now that we have an identification, we can get on to next of kin.'

'He has a husband,' says Harbinder. 'I've got his details.' She reaches for her notebook.

'You can fill me in on the case,' says Akinyemi. 'There's obviously more to this than meets the eye.'

'And there's quite a lot to meet the eye,' says Harbinder.

As dawn rises over Bleeding Heart Yard, it reveals the older form of the courtyard. The curved wall of the pub with the same name, the brick walls intersecting the modern structures, the hidden arch-ways and dark alleys. Harbinder and Akinyemi, whose first name is Daniel, sit at one of the pub tables and drink coffee from his flask.

'First rule of crime scene investigation. Bring a flask. Then find out where the nearest Costa is.'

'How long have you been a DI?' asks Harbinder.

'Eight years. I think I've hit the glass ceiling. The one for people of colour anyway.'

'It's amazing they let us work together. Does this mean there's a fault in the matrix? Somewhere, somehow, a white supremacist is dying.'

The crime scene manager has arrived and is supervising the erec-tion of a canopy over the body. The yard will remain sealed off, with just one exit and entry point. A family liaison officer has been dispatched to the home of Henry's husband, Stephen Hill.

'Do you really think this is linked to that other MP's death?' says Daniel.

'Different MO,' says Harbinder, blowing on her hands to keep them warm. 'Garfield Rice was injected with insulin. Henry Steep was stabbed. But they were friends. At least, they were friends once. They had recently attended a school reunion. Garfield used to meet his cronies here, at that restaurant behind us. There has to be a link.'

The logo of the restaurant shows a heart behind bars. Such a neat shape, the cartoon heart, thinks Harbinder. Nothing like the mess of blood and tissue on the cobbles, a few metres away, now with a neat crime scene number beside it. An expert from London Zoo is on the way to see if they can identify the species.

'The heart,' says Daniel. 'That's making the link for us.'

'Garfield Rice received anonymous notes saying bleeding heart,' says Harbinder. 'This place has to be significant.' She can hear Mette's cool Danish voice. 'A woman was murdered there and her heart was found on the cobbles, still pumping out blood'. She must trace the source of this legend.

'Or someone wants us to think it's significant,' says Daniel. 'Misdirection. Like in the magic tricks.'

Neil used to talk about misdirection, remembers Harbinder. What is it about men and magicians?

'Looks like the cavalry have arrived,' says Daniel.

Harbinder sees Kim's red hair gleaming in the weak morning light. She's accompanied by a uniformed PC carrying a cardboard tray from Costa. The rising sun slants through the high buildings, making them look like ministering angels.

★

169

Back in her office, Harbinder demolishes two blueberry muffins and another cappuccino with an extra shot. Then she googles 'Bleeding Heart Yard'. She learns that the place probably took its name from a pub sign showing the Virgin Mary pierced by five swords (Christian imagery really is weird) and was mentioned in *Little Dorrit* by Charles Dickens. In Victorian times the area was downmarket, even dangerous. Nearby Saffron Hill was where Fagin lived with his pack of child thieves. Dickens describes the yard as being inhabited by poor people but still retaining 'some relish of ancient greatness.' If you say so, Charlie, thinks Harbinder.

Mette's legend is slightly more difficult to find but eventually Harbinder locates a website called InBloodSteppedSoFar which tells her of a seventeenth-century beauty called Elizabeth Hatton who was wooed by the Spanish ambassador. When she jilted him, he killed her and her body was found in Bleeding Heart Yard. He would probably still get off with manslaughter today, thinks Harbinder, especially after claiming diplomatic immunity.

Another version has Elizabeth selling her soul to the devil for the usual gifts of untold wealth and a house in the SW1 postcode. The demon then whirls Elizabeth away in a fiendish foxtrot and, the next morning, her bleeding heart is found on the cobbles. A poet called Richard Barham immortalised this pleasing scene in a book called *The Ingoldsby Legends*.

Of poor Lady Hatton, it's needless to say,
No traces have ever been found to this day,
Or the terrible dancer who whisk'd her away;
But out in the court-yard — and just in that part
Where the pump stands — lay bleeding a LARGE HUMAN HEART!

Was Henry's body found near where the pump used to stand? wonders Harbinder. Had the murderer read this poem? At any rate, there's clearly a significance to the place where the victim's body was discovered. Forensics will have to discover if Henry was actually killed there or transported from another location. Harbinder remembers the brown lace-up shoes. She's betting that Henry Steep was still wearing his work clothes. What did he do between politicking at the House of Commons and being found dead in Holborn?

And she hears the voice of Pete, Cassie's husband. 'You've had a few missed calls.' And the name 'Henry Steep' appearing on the cracked screen. Henry's phone had not been found with his body.

A knock on the door. 'Boss?' Kim's head appears. 'The team are all in the incident room.'

Harbinder brushes off crumbs. 'Let's get on with it then.'

Chapter 26

Cassie

Tuesday evening

'Are you all right?' Pete asked me, as we stood at the door watching the slight figure in a leather jacket dodging the gridlocked traffic on our street and disappearing into the night.

'Yes,' I said. 'It's just all so horrible. Gary dying like that. And now my own team are investigating it.'

'Are they sure he was murdered?' said Pete. 'On the news they just said the police were treating it as suspicious.'

'That means murder,' I said. 'They've given it a name and everything. And now they've found a syringe at the site and I'm a person of interest.'

'A suspect?' Pete had picked up enough police jargon to know what that meant. 'Surely not? I mean, they know you. You're one of the team.'

'Harbinder doesn't know me,' I said. 'And she suspects everyone. She's right to, of course.'

'What was she saying to you when I came upstairs?' said Pete. 'You sounded upset.'

'She was asking about David,' I said. 'You know, the boy in our year who died? It still gets me. You know, his mum killed herself a year later? I'm still in touch with his dad. I send him Christmas cards.'

I sent Mr and Mrs Moore a condolence card. I hadn't wanted to but my mum insisted. She even bought the card, white lilies on a green background. I was in my second year at Sussex when Mum rang to tell me that Barbara Moore had committed suicide while I was sitting on Brighton beach, celebrating the new millennium and drinking Champagne from the bottle. The next day I ran for miles along the misty coast road, wanting to outrun my memories. When I reached Newhaven I collapsed and had to be driven back to the flat in an ambulance. Freddie was angelic. He didn't know about David, of course, only that a friend's mother had died. He made me soup and we watched *Friends* on the TV. 'Cassie's so sensitive,' I heard him saying on the phone, 'she takes everything to heart.'

Now Pete puts his arms round me. He's so big that his hugs are both stifling and incredibly comforting.

'You're so soft-hearted, babe,' he said. 'It's in the past. Let it go.'

Pete knew about David's death. Everyone did. But Pete had left school by then and was away at university in Loughborough. He found out about it when he was working out at the university gym. This was in the days before you could listen to music on your mobile phone, plugged into the treadmill. There was one screen showing the day's news with subtitles. Tragic Death of London Schoolboy. Something like that.

What with everything that had happened, you might have thought that I'd run a mile from someone who'd attended the Manor. But that, too, was part of the attraction. Pete knew me by sight (he said he'd always fancied me) but he didn't know any of The Group. He occasionally saw Gary at sports reunions, but that was it.

I felt safe with Pete. He was familiar. He came from the same part of London and from a similar middle-class family, although his was Irish Catholic. His father had been in the army and was now a civil engineer. His mother was a dental nurse. They liked me. Apparently his previous girlfriend, a fellow student who played women's rugby, was 'too opinionated'. I was the opposite, I rarely spoke in their presence except to agree with his mother's views on feminism going too far. I agreed to convert to Catholicism and to have the children baptised. I was also, in his father's often-expressed opinion, a 'pretty little thing'.

Pete's size and strength made me feel safe too. On one of our first dates we came across a crowd gathered outside a hotel.

'Who are they waiting for?' I said. 'Do you think it's someone famous?'

'Do you want to see?' said Pete. And he lifted me up, right over the heads of the rubber-neckers, just in time to see Geri Halliwell's red hair disappearing into a taxi.

Freddie, my university boyfriend, had been kind and gentle. He was just what I needed after David and the one-night stands who had followed. But he didn't really stand a chance against Pete. I finished with him the day Pete stopped me by the rowing machine and asked if I'd been to Manor Park.

★

It helped that I had to keep busy that evening. I made pizzas for Lucy and her friends. I consoled Sam after a bruising day at football and saved the pepperoni one for him. Pete and I had margheritas and a glass of wine each, breaking our normal midweek rule. When Sasha and Rosie's parents came to collect them, I offered them drinks too and we all sat in the kitchen talking about GCSE choices and whether the head of year was having an affair with the caretaker. I remembered Harbinder's look of horror when she saw the mess in our hall and heard the noise coming from the kids in the playroom. She's single with no children. She probably lives in a minimalist flat with monochromatic furniture and soundproof walls. Does she have a boyfriend? No one knows. Pete said that he thought she was quite attractive but I'd never really considered Harbinder in that way. She's the boss, every bit as sexless as Dean Franks before her.

Later, I persuaded an overexcited Lucy and a still rather tearful Sam to have baths and get into bed. Pete was finishing the leftover pizza when I got downstairs. I picked up a crust and ate it.

'Now I'm really worried,' said Pete. 'What happened to the calorie-controlled diet?'

'I know,' I said, because I'm normally very careful about what I eat because of the diabetes. 'I don't know what I'm doing today.'

'Cup of tea?' Pete reached for the kettle.

'Yes please.' I really wanted more wine but knew that wasn't a good idea. 'I'd better have herbal,' I said. 'I think I'm going to have an early night.'

'We've got to watch *Game of Thrones* first.'

Pete and I had become obsessed with the series, although I normally hate anything with sword-fighting or dragons in it. But even Tyrion couldn't distract me tonight. I went to bed at ten. Lucy was still texting her friends. 'Go to sleep,' I said, kissing her. 'No screens after nine.' I don't know why I keep pretending we have this rule because no one sticks to it. Sam was well away, mouth slightly open, one arm round the teddy he still slept with. I dropped a kiss on his forehead, noticing that the bath hadn't completely obliterated all traces of mud. Suddenly my love for my son was so fierce and so protective that I wanted to go round and arrest the boy who had tackled him roughly, causing Sam to cry and be laughed at by everyone, even his so-called best friend Rhys.

I climbed the stairs to our luxurious attic bedroom thinking of custodial sentences for Rhys. I was still awake when Pete came up, slightly unsteady after finishing the wine. I shut my eyes so that he wouldn't try to initiate drunken sex. He did kiss my neck and cup my breast, but I kept my breathing even and Pete turned back to his phone, the blue light reflecting on the ceiling.

He stirred briefly when I got up, a few hours later.

'Where are you going?'

'I'm going to sleep on the sofa.'

'Can't you take a sleeping pill?'

'I've run out,' I lied. The pills had been given to me after a previous bout of anxiety, but I didn't like taking them. Pete grunted and turned over. I crept downstairs, past the children's rooms – Lucy muttering in her sleep – took a picnic rug from the cupboard under the stairs and lay down on the sofa in the sitting room. Kevin, who gets shut into the kitchen at night, heard me and whined softly. I let him in and he heaved himself up beside me. I think I slept but it was fitful, disjointed, Kevin twitching beside me.

'I feel there's something you're not telling us, and I think it's about David Moore.'

I saw David falling to his knees in front of me, heard the rush and roar of the train, like one of Daenerys's dragons emerging from its lair. All night, in my dreams, I heard the door opening and shutting and my friends appearing, one by one. Henry, Izzy, Anna, Chris and, finally, Gary.

'I know what you did that day,' said Gary.

I invited all The Group to the wedding. I don't know why unless it was just a way of keeping tabs on them. As I said, I liked to know where everyone was. My Christmas card list was a way of doing that.

I sent them all cards, carefully chosen: nativity scenes, robins in the snow, London by night with snow falling against red buses. Henry was the one who replied most. He was doing his solicitors' exams after studying law, but I knew he wanted to get into politics. That was Gary's ambition too, we all knew that. But we didn't know then that he would stand as a Conservative. I'd been close to Izzy at school, in fact I thought of her as my best friend, but we hadn't stayed in touch very well. She came to Sussex once and professed herself shocked at the size of my bedroom. I never visited her at RADA although I did go to see her in a production of *The Tempest*. Izzy played Prospero, not Miranda. It was one of those shows.

In the end, only Henry, Izzy and Anna came. Sonoma was in America and Gary was 'working'. Chris was on tour with The Cubes. They weren't that famous then. I was surprised to see Anna. She was living in Italy but was apparently in England for her sister Sophie's graduation. I remember that she looked different, more sophisticated somehow, with her hair up and wearing a tight-fitting black dress, not very suitable for a wedding, in my opinion. 'She looks quite Italian,' said my mother, not meaning it as a compliment. I'd always thought that Anna was rather cool. We could wear our own clothes in the sixth form and most girls favoured low-waisted jeans and skimpy tops. Anna wore dungarees and long, lacy skirts. She had a butcher-boy hat and carried her books in a vintage satchel. And she was witty. I envied that. I used to sit in the canteen listening to her bantering with Chris and Henry and think: how does she always know the right thing to say, the perfect comeback? I would spend ages thinking of an appropriate retort, or honing a funny story, but somehow Anna could make everyone laugh with just a few words. 'Pinochet is a mass-murderer,' Gary would say. He was always getting angry about foreign politics. 'Well, nobody's perfect,' Anna would reply, taking a swig of her Coke.

I admired Anna but I wasn't always sure that I liked her. Sometimes I thought she waited a beat too long before coming in with her witty replies, just to make people look stupid. 'Where are you going to go?' I once asked her as we walked along the corridor, continuing our conversation about universities. 'To the loo,' Anna replied. Behind her, Chris and Henry almost died of laughter. Anna was always closest to Chris and didn't seem to feel the need of a female best friend. When Izzy and I talked about clothes and boys, Anna would make a great show of being bored, getting out her book or scribbling one of her stories. 'Anna's going to be a famous writer one day,' Henry kept telling everyone. Well, she isn't, is she?

Funnily enough, it was David who brought us together. When Anna made that remark about David trying to rape her at Molly's party, it gave me the strength to say what had happened to me. Or did I just want to cap her story and direct The Group's attention onto me? I've thought about this a lot. Well, both things might well be true.

Of course, Izzy had to come in with, 'He tried it on with me too, but I kicked him in the balls.' Of course, Izzy was *way* too street-smart to fall for something like that, unlike gullible Cassie. I was the one who actually slept with boys, believing their promises of undying love. I was the one who said 'no' to David but, afterwards, when he pretended not to hear, did not at first give the act its true name. I knew that, if I went to the police, they would ask how many sexual partners I'd had. If I replied, truthfully, 'Five', they would dismiss me as a teenage slut. Sonoma believed in pre-marital chastity and had a 'promise' ring to prove it. I think Anna was a virgin before Chris. Izzy wouldn't even sleep with Gary when they were going out together. Hence the sex against the garage wall on New Year's Eve.

Anna and I bonded over our hatred of David. We'd sit in her bedroom, on her naff flowery duvet, and devise punishments for him. Her mum would leave tea and Marmite sandwiches outside the door, never intruding the way my mother would.

'But I don't think I could actually kill him,' I'd say.

'I could,' said Anna.

Chapter 27

Anna

Wednesday

I hadn't been to Brighton for more than twenty years. Growing up, we couldn't afford foreign holidays (I know, I know) but sometimes we'd get the train to Brighton for the day. I'll never forget the excitement of seeing the sea for the first time, the long trek down from the station, the shops becoming progressively more colourful and more eccentric, walking along the pier and seeing the water between the slats, the ghost train, the bumper cars, the silver falls. Then, at the end of the day, the slog back up the hill, tired and happy, clutching a hideous toy won in the arcade. Once, we stayed at a B&B in Saltdean, a few miles outside of Brighton, and I fell in love with the rock pools, the 1930s houses, the curves of the Lido. Even my first trip to Florence, as a student, couldn't eradicate my affection for the White Cliffs Hotel.

Chris drove us to Brighton in, of all things, a Fiat 500. 'It's great for getting around London, low carbon emissions and so on,' he said, 'and it's kind of cool, don't you think?' I had to agree. From the retro dashboard to its Italian go-faster stripe, the Fiat was extremely cool. I managed to forget yesterday and Henry's disturbing comments. I just enjoyed the sensation of being driven, Croydon giving way to the Brighton Road, once famous for highwaymen and the scene of many a curricle race in Mum's Georgette Heyer books. Mum's friend Sapphire was spending the day with her so I had nothing to worry about. They had once been part of a short-lived singing act, Sapphire and Star, which had given Mum her nickname. It was ten o'clock. I calculated that the reminiscences would only just have reached 1973. They would keep going all day.

Chris had been the first in The Group to learn to drive. He was one of the oldest in the year. His birthday is in September and, according to Mum, he's a typical Virgo. I was one of the youngest. My birthday is in August (I'm not a typical Leo but, again quoting Mum, that's because my moon is in Pisces) and, of course, I couldn't afford driving lessons anyway. In those halcyon days in the sixth form before the A-level panic set in, Chris would sometimes borrow his mother's car and drive us to Richmond Park. I used to think that the sight of Chris's hands braced on the wheel was the sexiest thing in the world.

I didn't look at his hands as we took the M23 to Brighton. I no longer found Chris attractive, I told myself, partly because the world now seemed to share my teenage crush.

'Aren't you worried about being recognised today?' I said.

'I'm in disguise,' said Chris, indicating his dark glasses. 'And I've got a hat on the back seat.'

I twisted round to look.

'Bit like your butcher boy cap, isn't it?' said Chris.

'What did I tell you about reminiscences?'

'OK. OK. Let's have some music.'

The radio was playing The Cubes' latest hit, 'Subway World'.

'Christ,' said Chris, switching it off. 'Not this.'

'Don't you like listening to your own music?'

'I hate it. Izzy's the same about watching herself on TV.'

I felt a sudden pang at the thought of Chris and Izzy having this conversation. I remembered Izzy saying that she saw him sometimes at 'events'. I suppose it was only natural. They were both in the public eye and both under the same pressures. But I didn't buy that about Izzy for one second. I thought she probably recorded all her performances and watched them back in slow motion.

If I had ever managed to get published, would I feel the same about seeing people read my book or hearing the audio version? The question was too hypothetical to consider. I'd sent a few man- uscripts off to agents but had only ever received rejections back. I still wrote all the time – short stories, poems, plays – but I'd given up hope of ever seeing them in print.

'Shall we listen to Radio 4?' I said. I love this channel, which I can still get in Italy. It's like distilled England.

'Let's not listen to any news,' says Chris. 'No news, no reminis- cences. Let's not even look at our phones.'

'My phone doesn't give me news.' I brandished my Nokia.

'Jesus, Anna,' said Chris. 'Isn't that a listed monument?'

'It's sufficient for my needs,' I said. I didn't mention that the battery had already run out.

Chris parked near the peace statue and we walked past the shell of the old pier towards the surviving edifice. It was another beautiful day. It had rained last night in London but, here, the sky was the azure blue of a Renaissance painting. Chris wasn't the only person wearing dark glasses and a baseball cap to protect him from the sun. I took off my jumper and knotted it round my neck.

'Very Italian,' teased Chris.

'Italians are born knowing how to do this sort of thing,' I said.

'Do you have lots of Italian friends?' asked Chris.

'Yes,' I said. 'I've lived there almost twenty years now. I've got a few very close friends.' I thought of them: Simonetta, Fabio and Aurelia. Good, serious-minded people who cared about the world. Simonetta and Fabio were fellow teachers. Aurelia was Fabio's girlfriend, a cellist. What would they say if I told them that, as a teenager, I had watched a murder and then wiped it from my mind?

Chris said, looking away from me in a rather studied way, 'Any boyfriends?'

'Is that in the rules?'

'It's not a reminiscence.'

I sighed. 'I had a longish relationship with a man called Marco. We broke off because he wanted to get married and I didn't. So he married someone else and I think they're very happy.'

'Why didn't you want to get married?'

'What is this? Twenty questions?'

Chris laughed. 'Sorry. It's just that you're almost the only person I know who's never been married.'

'What about you? What about Stormy?' I said.

'Stormy?' Chris looked at me in surprise although I wasn't the one who'd come up with the ludicrous name. 'What do you know about Stormy?'

'Izzy mentioned her at the reunion.' I wasn't about to admit that I followed Chris in the gossip websites.

'I'm not in a relationship with Stormy,' said Chris, smiling as if at some secret joke. 'We've just been to a few events together.' Those 'events' again.

'So you've never brought her to Brighton?'

'No.'

As it was a weekday in September, the pier was almost empty. I wondered if Chris ever brought his children here. Seeing Izzy with Annie/Anna had made me think about my contemporaries who had managed the incredible feat of becoming parents. But Chris clearly didn't want to talk about Harriet and Connor. I'd seen several photos of them in his flat and Chris had, while we were eating curry that evening, broken off to answer a text from his son, rather rudely, in my opinion, smiling down at his phone. At the time, I hadn't asked what it was about.

We walked past the penny arcade and the shrouded fairground rides to the very end of the pier. I pointed eastwards, to where Roedean School brooded over the cliffs and the ugly marina.

'Saltdean's that way. We stayed in a B and B there once. Me, Mum and Sophie.'

'Shall we drive there for lunch?'

I wasn't ready to let Chris so far into my memories. Or start a conversation that would lead to Mum. 'Let's stay in Brighton,' I said.

In the end, we bought fish and chips and ate them on the beach. The seagulls sat around us in a fascinated circle.

'Probably Cube fans,' I said.

But no one recognised Chris Foster as Kris Foster, not even when he paddled in the sea with his trousers rolled up like a 1950s dad.

We walked back to Hove, past the new installation called the i360, almost embarrassingly phallic. Then we got coffees and sat on the pebbles again. It was, mysteriously, almost twilight. We could see the lights of the windfarm, far out to sea. Nearby some teenagers were lighting a barbecue and playing hip-hop.

I closed my eyes. I hadn't been sleeping well and the sound of the waves on the shingle, combined with the rapping, was having a soporific effect.

'Anna?' said Chris.

I opened my eyes. It was like the day in Hyde Park, only reversed. I could see Chris's face above mine and, suddenly, it was summer in London and we were eighteen again. I held my breath.

Chris straightened up. It was a few seconds before I realised that he was looking at his phone.

'What is it?' I sat up too, feeling foolish.

'Izzy. A voicemail. Do you mind if I check it?'

'Of course not,' I said. 'Feel free.'

I stared at the ruins of the pier. Starlings were swooping around the iron birdcage, now clustering together in dark clouds, now separating and reforming. Murmuration. The word spoke itself in my head.

'My God,' said Chris.

'What's happened?'

It was as if I was braced for bad news, as if our golden day was always leading to this, like the last day of peace, or 10 September 2001.

Chris's face was blank with shock. 'Henry's been murdered.'

'*What?*'

'Excuse me.' It was one of the kids from the barbecue. 'Aren't you that singer? The one from the TV?'

Chapter 28

Anna

Wednesday evening

We drove home almost in silence, past the Brighton gates, supposedly haunted by the ghost of a hitchhiker, and onto the motorway. Izzy had said only that Henry had been found dead in the early hours of the morning and DI Kaur had paid her a visit. Chris had several missed messages from the police. My phone was, of course, silent.

'Izzy sounded quite hysterical,' said Chris, as we reached the outskirts of London. Sprawling supermarkets, the IKEA towers, large houses, set back from the road, probably desirable residences before they were strangled by the Brighton Road and the Purley Way.

'And we don't know any more?' I asked, for the umpteenth time. 'Just that he was found dead? God, I only saw him yesterday.'

Chris had tried to ring Izzy back but having planted its bombshell, her phone was now going straight to voicemail. Chris hadn't returned DI Kaur's calls. We tuned the radio to a news channel but there was nothing about Henry.

'It's a nightmare,' said Chris. 'First Gary, now Henry.'

Both the MPs, I thought. The two brilliant political minds in The Group. Maybe that was the link? Maybe it was nothing to do with David at all? I remembered what Henry had said about Gary. 'He thought he could manipulate us all. Maybe that's why I started reading Machiavelli. To get the measure of him.'

It was nearly nine o'clock when Chris turned into the car park of Attlee Towers but, somehow, I wasn't surprised to see a police car waiting for us. DI Kaur got out. She seemed to have got taller since I last saw her.

'Mr Foster? Ms Vance? I'd like to talk to you both, if you don't mind.'

'I've got to check on Mum,' I said. 'I've been out all day. She isn't well.' I saw Chris start slightly. This was news to him.

'We've just been up there,' said Kim, emerging from the back seat. 'Her carer is with her. Nice woman called Roxy.'

'I need to check.' I could hear my voice sounded hysterical.

'OK,' said DI Kaur equably. 'We'll wait.'

I took the lift, trying to catch my breath.

'Is that you, Anna?' called Mum from the bedroom.

'Yes,' I said, panting slightly.

'Roxy's just getting me into bed.' Mum preferred me not to see this bit, so I waited until Roxy's cheerful 'All decent!' before coming in.

Mum was sitting up in bed, looking tired but comfortable in her pink negligee. I bet most of Roxy's clients wore sensible cotton pyjamas.

'Someone was asking for you just now,' said Roxy. She got a note out of her pocket. 'Woman called Kim Manning.'

'Wasn't she one of the police officers?' said Mum. 'Well, don't worry about that now. How was Chris? How was dear old Brighton?'

'Both were lovely,' I said. 'I'm afraid I'm going to have to pop out now to talk to this Kim. I won't be long.'

'Don't worry,' said Mum. 'Roxy's going to leave me with *Celebrity Antiques Road Trip*.'

DI Kaur suggested that we talk at the police station. 'It'll be easier,' she said. Neither of us liked to disagree. Somehow, I found myself in the car with Kim and DI Kaur while Chris followed in the Fiat.

'I hear you've been to Brighton,' said Kim. 'I do like that town. Spent my honeymoon there. The Old Ship Hotel, right on the seafront.'

'I used to go on day trips to Brighton as a child,' I said.

Unexpectedly, DI Kaur joined in. 'I grew up in Shoreham. Brighton was like Las Vegas to us.'

'I've never been to Shoreham,' said Kim.

'Don't bother,' said DI Kaur. She was in the front seat and I could only see her profile. She had one of those very straight noses, like the statue of a crusader. I realised that I was scared of her.

At the station, we walked through the reception area, which had high counters like an old-fashioned bank and a collection of sad-looking people sitting on nailed-down chairs. Kim escorted me up some stairs and into an 'interview suite'. She offered me tea or coffee, as solicitous as ever, but I still couldn't escape the feeling that I was under arrest. I asked for tea although what I actually wanted was something to eat. How long ago was it since I'd eaten fish and chips on the beach? Too long. The room was so bland as to be almost sinister: cream walls, green plastic chairs, a table with a plant (possibly plastic), a painting of horses in a field. Or were they cows?

Kim returned with the tea and two biscuits. I was almost pathetically grateful.

'Where's Chris?' I asked.

'DI Kaur's just talking to him now,' said Kim. They were keeping us apart, I realised, with a slight shiver. 'Everyone's very excited, having a real pop star at the station. I suppose it doesn't seem so exciting to you. You're probably used to it.'

Her tone was cosy, confiding, with those gentle East London glottal stops. But she was clearly getting at something.

'I haven't seen Chris for a long time,' I said. 'I keep forgetting how famous he is.'

'Was he good at music at school?'

'He used to play the guitar in assembly sometimes,' I said. 'But art was his thing then.'

'Were you close at school?'

'Quite close,' I said. The room seemed suddenly very hot. Was the plant edging nearer?

'What about Henry Steep?'

'We were friends, yes.'

'You saw him yesterday, didn't you?'

'How did you . . .' This seemed almost diabolical second sight.

'We spoke to his husband.'

'Stephen? I've never even met him. I still can't believe Henry's dead.' I realised that I was shaking. Kim took the mug of tea from me.

'This must be an awful shock for you,' she said.

★

DI Kaur appeared about twenty minutes later. She was accompanied by a man I recognised from the reunion: dark hair, brusque manner, Geordie accent.

'This is DS Jake Barker,' said DI Kaur. 'We've just got a few questions for you.' I wanted Kim to come back into the room but I realised that she was probably now with Chris, chatting cosily about school and just how well he knew Anna Vance.

'Is this a formal interview?' I asked. I didn't want to ask the clichéd question about whether I needed a lawyer but, all the same, I wondered if I *did* need one.

DI Kaur looked shocked. 'Oh no. You're here voluntarily. You can leave any time.'

Was I? Could I? I remembered the car journey and the way I'd been separated from Chris. But I forced myself to say, 'I want to help. It's a terrible shock.'

'You saw Henry Steep yesterday, didn't you?' says DS Barker, flicking through his notes in a way that looks too theatrical to be genuine.

'Yes. We had tea at the Houses of Parliament.'

'Very nice too,' says DI Kaur, managing to sound disapproving all the same. 'Was there any particular reason for meeting that day?'

'Not really,' I said. 'We'd talked about having tea on the terrace ever since Henry became an MP.' Well, I'm sure we talked about it once.

'What did you talk about?' asked DS Barker. Neither of them could do casual chatting in the way that came so easily to Kim Manning. Every question sounded like the Spanish Inquisition.

'Life,' I said. 'Italy. Henry's job. His marriage. I've never met his husband.'

'Did you discuss the reunion?' asked DI Kaur.

'Just briefly. I don't think either of us really wanted to talk about it, after what happened to Gary.'

'Did you talk about David Moore?'

'No.'

'When did you leave?'

'About three-thirty.' I wondered if anyone would remember me standing up, clearly upset and knocking over a cup. *Don't go.* Those had been Henry's last words to me.

'What did you do then?' DS Barker took over.

'I went home. My mum isn't well and I wanted to get back to her. I made supper and we watched TV.'

'What did you watch?' asked DI Kaur.

'Some travel programme with Michael Portillo.'

'I can't stand him. When did you go to bed?'

'Early. About ten.'

'And when did you get up?'

'Seven-thirty. Chris was collecting me at nine-thirty to drive to Brighton and I wanted to get Mum sorted for the day. A friend of hers was coming round to sit with her.'

'And you spent all day with Mr Foster?'

'Yes.' Like a diorama, the day spooled in front of me: the pier, the beach, the walk along the promenade, Chris saying 'Anna'.

'Anna,' DI Kaur chipped in, using my first name for what felt like the first time. 'Do you know a place called Bleeding Heart Yard?'

'What?' I wondered if I'd heard right.

'Bleeding Heart Yard. It's in Holborn.'

'No.'

'Chris didn't mention having lunch at a restaurant there?'

'No.' I was beginning to get hot again. 'Look, how long is this going to take? I need to get back to my mum.'

'Of course.' DI Kaur actually smiled at me. 'Let's finish for now. Do you need a lift home?'

But a lift was not necessary. Chris was waiting for me on one of the nailed-down chairs in the reception area. There was only one other occupant now and he seemed to be asleep. Or dead.

'Finished?' said Chris.

'I think so. Do we need to sign out or anything?'

There was no sign of life behind the high wooden counters.

'Let's get out of here,' said Chris.

In the cool little car, Chris didn't turn on the engine. Instead he leant back in his seat and closed his eyes. 'Jesus.'

'Yes,' I said.

'What did they ask you?'

'Where I was last night. That sort of thing.'

'We must be the prime suspects. Jesus.'

'Did they ask you about a place called Bleeding Heart Yard?'

'Yes.' Chris turned to look at me. 'Why would they ask you that?'

'Where is it? Have you heard of it before?'

'It's a place where I once had lunch with Gary. How could it be connected to Henry?'

'Do you know what actually happened to Henry?'

'No. I've been scared to look it up on my phone in case they get hold of my records.'

Chris laughed uneasily but I knew exactly what he meant. I was consumed with the fear of looking guilty. What could they tell from the way I walked and talked? Was it suspicious that I'd eaten both biscuits?

'No good looking at your phone, of course,' said Chris, starting the ignition. 'Unless they want to play a retro game of Tetris.'

'My battery died hours ago,' I said.

Chris switched on the radio and, before we had reached the traffic lights, we heard that Labour MP Henry Streep had been found dead in London. 'Police have yet to release any further details.'

'They wanted to talk to us before we heard it on the news,' I said.

'At least we can give each other alibis for today,' said Chris.

'Alibis,' I said. 'Murders. What has our life become?'

'It's like living in bloody Midsomer,' said Chris. 'Our friends dying one by one.'

'Poor Henry,' I said.

'Yes. That's almost the worst thing. I haven't really felt any uncomplicated grief for Henry. Or for Gary either.'

'It's hard to feel two things at once,' I said. 'At the moment, for me, fear is stronger than grief.'

We'd reached Attlee Towers. Chris parked by the recycling bins. We were both silent for a full minute after he turned off the engine. I was wondering how we'd say goodbye. Would a kiss seem inappropriate?

'Why didn't you tell me your mum was ill?' said Chris.

'I didn't want to talk about it,' I said.

'I can understand that. I'll see you tomorrow, though, won't I?'

'Yes,' I said.

'I'll pick you up here at ten. Don't want to text. Just in case the Stasi are watching.'

'OK,' I said.

And, despite everything, as I walked up the stairs to the flat, I found myself smiling.

Chapter 29

Cassie

Wednesday

I got up as soon as light filtered through the sitting room curtains. I let Kevin out into the back garden and made myself a cup of tea. Then I unloaded the dishwasher, tidied the kitchen and made wholesome sandwiches for the kids' lunchboxes. By the time Pete appeared, yawning and dishevelled in tracksuit bottoms and a London Irish T-shirt, I was on to coffee, black with sugar.

'How did you sleep?' he said.

'OK,' I said. 'Kevin kept me company.'

Hearing his name, Kevin came clattering in, muddy from digging in the flower beds.

'Sleeping with another man,' said Pete, fending off the dog with one hand.

'What would Father Kevin say?' I answered.

'Are you OK, Cass?' said Pete. 'Why don't you ring Harbinder today? See what's going on?'

I noticed that he was now on first-name terms with my boss. That was Pete all over.

'I'll see,' I said, in the same tone that I use with the children. 'Can you give the kids a shout? They ought to be getting up.'

Lucy and Sam appeared at the last possible moment, complaining about the contents of the wholesome sandwiches and telling me about previously forgotten play dates, homework, letters from school. I was glad that Sam seemed his usual cheerful self and was talking about going to Rhys's house on Saturday. I decided to shelve my midnight plan to have Rhys sent to a juvenile detention unit.

Lucy set off for the bus in a flurry of gym bag, violin and trailing headphones.

'Don't forget your coat,' I shouted after her.

'There's nowhere to put it at school,' she said.

'What about your locker?'

'I've lost the key.'

I let it go. The weather was still mild for September. Time to have that battle later. I walked Sam to school, keeping the conversation light and confined to things we saw on the way: cats, unusual cars, a woman walking her dog whilst wearing what were clearly her pyjamas.

'Jupiter's mum drives him to school in her pyjamas.'

'There you are. I'm not the most embarrassing mum at school.' And I didn't give you a ridiculous name, I added silently.

Sam grinned but said nothing. He did allow me to kiss him, though, just as we reached the corner by the school gate.

'Have a good day, darling.'

'I will. Bye, Mum.' Kevin strained at the leash to follow Sam but

I told him not to be clingy. Nevertheless, I watched until Sam was absorbed into a group of boys who swept him along towards the entrance. Then I turned back.

The kitchen was eerily quiet, the gleaming surfaces seeming to mock me. I know that Pete would like me to work less, or give up completely, now that he's running his own company, but I find being alone too oppressive. 'I'm a home-maker,' my mother used to say, 'that's enough career for me.' I once asked her if she missed working as a nurse and she just shuddered. Maybe the house was enough for Mum although I never got the impression of a wonderfully contented woman. It was more like she was fighting a constant battle against the rambling old building, against me and my sister, Emily, and, especially, against my dad. I didn't want that for my marriage. Plus, being at home gives you too much time to think.

I made myself another coffee and sat at the kitchen table. The silence was louder than ever. What should I do next? Vacuum the upstairs rooms? Put some washing on? Relive the day I killed a man?

By midday the house was spotless. I wasn't hungry but I need to eat regularly so I made myself cottage cheese on half a bagel. Kevin put his head on my knee and gazed up, eyes limpid. I knew it was greed really but his devotion comforted me. At least Kevin still loves me, I told myself. The doorbell made me jump, heart pounding. Kevin went galloping to greet whoever it was. He has a more trusting nature than me. Two figures were reflected in the bubbled glass over the door. Should I put the security chain on? Don't be ridiculous, I told myself, it's a sunny weekday lunchtime.

You're in your own home with your loyal guard dog. There's nothing to be afraid of.

I opened the door.

'Hallo, Cassie,' said Harbinder. 'Can Kim and I have a word?'

Chapter 30

Harbinder

The room is quiet while Harbinder describes the discovery of the body.

'We'll have to wait for the post-mortem results but it looks as if Henry was killed by a knife blow to the heart. In addition, entrails were found a few metres away. An expert from London Zoo identified them as a cow's heart.'

'A cow's heart?' Predictably, Tory seemed to find this more shocking than another murdered man. 'Who would do something like that?'

'How would you even get hold of a cow's heart?' says Jake.

'Butchers sell them,' says Harbinder. 'My parents buy them for their dog. We need to ask at all local butchers and supermarkets. House-to-house will be key, and we need to get started as soon as possible. We've got the body-cam film from the PC who first attended the scene but there should also be CCTV. Someone must have seen something.'

'Was Henry murdered in BH Yard?' asks Jake. It's a very good question but Harbinder wishes he wouldn't reduce everything to initials. It makes her want to tell him to FO.

'We don't know yet, but I think we have to assume that the site itself is significant. I've been looking it up and there are lots of legends about the place, including a murder in the seventeenth century.'

'It sounds really spooky,' says Tory.

'It's not really,' says Harbinder, although she had been glad of Daniel's company in the grim hours before dawn when the shrouded figure lay in the doorway. 'It's really just an upmarket dining place now and this is still our most likely connection. Bleeding Heart Yard is where Garfield Rice met his mates and chatted about climate change. Jake, I want you to reinterview all the members of Garfield's dining club.'

'You can't think that one of them did it?'

'I'm not assuming anything, but another MP has been killed and I think we have to consider political motives. I'm also waiting on handwriting analysis of the "bleeding heart" notes send to Garfield.'

'What sort of political motives?' says Jake.

'I don't know,' says Harbinder. 'But there will have been rivalries and resentments. There are in any workplace. Garfield Rice certainly had his enemies at the House of Commons. Henry Steep was one of them. Now they're both dead.'

'What about The Group?' says Jake. 'Are they off the hook?'

'Not at all,' says Harbinder. 'We need to find out where they all were last night. I've asked for a twenty-four-hour news blackout. That'll give us time to catch them off guard. But Kim and I must speak to Henry's husband first.'

'Poor thing,' says Tory. 'They hadn't been married long. Henry seemed so nice when Jake and I interviewed him.'

'Well someone didn't like him,' said Jake, callously but unanswerably.

'Steep Hill,' says Stephen Hill. 'You can see why we didn't double-barrel our names.'

Stephen, who is sitting between his sister and the FLO on a stylish-looking sofa, alternates between tears and gallant attempts at humour. Harbinder has seen enough bereaved relatives to know that this is fairly standard. Or, rather, that there is no one way of expressing grief.

'I'm so sorry,' she says. 'This must be a terrible shock.'

'It is rather,' says Stephen. 'It's not . . . it's not what you'd expect.'

This touching understatement makes Stephen's sister, Connie, wipe her eyes and pat her brother's hand.

'Are you up to answering a few questions?' says Kim. 'It's just that, the sooner we can start the investigation, the quicker we'll find the person who did this to Henry.'

'Of course,' says Stephen, sitting up straighter.

'How long had you and Henry been together?' asks Kim.

'Ten years. We met at law school but didn't get together until a few years later. We got married two years ago.' Harbinder knows that Stephen is a solicitor specialising in corporate finance. Henry Steep was a qualified lawyer too, although he'd been an MP since 2010.

Kim admires the wedding photo on the mantelpiece. It shows the two men in matching morning suits with pink ties. Connie volunteers that she was best man, 'best person, I called myself,' and that lots of friends attended.

'Any of Henry's old schoolfriends?' asks Harbinder. 'Garfield Rice? Chris Foster?'

'Henry wouldn't have invited Garfield,' says Stephen. 'He loathed him. But Isabelle Istar was there. Apparently, she and Henry were close at school. Chris was on tour but he sent a present.' He still sounds proud of this fact.

After a few more minutes of wedding chat ('I had the full meringue dress,' Kim told him. 'My kids think it's hideous.'), Kim asks when Stephen last saw Henry.

'Yesterday. We had breakfast together and then we both went off to work. '

'You didn't see him last night?'

'No. I assumed he'd stayed with a colleague who has a flat in Dolphin Square. He often does that when he's working late.'

'Do you know what Henry was doing yesterday? Besides working?'

'He was meeting an old schoolfriend, Anna Vance. They had tea at the House. Henry hadn't seen her for years because she lives in Italy. He wanted to catch up with her.'

'Did you hear from Henry yesterday? A text or phone call?'

'Just a text at eleven to say goodnight.'

'Stephen,' says Harbinder, 'does the name Bleeding Heart Yard mean anything to you?'

'No,' says Stephen. 'Wait. Is it a place in London? Near Holborn?'

'That's right. Do you remember Henry mentioning it?'

'I don't think so. Why are you asking? Is that where . . . where he was found?'

'Yes,' says Harbinder. There's no point hiding this from Henry's next of kin.

'Helen,' Stephen gestures towards the FLO, 'says that he was stabbed. Is that right?'

'We think so. We'll know more when we have the forensics results.'

'Can I see him?'

'Very soon,' promises Harbinder. 'Helen will organise that for you. Kim and I will leave you in peace now.'

'Thank you,' says Stephen.

The thanks are always hardest to bear.

Harbinder and Kim drive straight to Anna's flat. They are met by a pink-haired woman of uncertain age who introduces herself as Sapphire.

'Anna's out, I'm afraid. I'm keeping my old friend Star company.'

'Do you know where Anna is?' asks Harbinder. 'We're very keen to talk to her.'

'She's gone to Brighton,' says Sapphire. 'With *Chris Foster*. They're still very good friends. Star thinks that they might get back together again.'

Which is interesting but doesn't get them very far. Harbinder decides against following Anna to Brighton or informing her old pals at Sussex police. Sapphire says that Anna is expected back that evening. 'She won't want to leave her mum alone for long. Even though the carer's coming to help her to bed.' Harbinder rings Chris Foster but the phone goes straight to voicemail. She leaves a tersely worded message and turns to Kim.

'What now?'

'Isabelle Istar? The wedding guest?'

'Good idea. Then we need to talk to Cassie.'

'Sandwich first?'

'Definitely.'

Harbinder has been flagging slightly but, after a cheese sandwich and a Diet Coke from one of Kim's favourite backstreet cafés, she feels re-energised. They drive to the tasteful house in Ladbroke Grove and knock on the green front door.

To Harbinder's surprise, Isabelle herself answers the door. It must be Maria's day off.

'You,' she says. She's wearing what look like exercise clothes, pink and green Lycra. Harbinder has a sudden flashback to Mette in cycling shorts.

'Can we come in?' says Harbinder. 'I'm afraid we have some bad news.'

'Not Anna?' Isabelle puts her hand to her mouth.

For a moment, Harbinder thinks she's referring to Anna Vance then she remembers the name of Isabelle's daughter.

'No,' she says hastily. 'It's Henry. Henry Steep. I'm afraid he's dead.'

'Oh.' Isabelle lets out a long sigh of what sounds like relief.

A yoga video is still playing when they go upstairs to the sitting room.

'Inhale, reach the fingertips all the way up . . .'

Isabelle presses a button and the screen goes black.

'What were you saying about Henry? I can't take it in.'

No offer of refreshment. Maria really must be off duty.

'I'm afraid Mr Steep was found dead last night,' says Harbinder carefully.

'Found dead? You mean killed?'

'It looks that way, yes.'

Isabelle collapses onto a chair in a jointless, yogic way. Harbinder and Kim take this as their cue to sit too.

'When did you last see Henry?' asks Kim after a tactful pause.

'At the reunion. God, was it only on Saturday? It seems like centuries have passed.'

Harbinder knows what she means. It's Wednesday now.

'Did you receive any messages from him between the reunion and last night?'

'Messages? No. Why would I?'

'I understand that you were pretty good friends. You went to his wedding.'

'We were friends, I suppose, but we didn't see each other much. I was surprised to be invited to the wedding, to be honest.'

'But you went?'

'Like I say,' Isabelle sweeps her hair into a ponytail, tying it with a scrunchy from around her wrist, 'we'd known each other a long time.'

'What did you do last night, Isabelle?' Harbinder thinks it's time she chimed in.

'Last night? Why do you want to know?'

'We're asking everyone.'

'I had dinner with my agent, Jill Browning. I got back home at about ten. Oliver was still up but Annie was in bed. We watched TV and then we went to bed at about midnight.' The recital, complete with names, seems to have calmed Isabelle. She faces them almost defiantly.

Harbinder presses on. 'Have you ever heard of a place called Bleeding Heart Yard?'

'Yes,' says Isabelle surprisingly. 'I was in a historical drama once playing Lady Elizabeth Hatton. You know she was the wife of Sir Christopher Hatton, of Hatton Garden?'

'Wasn't she the one who was murdered?' says Harbinder. 'And her heart cut out?'

She watches the realisation and horror dawning on the actress's face.

Cassie opens the door as if expecting an armed assassin to be outside. Interesting, thinks Harbinder. She knows that Cassie is probably on edge – she's on leave from work, her boss called round yesterday to ask intrusive questions – but is there any reason for her to look quite so haunted?

'Hallo, Cassie,' says Harbinder. 'Can Kim and I have a word?'

'What about?' says Cassie.

'Hallo, Kevin,' Kim reaches past Cassie to pat the dog, who is wagging his tail so hard that his entire back end moves. Harbinder supposes that Kim has visited the house before, possibly for a dinner party. Malcolm and Kim, Cassie and Pete. The two couples discussing hetero things like house prices and schools. Candles on the table, the latest Nigella casserole in the oven. The scenario makes her feel uneasy somehow.

'Can we come in?' says Kim. 'Are the kids at school?'

'Yes,' says Cassie. 'But I've got to pick them up in a minute.'

As it's not yet one o'clock, Harbinder assumes that Cassie is searching for excuses, but she stands aside and lets them enter the house.

It's much tidier than Harbinder remembers from yesterday, floorboards gleaming, hall free from clutter. This time Cassie leads them into the kitchen, which is a large airy room with a dark blue Aga and doors opening onto the garden. Again, every surface is shiny and clear except for a half-finished bagel on the scrubbed pine table. But, although pristine, it's still a family room: children's paintings on the walls, letters from schools attached with magnets to the fridge. Harbinder squints to read one of them. St Bede's Catholic Comprehensive. It seems that Cassie, like Sonoma, has avoided sending her offspring to Manor Park.

'Blimey,' says Kim. 'It's very tidy in here.'

So she has obviously been in the kitchen before.

'I've been doing some housework,' says Cassie. 'It's not as if I've got anything else to do.' She shoots a rather unfriendly look at Harbinder.

'Cassie,' says Kim. 'Why don't you sit down? We've got some news for you. It might come as a shock.'

If Cassie looked pale before, now her face seems to drain of blood.

'What?' she whispers.

'It's Henry.' Kim sits at the table, facing Cassie. 'He's been found dead. We've opened a murder enquiry.'

'A murder enquiry?' echoes Cassie.

'We can't give you the details,' says Harbinder. 'But it's definitely a suspicious death.'

As she says this she thinks of the bloodstained cobbles, the body lying in the doorway, the ace of hearts on the white shirt.

'Oh my God,' says Cassie. 'That's awful.'

'I know you were old friends,' says Harbinder, although 'friends' doesn't seem the right word to describe the ex-pupils of Manor Park school. 'Had you seen Henry recently?'

'Not since the reunion,' says Cassie. 'And we didn't talk much that night.'

'Why not?' asks Kim, in her gentlest voice.

'He was too busy chatting to Anna. They were always close.'

Not another one who was obsessed with Anna Vance, thinks Harbinder.

'Where were you last night, Cassie?' she says. 'We're asking everyone who was at the reunion.'

'I was here,' she says. 'You saw me at six-ish, when you came round. I didn't go out after that.'

'I'm sure Pete can vouch for that,' says Kim chummily. 'I expect he was with you all the time, snoring, taking up all the bed.'

This seems a bit too familiar, even for Kim, thinks Harbinder. Maybe Cassie thinks so too because she pauses before replying,

'I slept on the sofa. I do that sometimes.'

'When I was here,' says Harbinder, 'you had a missed call from Henry. What was that about?'

The flush looks almost painful on Cassie's pale skin. 'How did you . . . Oh, you must have seen my phone.' Her voice is dull.

'Well, I am a detective,' says Harbinder, half in apology.

'He did ring,' admits Cassie. 'I didn't have time to call back. Lucy had friends round so I had to cook them supper. Then I was overseeing homework, organising bedtime, that sort of thing.'

This is addressed to Kim because, of course, Harbinder knows nothing about that sort of thing.

'Have you any idea why he might have called you?'

'No.' This is said flatly, as if Cassie no longer cares if they believe her or not.

'Cassie,' says Harbinder. 'Have you ever heard of Bleeding Heart Yard?'

'I think Gary mentioned it once,' said Cassie. 'He popped round after one of the rugby reunions.'

How many reunions can one team have? wonders Harbinder. It makes her feel glad that she never even made the primary school rounders squad.

'What did Gary say about Bleeding Heart Yard?' she says.

'That he used to meet some of his Tory friends there. Pete said that it sounded just the right sort of bloodthirsty place for them.'

'Who else was at the rugby do?' asks Kim. 'Was Henry?'

Harbinder is surprised at the question and even more so by Cassie's careless answer.

'Oh yes. You wouldn't think he could play rugby, would you? But he was apparently quite a useful fly half.'

By evening, Harbinder is flagging but she is determined to wait it out for Anna Vance. After another sandwich stop, they drive back to Attlee Towers and Kim makes the journey up in the lift.

'The carer was there,' she says, when she arrives back at the car. 'She says they're expecting Anna soon.'

'She hasn't rung to say she's on her way?'

'No. Apparently her phone's not very reliable.'

Harbinder remembers the Nokia that Anna showed them, with some pride, that day in her room. She thinks again of the arrogance of a person who considers themselves above the latest technology, even if it means inconvenience, or even distress, to others.

It's nearly nine o'clock when a small white Fiat noses into the car park.

'That's *not* the car I expected Chris Foster to drive,' says Kim.

Harbinder gets out. 'Mr Foster? Ms Vance? I'd like to talk to you both, if you don't mind.'

Anna looks slightly wild, her curly hair standing on end.

'I've got to check on Mum,' she says. 'I've been out all day. She isn't well.'

'We've just been up there,' says Kim, reassuringly. 'Her carer's with her. Nice woman called Roxy.'

'I need to check.' She's almost hysterical now.

'OK,' says Harbinder. 'We'll wait.'

As Anna sprints across the car park, Chris Foster emerges from the Fiat. He's wearing a ridiculous baseball cap which he takes off and ruffles his hair. Don't worry, Harbinder tells him silently, you're still hot. Possibly thinning slightly, though.

'Good day?' she says.

'Yes. We went to Brighton. Look . . .' He tries for a matey tone. 'This is all a bit of a shock. I got a voicemail from Isabelle. She says Henry's dead. Is that true?'

'Let's discuss it back at the station,' says Harbinder.

'Discuss what?'

'All in good time,' says Harbinder. She's hoping to provoke a reaction but Chris just gives her a glance that teenage magazines would probably describe as 'smouldering'.

'We'll take Miss Vance in our car,' says Harbinder. 'You can follow in yours. I like it, by the way. Very cool.'

'Thanks,' says Chris. He doesn't argue about Anna and, when she emerges a few minutes later, Kim ushers her into the back of the squad car.

They chat inconsequentially about Brighton on the way to the station and, once there, Kim takes Anna upstairs to interview room one while Harbinder detains Chris in the reception area.

'Tea? Coffee?'

'No thanks. Look, what's all this about?'

'We've just got a few questions for you.' At just the right moment, Jake appears, trying to look intimidating.

'If you'd just follow DS Barker,' says Harbinder.

'Look,' says Chris Foster. He has a Tony Blair-like fondness for starting sentences like this. 'What's this all about? Do I need to get my lawyer?' He laughs slightly to show that it's a joke but also, possibly, to remind Harbinder that he could afford the best legal representation in the land.

Harbinder tries to sound shocked. 'Oh no. This isn't a formal interview. You can leave any time. It's just that we're very keen to follow up all of Henry's contacts so that we can catch the person who did this.'

'Of course,' says Chris, smoothing his hair. 'I want to help.'

Harbinder nods at Jake. She wants to see how Chris responds to a man asking the questions when he won't be able to go into his 'look how attractive and approachable I am' act. Or maybe he will.

'When did you last see Henry?' asks Jake. His flat northern voice (nothing like Ant or Dec) seems to have a calming effect on Chris. He leans back in his chair.

'At the reunion. God, was it only a few days ago? Last Saturday.'

Isabelle said almost the same thing and Harbinder supposes that it has been quite a week for the Manor Park alumni.

'Can you remember what you talked about that night?'

'The usual things. The old days. Work. I told him I voted

Labour.' Chris attempts a smile, probably assuming that Jake shares this political preference.

'And have you heard from him since? Texts? Phone calls?'

'No.' Harbinder doubts that he'd lie about this. Chris probably assumes that they have Henry's phone and can check the records.

'What did you do last night?'

'I was at home. In Clerkenwell. DI Kaur has been there.' Another comradely grin.

'All night?'

'Yes. I listened to some music. Watched something on Netflix. I woke up at eight. Had a shower and some breakfast, then went to call on Anna. We went to Brighton for the day.'

'Nice place, Brighton,' says Jake. 'Did you go on the pier?'

'We certainly did. It's obligatory, isn't it?'

And presumably the pier has CCTV, thinks Harbinder. Being a local Sussex person, she doesn't visit the tourist spots much.

'Mr Foster,' says Harbinder. 'Chris. When DS Manning and I called on you that time, you told us that you'd met Garfield Rice at a restaurant in Bleeding Heart Yard.'

Chris frowns. 'Yes.'

'Do you know if Henry Steep ever attended any such lunches?'

'I wouldn't think so. They were very much on opposite sides of the political divide, Henry and Gary.'

'But they were friends at school?'

'We were all friends at school,' says Chris. 'It seems a lifetime ago.'

Anna Vance is both more nervous and more forthcoming. She says that she had tea with Henry at the House of Commons yesterday.

Then she went home, alone, and spent the evening with her mother. This, Harbinder thinks, will be easy to check. Anna woke up at seven-thirty, 'got Mum sorted for the day' and then swanned off to Brighton with Chris Foster.

Harbinder asks Anna if she has ever heard of Bleeding Heart Yard and she says no, sounding suitably puzzled. She then asks if she can leave, playing the sick mother card again, and Harbinder says of course she can.

'What do you think?' says Harbinder to Jake after Anna has left the room.

'Anna's alibi is better. She was with her mother all evening. Chris was alone.'

'Anna's mother is ill. She probably goes to bed early. Plenty of time for Anna to creep out and kill Henry Steep.'

'Is that what you think she did?'

'I don't know but it's a possibility.'

'Is Anna strong enough to stab a man?'

'It wouldn't take much strength if you took him by surprise. And Henry wasn't a big man.'

'Why, though?'

'I don't know but I'd like to find out what they talked about on the House of Commons terrace. Let's send someone there tomorrow. We need to track Henry's last movements. The area around Parliament will be full of CCTV. We need to know what Henry was doing between eight p.m. and two-thirty a.m., which was when his body was discovered.'

'Meeting a lover?'

'Always a possibility. And all that bleeding heart stuff could point to a crime of passion. I always think it's odd, on Valentine's Day, to see dismembered hearts everywhere.' She thinks of the caged heart on the restaurant sign, of Deborah, Garfield's agent, saying, 'Some of the letters just had "bleeding heart" written on them, and some had a drawing of a heart with an arrow through it.' She's seen those images on cards. Cupid's arrow. The blood dripping down.

'Bloody hell, boss,' says Jake. 'That's dark.'

'The world is a dark place,' says Harbinder. She looks at her watch – there are no clocks in the interview suites. Nearly eleven. 'Let's call it a night now,' she says. 'I'd like to give you and Kim the morning off but we need everyone on the case. I promise I'll get you some leave soon.'

'Don't worry,' says Jake. 'I'm like Napoleon. I don't need much sleep.'

Napoleon. Harbinder has heard it all now. Well, she supposes that he was short too.

Unlike Napoleon, Harbinder is exhausted when the car drops her off at Barlby Road. She's too tired to eat and, anyway, she's full of Kim's sandwiches. She has a quick wash, changes into pyjamas and collapses onto the bed. She sleeps soundly until eight when she hears her flatmates leaving for work. In the kitchen she finds a silver foil parcel containing a piece of rye bread covered with thin slivers of chocolate. There's a note from Mette. *The Breakfast of Champions. Go get 'em tiger and all that shit. Mx.*

Chapter 31

Harbinder

Thursday

Harbinder arrives at work at nine to find the super, Simon Masters, waiting for her in her office.

'Ah, Harbinder,' he says, managing to convey the impression that she's late which, technically, she isn't. 'Bad business about Henry Steep.'

'Yes,' says Harbinder. 'Especially for his family.'

Freya, Harbinder's PA, appears with coffees. Harbinder thanks her profusely. The super less so.

'Do you think it's linked to the other MP's death?' asks Masters.

'It's a line of enquiry,' says Harbinder. 'And there is a connection.' She tells her boss about the Bleeding Heart dining club. He looks positively appalled.

'But these are important people. Very influential people.'

'We'll be tactful,' says Harbinder, thinking doubtfully of Jake and Tory.

'Not a word of this must reach the public.'

'No, that wouldn't be helpful.'

'The news broke last night. There'll be a lot of press interest. You'll need to do a press conference today. Do you want any help with that?'

'No thanks,' says Harbinder.

'No need to be nervous.' Masters tries what, in the right light, might be considered a fatherly smile.

'I'm not nervous,' says Harbinder. She thinks of Jeanne. 'Nervous and excited are two sides of the same thing'.

'It could be that the two cases are quite separate,' says Masters. 'Different MO, for one thing. Henry Steep could have been meeting someone . . .'

Go on, say it, thinks Harbinder. Henry was gay so he must have been meeting some rough trade lover.

Masters catches her eye. 'Someone insalubrious,' he concludes.

'We'll conduct a very thorough investigation,' says Harbinder. 'I could do with some more intel people. I need to trace a lot of CCTV.'

'I have every faith in you,' says Masters, not promising about the extra staff.

'Superintendent Masters has every faith in us,' Harbinder tells the team.

This is met with a few rueful grins. Masters is not that popular, despite allegedly singing 'Watching the Detectives' at every Christmas party.

'We need to work quickly,' says Harbinder, 'but we must be meticulous. We can't afford to cut corners.' She turns to the whiteboard. 'Henry Steep left the House of Commons at eight on the night of Tuesday the twenty-fourth of September. He shares an office with another MP. CCTV shows him hailing a taxi on Westminster Bridge at eight-fifteen. We've got the cab number so that should be easy to trace. We need to account for his movements between eight-fifteen and around midnight, when forensics estimate the murder occurred. They also think he was probably killed at the scene. Annoyingly, there's no CCTV in the yard itself.'

'The killer must have known that,' says Kim.

'Possibly. Or maybe they just got lucky.'

'So, Henry may have arranged to meet his killer,' says Jake. Harbinder wonders if his thoughts are going in the same direction as the super's but she has misjudged the DS.

'It must mean that it was someone he knew well,' he says. 'Maybe one of The Group.'

'We know Henry rang Cassie at approximately six-thirty p.m. on the twenty-fourth,' says Harbinder. 'That must have been before he left his parliamentary office. She says she didn't call back. We don't have Henry's phone but I've got on to the data people. They can do cell site analysis to work out where he was calling from. Cassie says she was home all night but she slept on the sofa so doesn't have a watertight alibi.'

There's that slight ripple of unease amongst the team that always accompanies any mention of their colleague.

Tory says, as ever, 'Surely Cassie isn't a suspect?'

'She's a person of interest,' says Harbinder. 'I know she's a colleague and a friend, but we can't forget that she has links with both dead men and her fingerprints were found on the murder weapon in the Garfield Rice case.'

'Anyone could have taken the syringe from her bag,' says Tory.

'That's true,' says Harbinder, 'but there's still the message Garfield left for Isabelle Istar about David Moore's death. Gary said that he thought David had been murdered and, what's more, he knew who did it. I'm convinced there's something Cassie isn't telling us about that.' She looks at the slightly mutinous faces in front of her. 'Let's put that aside for now. Priorities today are interviewing the Bleeding Heart diners and tracking Henry Steep's movements. If we could find his phone that would be a great help. It's linked to his husband's but seems to have been switched off at around midnight. The last message was sent at eleven from somewhere in the Strand area.'

'The goodnight text to Stephen,' says Kim.

'Yes,' says Harbinder. 'After that, nothing. Now let's get going. Jake, you carry on with the Bleeding Heart MPs. Kim, you're in charge of door-to-door at the scene.'

'Trouble is,' says Kim, 'there aren't many doors. Domestic ones, that is. It's all offices around there.'

'Do what you can,' says Harbinder, remembering that Mette worked on a development in the area. 'There may be builders, construction workers, night watchmen.'

'OK, boss,' says Kim.

Harbinder feels real satisfaction at the sight of her team setting off on their different missions. Part of her wishes she was going with them, but her job is coordination, triangulation and trying not to mess up the press conference. She's just scribbling down some notes when she gets a message from Trish, the civilian officer in charge of tracing CCTV.

'There's something you'll want to see.'

Harbinder goes into the main area to find Trish enlarging a picture on her screen.

'I contacted all the twenty-four-hour cafés around the Holborn area. This is from a place near Temple Tube station. Eleven-fifteen last night.'

The image is grainy and pixilated, but it shows Henry Steep talking intently to a woman who can only be Sonoma Davies.

It's mid-morning break time when Harbinder arrives at Manor Park school. The grass of the playing fields has turned purple with blazers and there's a sustained roar that can be heard several streets away. Harbinder gives her name at reception and is asked if she's there to give a citizenship talk to Year 8.

'No,' says Harbinder grimly, thinking of Jeanne's comments about Year 8. 'I'm here to see Ms Davies.'

A few minutes later, Sonoma herself appears, blindingly smart in a red trouser suit. She really does like that colour.

'This way, Detective Inspector.'

In the headteacher's office, surrounded by silver cups and certificates of achievement, Harbinder gets straight to the point.

'Did you meet Henry Steep late on Tuesday night?'

If Sonoma denies it, Harbinder plans to show her the CCTV. She's slightly disappointed when Sonoma replies, in a quiet voice, 'Yes.'

'Why?'

Sonoma pauses before replying, 'Henry said that he wanted to talk to me urgently.'

Harbinder waits. A bell rings and, a few seconds later, there's a thunder of footsteps in the corridor outside. Then all is silent again.

'Let the witness speak,' Harbinder hears the voice of Donna, her old boss, in her head. 'Then you can ask for clarification.'

'Henry was worried,' says Sonoma at last. 'He'd just seen a mutual friend, Anna, and he was worried about her state of mind. Anna's a lovely person but she can be slightly strange. Even at school she had these moments when she was odd. Distant.'

'Distant?'

'Yes, as if she had separated herself from reality. There were whole conversations – even events – that she didn't remember. She was always writing these stories and it was as if they were more real to her than what was going on around her. Henry met Anna on Tuesday and they talked about a tragedy that happened when we were at school. Henry was concerned that Anna seemed to have blocked it out.'

'A tragedy?'

'Yes. David Moore's death. We talked about it last time we spoke. David died after falling onto a railway track. It was in our final year. Just after we'd finished our A levels.'

A levels you excelled in, thinks Harbinder. She remembers that Sonoma, unlike Cassie, had felt able to go inter-railing that summer. Harbinder remembers Sonoma referring to David's death as 'a terrible time for the school'.

'Why was that so important that you had to drive across town to meet Henry in the middle of the night?' she says.

Another silence. The sound of chairs scraping across floorboards. A whistle blowing from the football pitch.

'When Garfield rang me on the night of the reunion,' said Sonoma, 'he said that he thought that David had been deliberately killed. He wondered if he should confront the person himself. I told him that he should go to the police, but Gary was worried about how it would affect people.'

'People?'

'Well, people like Isabelle, who's very sensitive. And Anna.'

'Did Garfield say who the killer was?'

'No, but then he died that night. So, you can see why I didn't ignore Henry's call.'

'Where did Henry go after meeting you?'

'I don't know. He got a message on his phone and left almost immediately.'

Temple is not that far from Holborn, thinks Harbinder, with her newly acquired London knowledge. Henry probably left the café and walked to meet his killer.

Frustration bubbles over. 'Why didn't you tell this to the police immediately?' she asks.

'I didn't want my school dragged into it.' *My school.* Sonoma's fiefdom. Harbinder remembers Sonoma's earlier reluctance to share information and her assertion that Garfield hadn't gone into any details about his concerns.

'Your school is already in it,' she says. 'In it up to the neck.'

Harbinder is in a daze on the drive back, London sliding past her in a blur of sudden rain. Could Anna, the outsider, really be the murderer? Did she kill David Moore all those years ago, and murder Garfield and Henry to cover it up? If Gary had wanted to confront David's killer, that meant it was someone at the reunion. Anna could easily have stolen Cassie's syringe, during the tragic disco dancing, killed Gary and then thrown the object away, wearing gloves all the time. She could have left her mother's flat last night, met Henry in Holborn, stabbed him in the heart, and returned for a jolly seaside jaunt with Chris. Harbinder thinks of Anna emerging, wild-haired, from the Fiat. There is certainly something wired-up, almost unhinged, about her sometimes.

Was Henry trying to ring Cassie to share his worries about Anna? But, if she is to be believed, Cassie didn't answer the call. It was Sonoma, working mother with a demanding job, who crossed London at night to meet her old schoolfriend. Is this slightly suspicious?

At the station, things are moving fast. The cab driver remembers picking Henry up on Westminster Bridge and dropping him outside a pub on the corner of the Strand and Aldwych. CCTV shows him leaving the pub at ten and walking towards Temple. More CCTV has Henry leaving the café at eleven forty-five and he's picked up again on Fetter Lane at ten minutes past midnight. At that point he's only metres away from Bleeding Heart Yard.

There's also a message to call the handwriting expert.

'I think we've got a match.'

'For the bleeding heart notes?'

'Yes. Hard to tell with so few words but I think it's a match for sample two.'

Harbinder looks at her notes. Handwriting sample two belongs to Paula Rice, Garfield's wife. Was Harbinder right, then, about it being a crime of passion? But why would Paula kill Henry?

Harbinder is so deep in thought that she doesn't hear the knock on the door.

'Boss?'

She looks up. Cassie Fitzherbert is standing in front of her.

'I've come to confess,' she says.

Chapter 32

Cassie

Thursday

The next morning, I got dressed in what I think of as my work clothes, dark trousers, white shirt, black jacket.

'What's going on?' said Pete. He was about to walk Sam to school. Kevin was standing in front of the door so that he wouldn't be forgotten. Lucy had already left.

'Harbinder asked me to come in for a meeting,' I said.

'Do you think that means she wants you back on the team?' said Pete.

'I hope so,' I said.

'Remember,' said Pete. 'She needs you more than you need her.'

There wasn't much more we could say, with Sam fussing about a mislaid football boot and Kevin watching our every move. But I knew the subtext. Pete didn't think I owed anything to a job that made me stressed and where – in his opinion – I had been passed over for promotion. He had no idea how much being a police officer meant to me.

'I'll text you,' I said. 'Let you know what she says.' I was thinking: will I be allowed a phone in prison?

Pete bent to put Kevin on the lead. I hugged Sam tightly, as I had done Lucy earlier. 'I love you.'

'You're hurting my ears,' said Sam. His ears stuck out and were very sensitive. The sight of them made my heart contract. When would I see them again, my brilliant, bolshy daughter and sweet-natured son?

'Why the tears?' said Pete, giving me a kiss. 'Are you dreading going back to work? Were you enjoying being a lady of leisure?'

I thought of cleaning the house the day before, of the thrill when I joined CID, of the inane chatter in the break room. 'Cheer up, Smoothie, it might never happen.' 'That's what she's afraid of, mate.'

'I'm crying because I'm happy,' I said. 'I'll see you later.'

I walked to the station. As I strode past the buses and cars, nose-to-tail in the familiar rush-hour snake, I thought of running along the seafront in Brighton, from the peace statue to the pier. Running had saved me then. I could still remember the feeling of the sea spray and fine sand on my face, the sound of the seagulls. But you can't run away for ever. There comes a time when you have to confess.

Confession was something that I struggled with when I first became a Catholic. The idea that you would go into a cubicle, the 'box' they called it, kneel down and list your sins to an invisible auditor on the other side of the grille. 'It's not like that now,' Father Kevin told me. 'You can sit face to face. It's just a chat really. A chat with God.' Because that was the thing; you were confessing to God, not the priest. 'Afterwards,' Father K promised me, 'you'll feel light and free. Almost transparent. Sure and being a Catholic is cheaper than seeing a therapist.' I did sometimes fantasise about confessing what happened with David. They're not allowed to tell the police, you know. Even if the person behind the screen confesses to murder or child abuse, the priest cannot break the seal of the confessional. The most they can do is refuse absolution until the person gives themselves up but, if they don't, the priest has to take that knowledge to their grave. But then I thought: was it fair to land Father Kevin, or one of his mates, with that responsibility? When I made my first confession – I insisted on a cubicle and an unseen priest – I felt only relief. I had got through it without being tempted to tell the truth. It was the best I could hope for.

But today I would be confessing not to God, or an unseen male cleric, but to Harbinder who was a woman of almost my own age (slightly younger, as Pete kept reminding me), a serious and formidable figure. As I neared the solid soot-stained building with portico and stumpy columns, I thought it was a shame that I wouldn't get to know Harbinder better. She wasn't the cosiest of bosses but she was efficient and knew how to delegate. I thought I would have enjoyed working with her. All the team liked her, and respected her, even Jake, who hadn't been pleased to get a woman boss.

'Hallo, Smoothie,' said Terry, the desk sergeant. 'Have you been on holiday? You're not very sun-tanned.'

'I've only been away a day,' I said.

'That's like a year in this place,' said Terry.

'You're not wrong there,' I said, pressing my key fob against the door to the upstairs rooms. I was slightly surprised that it still worked. As I crossed the open-plan area, I could see people bent over their computers, the intensity of an important case. Only Kim looked up and waved at me. I waved back, trying to smile.

Harbinder was in her office. She seemed deep in thought. She didn't hear my knock and only looked up when I said, 'Boss?' She has dark skin around her eyes that often makes her look tired but, today, I thought that she looked at the end of her tether.

'I've come to confess,' I said.

'Sit down,' she said, not even sounding that surprised. I sat opposite her and took a deep breath, the way I do when I'm trying to avoid a panic attack. In for four, out for eight.

'What exactly are you confessing to?' asked Harbinder.

'I killed David Moore,' I said. 'I pushed him onto the track and I killed him. Deliberately,' I added, in case she hadn't got the message.

'You'd better tell me about it,' said Harbinder.

'David raped me,' I said. 'I didn't give it that name at first but that's what it was. We'd been on a couple of dates. I wasn't in love with him. I was still in love with Gary, but David was an OK person to be seen with. I know it sounds shallow, but I liked having a boyfriend. I wasn't like Anna, who was happy going to parties on her own, scribbling in her little book and making jokes with Chris. But David raped Anna too. Or he would have done if they hadn't been interrupted.'

'David raped Anna?' says Harbinder.

'Or tried to. I guess he had problems with consent. Or something like that. We weren't taught much about these things in the nineties.'

'Tell me what happened to you.'

'David asked me to go back to his house. His flat. He wasn't rich like lots of the pupils at Manor Park. That was another thing I liked about him. I'd been to his house once before, for tea. His mum and dad had liked me. I liked them. I assumed his parents would be there this time but they were both out. 'My mum has to work,' David said, 'not like yours.' Mum had been a nurse before she'd met Dad but she gave up when she had children. I hadn't realised David resented that. He said he wanted to show me his bedroom. It was small but very neat. I remember thinking it was odd because he didn't have posters on his walls. We sat on the bed and he started to kiss me. That was OK but it started to get more serious. He undid my bra, unzipped my jeans. I said "no" but he didn't seem to hear me. I struggled a bit but – it sounds ridiculous – but I didn't want to make a scene. He held me down and he had sex with me. Afterwards he said, "How was it for you?" and sort of laughed. I rearranged myself and I left the flat. I thought he'd come after me, but he didn't. At home I had a shower, then I went to my room and wrote a letter to David saying that I didn't want to go out with him again. I think I even said sorry. I gave it to him at school the next day and he said, "Why?" I tried not to think about it again – I'm good at that – but, one day at Gary's house, Anna was talking about David and I said that he'd raped me.'

'Didn't you tell anyone else? Your parents?'

'No. I was ashamed. David wasn't my first, you see. I thought that people would judge me.'

'What happened when you told your friends?'

'Some of them didn't believe me,' I said. I thought of Izzy. 'But some of them did. Gary – Garfield Rice – was angry.' Even now that gave me a glow of satisfaction. 'And he said we should teach David a lesson.'

'What sort of lesson?'

'We were going to take David to the old Tube station, Imperial, and tell him we knew what he'd done. Then Gary was going to pretend to push him under a train.'

'Who was "we"?'

'Me, Gary, Henry and Chris. I was meant to get David to the station. I told him there were drugs there. Everyone went to Imperial to take drugs. Well, not me, but all the cool kids. I knew it wouldn't be difficult to get David there. He always wanted to be part of the in-crowd and . . . well . . . I knew he still liked me. Chris would be waiting by the entrance and Gary and Henry inside the station.'

'And Anna?'

'Anna was meant to be there, but I don't think she was. I think she had a row with Chris. They broke up soon afterwards.'

'So, what happened in the Tube station?'

'Nobody was there. Well, Henry was but I didn't know that until later. David said something to me, something flirtatious. I snapped. I pushed him. I don't remember much after that. I think we struggled. I've got a memory of him kneeling at my feet but I don't think that really happened. But I remember the train coming, this explosive noise, and Henry telling me to run.'

'Why did he say that?'

'We all knew I couldn't be at the scene because of my history with David. Gary saw it all. He was on the bridge on the way to the station. He told the police that David had fallen by accident. Chris said that he'd gone to Imperial to buy drugs. Everyone assumed David was high. I wasn't even questioned. Nor was Henry. But I killed him. When I was eighteen, I killed a man. I've tried to put it out of my mind but, when Gary died, it all came back. I can't run away from it, however fast I run. So, I'm confessing.'

There was a silence. I could hear chatter in the open-plan office outside. I thought of Pete working on his computer at home, the kids at school.

'Cassie,' said Harbinder, her voice very gentle. 'I think you should talk to someone. A counsellor. I don't think you're clear in your mind about what happened that day. It was twenty-one years ago, after all. I think you might be suffering from PTSD.'

'I know what happened,' I said. I felt strangely insulted that Harbinder didn't believe me. 'I think it's linked to Gary's death. And Henry's.'

'How?' says Harbinder. 'Who killed them?'

'I think it might be Chris,' I said.

'Chris?' said Harbinder. 'Chris Foster? Why?'

I'd had plenty of time to think about this.

'I saw him with Gary at the reunion,' I said. 'I went out to get some air and I heard Chris talking to Gary by the loos. Chris was saying, "I'll never forgive you."'

'What did Gary say?'

'I couldn't hear the words but he sounded placatory. A few minutes later I saw Chris go back into the library where the party was. I went back in too and, about twenty minutes later, someone shouted that they'd found Gary collapsed in the Gents.'

'And you think Chris could have killed him?'

'I didn't at the time but, thinking back, I think it's possible. He's a cool customer, Chris. Doesn't show much emotion. And he's a diabetic too. He would have had access to a syringe.'

Harbinder gave me one of her searching looks. I made sure that I stared back, not blinking. It was a game I used to play with Emily.

'Why didn't you tell me this before, Cassie?'

I lowered my eyes. Look penitent, I told myself. 'I was afraid you'd find out about . . . about David.'

'It would have saved us all a lot of trouble,' said Harbinder, 'if you'd just been straight with me from the beginning. The David thing, it's so long ago, I can't see any merit in reopening the case. It would cause distress to his family, his dad, for one thing.'

Now I had no problem staring at her. When you've lived in fear of something for so long, the idea that someone can dismiss it with a few words is oddly upsetting.

'Do you mean you won't charge me?'

'I can't see any merit in it,' Harbinder repeated. 'My priority has to be the murders of Garfield Rice and Henry Steep.'

'Are you going to bring Chris in for questioning?'

'I can't discuss the case with you,' said Harbinder. 'You know this, Cassie. I'll have to ask you to give a statement about what you overheard at the reunion but, for the moment, you're on leave. Go home.'

Again, there was the feeling of a prison door being opened and the outside world awaiting me. It felt very cold.

Chapter 33

Anna

Thursday

Henry's murder was on Radio 4's *Today* programme.

'Labour MP Henry Steep was found dead in central London on Tuesday night. Police are treating his death as suspicious.'

Mum was having a good morning, so we were having breakfast in the kitchen. There was barely enough room for a folding table, but I preferred it to Izzy's marble palace or Chris's chrome operating theatre. The units were old-fashioned Formica, but Mum had painted them bright pink and added stencils of flowers and butterflies.

'That's your friend, isn't it?' said Mum. 'You went to see him the other day.'

'That's right,' I said, pushing the cafetière plunger down to avoid looking at her.

'What the hell's going on?' said Mum.

The announcer was talking about Henry's work as shadow environment secretary. 'Steep was passionately committed to environmental causes. In this, he differed strongly from his old schoolfriend, Garfield Rice MP, who also died recently.' This was as near as the BBC would get to suggesting a link. Mum had no such qualms.

'Is someone killing off MPs one by one? Or is it something to do with Manor Park? I never did like that place.'

'Why did you send us there then?'

'It had good results,' says Mum. 'And it was free. But, seriously, Anna, what's happening? Was Garfield murdered? Was Henry? That school has never been lucky. It's been cursed since that poor boy was run over by a train.'

Mum's conflation of the three events made me feel almost light-headed. I had to hold on to the chipped working surface. She'd been shocked about David at the time but, when she saw how upset I was, she hadn't mentioned it again. Just as she hadn't mentioned the sudden absence of Chris and my flight to Edinburgh and then Florence.

'I don't know,' I said, falling back on the truth. 'The police questioned me and Chris last night.'

'The policewoman who came here, the Indian woman? She was nice, I thought.'

'She's tough,' I said. 'And she obviously thinks the two deaths are linked. Chris is calling for me later. We're going to see if we can make sense of it.'

'Tell him to come up and say hallo,' said Mum. 'I'm feeling almost human today. And change the channel, for God's sake. I like Radio 1 in the mornings.'

'Hallo, Star,' said Chris. 'It's good to see you again.'

I was glad that he didn't say anything crass like 'you haven't changed at all'. The contrast between Mum in 1998, still black-haired and glamorous, and the emaciated figure in the chair by the window, was heartbreaking, even though I was used to it now. Mum was now bald, her head swathed in a jaunty red scarf, and you could see the bones of her skull. I watched Chris closely for signs of shock, but he just said, again, 'It's good to see you.'

'Come closer,' said Mum. 'You're still as good-looking as ever. And you're so famous now.'

'I'm no Bryan Ferry,' said Chris.

I was amazed that he remembered Mum's love of Roxy Music.

'Oh, I did love Bryan,' she said. 'Shame he turned out to be a Tory. You didn't, did you?'

'Definitely not.'

'No fox-hunting children?'

'No. My kids feed the foxes at home in Chichester. They've got a cat called Foxy.'

He had never mentioned his children or their species-confused pet to me.

'Are you married?' asked Mum, taking advantage.

'No,' said Chris. 'And I'm not with the children's mother any more.'

'I've never been married either,' said Mum. 'And nor has Anna. Maybe these things run in families.'

'Maybe,' said Chris. 'But my parents are still together. They despair of me.'

'I bet they don't,' said Mum. 'I hear you two are doing some sleuthing today.'

'Just chatting,' I said. I already had my jacket on.

'You should be good at detective work,' Mum told me. 'When you think of all those murder stories you used to write.'

'"Murder Made Easy",' said Chris, referring to the story I'd written for the school magazine.

And, suddenly, I thought of Chris's A.E. Housman lampoon.

I'm just a cheerful Shropshire bunny. Murder is nice and suicide funny.

Chris drove us back to his penthouse in the Fiat 500. 'Don't hurry back,' Mum had said. 'I've had a good breakfast. I'll probably sleep until lunchtime. And Roxy is coming to make me some soup.'

We stepped out from the lift into the light-filled room. It was a rainy day but even that was exciting from this height, like being on board an ocean-going liner. I was surprised to see paper and pens on the table by the window, as well as a selection of pastries.

'Sleuthing supplies,' said Chris.

'Oh my God,' I said. 'Are you serious about us attempting to solve this thing?'

'Why not?' said Chris. 'After all, we know everyone involved. And with your crime-writing brain and my, er, song-writing brain . . .'

'We'll come up with the "Ballad of Reading Gaol".'

'It's either that or DI Kaur pinning it on one of us.'

'You've got a point,' I said. I sat at the table and took a bite of an almond croissant. Chris went to operate the space-age coffee machine in the kitchen and came back with espressos in tiny, shiny cups.

'Just like home,' he said.

This gave me a slight jolt. I've got so used to being back at Attlee Towers that it is becoming difficult to think of Italy as home. With an effort I made myself remember my flat with its tiled floors and uncomfortable furniture, the balcony overlooking terracotta roof-tops, the palazzos, the Vespas, the courtyards where you could come face to face with a sixteenth-century Madonna or a twenty-first century Ferrari, the cafés where you drank your coffee standing up.

Chris wrote 'Gary' on a sheet of paper. 'What do we know about Gary?'

'Tory,' I said, thinking of Mum.

'But he was a socialist at school.'

I thought of Henry saying, 'We were all socialist at school.' 'He's confused,' I said. 'Like your children's cat.'

Chris gave me a sideways look but wrote 'Conservative, once Labour.'

'Married,' I said. Once more channelling Mum.

'Married to Paula,' Chris wrote.

'Once in love with Izzy,' I said.

That went down on the list too.

'Lunches at Bleeding Heart Yard,' wrote Chris. His writing was pleasing, generous with big capitals and looping tails.

'Tell me about that again,' I said.

'Gary invited me to lunch once,' said Chris. 'He was a member of this strange right-wing dining club. They invited guests and had speakers. They met at a restaurant in Bleeding Heart Yard. When I went, the speaker was a climate change activist.'

'I thought Gary didn't believe in climate change.'

'But he did. That was obvious after the talk. He believed in it but was obviously being paid by his capitalist friends to pretend it wasn't happening.'

'Bastards,' I said. 'Death's too good for them,'

Chris put down his pen. 'Do you know, that's what Izzy said about David. All those years ago.'

'I don't remember,' I said.

'You're going to have to stop saying that,' said Chris.

He was smiling but suddenly I was so angry I couldn't speak. Why did everyone insist on me remembering everything? I could hear Henry's voice, sounding almost amused, 'I saw you. In the building opposite. I was looking directly at you.'

I stood up. 'I think I'd better leave.'

'No,' said Chris. 'Don't go.' That's what Henry had said too. Was I ever going to stop running away?

As I stood, irresolute, there was an electronic ping from somewhere. Chris picked up the entry phone. I remembered that moment on the beach at Brighton when the charged atmosphere had been interrupted by a phone message.

Somehow, I wasn't surprised that it was the same person this time.

'Izzy's outside,' said Chris.

Chapter 34

Anna

Izzy erupted out of the lift in a flurry of scarves and a bright green coat.

'Why didn't either of you call me?' she said. 'When you heard about Henry?'

'Things have been moving rather quickly,' said Chris. 'We were both questioned by the police last night.'

This stopped Izzy in her tracks, though she managed to slide out of her coat and hand it to Chris.

'Coffee?' he said, sounding like a butler.

'I'd love a coffee,' she said. 'Can you do me a macchiato with extra milk on the side?' Chris disappeared to pull levers and compress air. Izzy looked at me and said, 'Isn't this awful?' She was wearing a black jumper with black jeans and looked like a secret agent. Despite her words, I couldn't help feeling that she was enjoying the drama.

'I still can't believe it,' I said. 'First Gary, now Henry.'

'We have to solve it,' she said. 'The police obviously think one of us did it. They came to call on me yesterday. Harbinder and Kim. They know about me and Gary. They probably think I was having an affair with Henry too.'

I was slightly taken aback by this reasoning, also that Izzy was on first-name terms with the police. All roads really did lead to Izzy. But, then again, Chris and I had just been having a similar conversation.

'They must know Henry was gay,' I said, in reply to her last statement.

'Yes.' Izzy put her hand to her chest. 'Poor Stephen. I feel so sorry for him. He loved Henry so much.'

'What did the police say to you?' I said. Unlike Izzy, I wasn't on first-name terms with them.

'Oh, just asking where I was on Tuesday night, that sort of thing. The point is, they think it was one of us.'

Chris came in with a tray. Macchiato for Izzy, milk on the side as requested, and another espresso for me.

'Anna and I were just trying to work it out ourselves,' he said. 'Treating it like a murder mystery.'

'You should be good at that, Anna,' said Izzy. 'I remember the mysteries you used to write. "Murder Made Easy". When the clues were all in the recipe. And that other thing you wrote, where the woman kills the man because she loves him so much.'

I'd forgotten that I had shown Izzy my embarrassing teenage efforts.

Izzy drifted over to the table. 'Let's see how far you've got,' she said. 'Good idea to start with Gary. Conservative, once Labour. Married to Paula. Once in love with Izzy.'

'We were brainstorming,' I said, acutely embarrassed.

'He was still in love with me,' said Izzy.

I didn't look at Chris. I hadn't told him what Izzy had told me over the Chablis and brownies, perhaps because of the 'lovebirds' comment about me and Chris.

Now he said, very quietly, 'Were you having an affair with Gary, Iz?'

'It sounds so sordid put like that,' said Izzy. She sat at the table and started to doodle on the paper. 'We were in love. It was serious.'

'Tell Chris what Gary told you,' I said. 'When he rang you that time.'

'He said he knew who killed David,' said Izzy, drinking her coffee in one. 'And then he was killed.'

'Did he say who it was?' I admired the calmness of Chris's voice. He could have been enquiring about the *Strictly* results.

'No,' said Izzy. 'But he'd been at one of those rugby reunions when he rang. I thought it must have been something he'd heard there.'

'Henry said that Cassie killed David,' I said.

'You didn't tell me any of this.' There was something in Chris's voice that made Izzy look from him to me and back again.

'It was when I went to see Henry at the Houses of Parliament,' I said. 'He said that Cassie pushed David. He said he saw it.' I paused. 'He also said he saw me.'

'But you weren't there,' said Izzy.

'I didn't think I was.' Suddenly my legs seemed to give way and I sank onto Chris's L-shaped sofa. 'I didn't think I was there but maybe I was.'

And I started to cry.

In a way, my tears helped. Izzy came to kneel in front of me.

'Don't cry, Anna. It's OK. We're all together again.'

It wasn't OK and we weren't together again because half of us were dead but the warmth in Izzy's voice soothed me. I searched for a tissue. Chris handed me some kitchen roll. I wanted him to comfort me but all he said was, 'There must be some way of unlocking those memories.'

'Therapy,' said Izzy eagerly. 'I had therapy after David died.'

'Why?' I said. 'You weren't there, either.'

'It was just so awful,' said Izzy. She sat next to me on the sofa and tucked her feet under her. I'd forgotten about her ability to look at home in any situation. 'Someone had died. Someone our age. It made me think about death. For a time, I used to listen outside my mum and dad's bedroom at night to hear them breathing and think that, at any minute, they might stop.'

I thought of Mum. This was actually true of her now but, at eighteen, I'd thought her invincible.

'Did you ever think that we'd killed him?' asked Chris. 'The people at the station. Me, Henry and Cassie. Gary too.'

'Gary wasn't there,' said Izzy. 'He was above it all, on the bridge.'

This seemed to sum Gary up. He was 'above it all' in every sense. I thought of the day I'd looked down on London from the Houses of Parliament and thought about superiority complexes.

'How did you think David had died?' Chris persisted.

'I thought it was an accident,' said Izzy. 'That's what Gary said. That David slipped and fell.'

'But maybe that wasn't what happened,' I said. 'Maybe Gary saw Cassie push him.'

'Then why didn't he say so at the time?' said Izzy.

'He wouldn't have done that,' said Chris. And he spoke so

definitely that we both turned to look at him. Chris was standing by the window with the light behind him so I couldn't see his expression. The rain was still hurling itself at the glass, running down in rivulets of tears. 'Gary would never betray one of The Group,' said Chris. 'Remember how close we all were. And Gary thought of himself as our leader. He would have thought he was doing the right thing. Cassie needed protecting and, after all, David deserved it.'

This was what I'd thought at the time too but now the words rather shocked me. I thought of Henry saying, 'His parents didn't deserve to lose their son.' Henry had also described the events of that day as a 'dangerous combination'. 'Everyone a bit mad, Cassie wanting revenge, Gary in full messiah mode. We should never have been anywhere near a speeding train.'

'But then why did Gary suddenly decide that David was murdered?' said Izzy. 'In his phone call to me he said it like it was a new discovery.' She sounded almost resentful, as if Gary had duped her by leaving an ambiguous message and then selfishly getting himself killed.

'Henry said that Cassie pushed David,' I said. 'He told me the day I met him at the House of Commons. He seemed very sure but then he seemed sure he'd seen me there too.'

'What happened when you met Henry?' said Izzy. 'Were you the last person to see him alive?'

This was said with a certain amount of ghoulish pleasure.

'I doubt it,' I said. 'I left the Houses of Parliament at about four. Then I went straight home. Chris and I went to Brighton the next day. We didn't know about Henry until you called.'

'The police were waiting for us when we got back,' said Chris.

'Harbinder's quite scary, isn't she?' said Izzy. 'Kim's nice though, the one with the dyed hair and the East End accent.'

'I think she's scary too, in her own way,' I said, remembering our chat about Brighton in the car last night. 'All that "I'm your best friend" stuff.'

'What did they ask you?' said Izzy. 'Did they ask about Bleeding Heart Yard?'

I stared at her. 'Yes, they did. Did they ask you?'

'Yes. I said I filmed a historical drama there once. I was Lady Elizabeth.'

I had no idea who Lady Elizabeth was but I was pretty sure that she was the heroine of this particular drama.

'They asked us too,' said Chris. 'It must mean that Henry's death is connected to that area. Do you think his body was found there?'

It sounded so cold put like that. *His body.*

'Should we go there?' said Izzy. 'Have a look at the place. It's quite boring, as I remember, though some of the alleyways are interesting.'

'Jesus, Izzy,' said Chris. 'If he was killed there, the place will be swarming with police. How do you think it will look if the three of us turn up on a sightseeing trip?'

'Murderers always return to the scene of the crime,' I said.

'Is that from one of your stories?' asked Izzy.

'No. I think I read it somewhere.'

Izzy got up and walked the length of the room, past the sofas and the modern art and the modestly concealed awards. I thought she must be getting bored but, when she turned to face us, her eyes were full of tears.

'I still can't believe they're dead. Henry or Gary. Do you think we're under a curse?'

'That's what my mum said this morning,' I said. 'She said that Manor Park was cursed.'

'We have to break the curse,' said Izzy. 'By solving this thing.' She got up and went to the table. 'Let's carry on brainstorming.'

I looked at Chris. He raised an eyebrow. Something he'd perfected at school.

'Henry,' said Izzy. 'What do we know about Henry?'

'MP,' I said.

'Shadow Environment Secretary,' said Chris.

'Married to Stephen,' said Izzy. 'I went to their wedding.'

'Did you?' I said. I'd been invited but didn't make the trip.

'I go to all the weddings,' said Izzy. 'I went to Cassie's. And Gary's. Paula wore a really odd dress.'

'You haven't been to mine,' I said. 'Or Chris's.'

'Oh, I think I went to Chris's,' said Izzy. 'Wasn't it when you were a student? Chelsea Register Office?'

'Why didn't you tell me?' I said. We were driving back to Mum's after a day of listening to Izzy talk about murder and trying not to look at each other. 'You actually said to Mum *this morning* that you weren't married.'

'I'm not,' said Chris. 'Siobhan and I were only together for a few years. We got married because she was pregnant. That's how it was back then.'

'Back then? It was only about fifteen years ago not the nineteenth century. My mum didn't get married when she was pregnant and that was in 1979.'

'Your mum's a one-off.'

'I know she is but that's not the point. You deliberately let me think you'd never been married.'

'I know,' said Chris. 'I'm sorry.' He turned to look at me. The Fiat swerved and the car behind hooted.

'Keep your eyes on the road,' I said. 'We don't want another two corpses for the Manor Park curse.'

We were silent as the little car zipped in and out of the rush-hour traffic.

'I can't believe the gossip websites don't know,' I said at last, no longer caring if Chris guessed that I was stalking him.

'It was so long ago,' said Chris, once again under the delusion that the noughties were the middle ages. 'Only a few people were there. Just our parents really.'

'And Izzy.'

'Yes. And Izzy. We saw quite a lot of each other in those days. We were both in London. I was at the Slade and she was at RADA. I didn't plan to invite her, but she found out about it somehow. You know how she likes drama. And weddings.'

This was an invitation to smile but I didn't take it.

'Siobhan and I were never well-suited,' said Chris. 'I mean, she's a lovely person but we were never meant to be together. We tried to make it work for the kids but we finally split up when Connor was two.'

'Yeah. My dad left when Sophie was two. It's the ideal time really.'

I meant to hurt him and I think I did. He said, quietly, 'I have tried. I've tried to be a good father.'

'Whilst whizzing round the world being a famous pop star.'

'I never wanted to be famous,' said Chris. 'I never expected it. I expected . . .'

'What did you expect?'

'I expected that you and I would get married.'

This silenced me for the rest of the journey. Once, those words would have made me so happy. Even now there was some gratification that Chris, too, had had the regressive wedding fantasy: the white dress, the beaming relations, the honeymoon in Tuscany. Except he'd had his wedding, to someone else at Chelsea Register Office.

When Chris parked outside Attlee Towers, I opened the door immediately. 'Bye,' I said. 'Thank you for the coffee and the croissants.'

I thought that Chris would reply – plead with me, shout, make me laugh – but he simply turned the little car in a neat circle and drove away.

Back at the flat, I made poached eggs on toast but neither Mum nor I ate much. Roxy came to help Mum get to bed and I went into my room and searched under the bed for the cardboard boxes containing my old life.

The sight of the Manor Park crest brought back all sorts of feelings: nostalgia, regret, sadness, even fear. *Anna Vance. Form 10PR. Science.* Our teacher had been Mr Price, middle-aged, strict-but-fair with a slight Welsh accent. We did combined science at school, which was an amalgam of physics, biology and chemistry with all the interesting bits left out. You got two GCSEs at the end of it. I'd only managed two Cs and the work in the book was half-hearted, to say the least. 'You must try harder, Anna,' Mr Price had written. At the end of the book, there was the start of the story I had obviously discussed with Izzy. It was written in green ink with my sixth form handwriting.

The Heart Has Its Reasons by Anna Vance.
Some are born murderers and some have murder thrust upon them.
That's how I justified it, at any rate, the day I joined the illustrious band of killers . . .

I put this literary work to one side and, underneath the textbooks, I found what I was looking for: three diaries tied together with an elastic band. The books ranged from a Hello Kitty Appointments Diary 1996 with illustrations of the eponymous feline, to a proper page-a-day hardback. I opened the 1998 diary and the first thing I saw was the signature: Mrs Anna Foster. Dear God. And I had thought of myself as a feminist. *I expected that you and I would get married.*

I didn't have to think of the date David died because it was engraved on my heart.

24 June 1998.

I'd written FINAL EXAM in red ink and, underneath, in my favourite green:

I feel like my life is over. Chris said that he didn't think we should see each other anymore. 'See each other'. What a stupid euphemism. I hate him. I love him.
Then The Accident. What a day. The worst ever.

247

I sat back on my heels. No mention of the exam. It had clearly been overshadowed by my stupid teenage heartbreak. And by 'The Accident'. I wished I'd written something like, 'I heard about a fatal accident that happened when I definitely wasn't there'. *Then The Accident.* Those three words were gnomic and unhelpful. What was the significance of the capitals? They seemed to make the subject of the sentence appear somehow ironical, like quotation marks. Or maybe I was just given to random capitals in those days?

I was so absorbed that I didn't hear the knock on the front door. 'Anna!' Mum shouted. 'We've got visitors.' Typical of her to put it that way. Anyone else would think of burglars, or worse. I thought of 'The Monkey's Paw'. Of the couple praying for their son to come back from the dead and then praying for the monster to go away.

I put on the security chain.

'Who is it?'

'It's me. Chris.'

I opened the door and, just like a love song, I walked into his arms.

Chapter 35

Anna

We'd had sex in this bed once before. After that first time, in his parents' spare room, Chris and I couldn't get enough of each other. We also had an unusual amount of freedom because of our so-called study leave. Chris's parents were at work all day and his younger brother, Callum, was at school. We had the run of the house in Chelsea; eating McDonald's hamburgers in the space-age kitchen, watching French films on TV, having baths in the decadently sunken tub. But the weekends were a problem. Chris's parents would selfishly insist on hanging round their own house reading the *Guardian* and drinking wine. They were always very friendly to me, Petra and Anthony Foster. They might even have let us sleep together if we had asked. We were both over sixteen, after all, though I (pesky August birthday) wasn't yet eighteen. But we didn't ask. We loitered, burning with frustration, while Callum monologued about *Star Wars*. He's a doctor now.

One Saturday, when we couldn't stand it any longer, we took the bus to Attlee Towers. My mum was working at Boots and Sophie was out with a friend. Chris and I made love on my single bed while the drug dealers in the flat below played 'I Want You Back' by NSYNC on repeat.

Now, I called through Mum's door, 'It's Chris.'

'Say hi from me.'

'What will she think?' said Chris.

'That we're having sex,' I said.

'Is that what we're doing?'

'I think so, don't you?'

We took up more space than we had as eighteen-year-olds. I was pressed up against the wall, the wood chip pressing into my face. Chris's arm was across me and he muttered in his sleep. When I eventually slept, I dreamt of the film *Titanic*, the band playing, the elderly couple in each other's arms, Rose on her life raft while Jack floundered in the water. I was ashamed, even in my subconscious, at having such a clichéd dream.

I was woken up by loud knocking on the door. Maybe this time it really was masked assassins. I climbed over Chris and pulled on my dressing gown.

I reattached the security chain. 'Who is it?'

'The police,' came the answer.

I opened the door, with the chain on, to find two uniformed officers proffering warrant cards.

'Is Chris Foster here?'

'Yes. No.'

'We've got a warrant for his arrest.'

'What are you talking about? You can't have.'

'It's OK, Anna.' Chris appeared behind me, fully dressed. 'Can you ring my solicitor? I've written the name down.'

'Don't go.'

'It's all right.' He gave me a brief kiss on the head. At the door, he turned. 'I want you back,' he said.

I checked on Mum but she was still asleep. Going closer, I saw that she was wearing earplugs. Very tactful. Chris and I had tried to be quiet but sound travelled in the flimsy-walled flat. I went into the kitchen and made myself a cup of tea. I'm not a good sleeper at the best of times and there was no way I'd get back to sleep now.

My room looked like a crime scene. My Laura Ashley duvet was crumpled at the foot of the bed, the fitted sheet half off, revealing a stripy, stained mattress. My old schoolbook and diaries had somehow fallen on the floor. On 10PR Science, Chris had scrawled 'Linden Grey', with his loopy Y. There was also a mobile phone number. I had no idea if a man or a woman would answer. Or if anyone would at ten-thirty at night. But, on the second ring, a posh female voice said, 'Yes?'

'Hallo,' I said. 'I'm calling on behalf of Chris Foster.'

I explained it very badly, starting at the wrong point, 'I'm an old schoolfriend,' but Linden Grey asked a few quick questions and ascertained the police station and the name of the officer in charge.

'I'll be there,' she said.

Her brisk efficiency made me feel slightly better, but I still couldn't sleep. I drank my tea sitting on the floor and, eventually, reached for the diaries again.

19 June 1998

Sometimes I really think that Chris and I are the same person. Today we caught a bus to Catford, just because it was the last stop on the route. There's an actual giant cat there, on the top of some building. We sang nursery rhymes all the way, changing the words to include our favourite bits from Housman. Later we MTBWTB at his parents' house.

Jesus Christ. I sent out a silent apology to the other occupants of the bus. Imagine the irritation of sitting near two teenagers intoning 'Is My Team Ploughing?' to the tune of 'Boys and Girls Go Out to Play'. I had no problem with the acronym. It came back to me, unscathed, across the years. Made The Beast With Two Backs. I'd come across this euphemism for sex in one of Mum's raunchy romances and we both thought it was hilarious. But, a week later, Chris had thought we ought to stop seeing each other.

Had I said anything about David?

2 June 1998
Worked at the shop. In the evening Cassie came around and we talked about David. She said, 'Would you kill him if you knew you could get away with it' and I said, 'yes'.

Jesus.

11 April 1998
Molly's party
OK party. Got separated from the group early on. Izzy and Gary snogged on the sofa. Cassie got off with someone's friend from Latymer Upper. Chris wasn't there because he had some family do. I messed around with David Moore, laughing and pretending to snog. Then he suggested going into the basement where there was a

snooker table and, apparently, more booze. I didn't really want to go but I did. Then, it was horrible, D was kissing me but with his teeth bared so it was a sort of bite. Then he put his hand down my trousers, undoing the zip. I said 'no, no' but he laughed more and pushed me onto a sofa bed thing. Then someone came in and switched on the lights. Someone else laughed and said, 'No fornication in the snooker room.' I ran away and cried in the loo for a bit. Then I came out and played snog, marry, avoid with Izzy and Gary. Caught the night bus home.

An 'OK party'. Really? An attempted rape and then a game of Snog, Marry, Avoid. Crying in the loo, Cassie getting off with some random boy, Chris absent, then the night bus, undoubtedly full of drunk men and girls like me being sick. Happy days.

16 May 1998

We were all in the Crow's Nest after school. I was looking out of the window when someone said something about Caliban. I thought about Caliban trying to rape Miranda. 'Thou dids't prevent me. I had peopled else This isle with Calibans.' If someone hadn't interrupted David would he have raped me, even made me pregnant? I suddenly saw David as an awful misshapen creature, hardly human, the way Miss Jones told us not to write about Caliban. I heard myself telling The Group about what happened. Izzy made some fatuous comment. Sometimes I hate her. But then Cassie said that David had actually raped her. Gary said he wanted to kill David. I have an awful feeling that nothing will ever be the same again.

Well, I was right about that, wasn't I? I had completely forgotten that it was *The Tempest*, our set play for A level, that had reminded me of David and the infamous party. If I hadn't said what I did, would Cassie ever have told us about her experience? I can see her now, lying on the floor, reading a book. Probably *The Tempest*, now I come to think of it. Chris was strumming on a guitar, one of his more irritating habits. Henry was probably writing a few million cue cards, Sonoma calmly recollecting every date in the Wars of the Roses. Gary and Izzy were mock fighting on the sofa with lots of squeals and giggles. I remember catching Henry's eye and him making a vomit gesture. When Cassie spoke, she looked directly at Gary. 'Changed eyes' is the phrase that occurs to me now. I think it's from *The Tempest*. 'I'd like to kill him,' Gary said. He may have squirmed on the sofa with Izzy, he may even have snogged her by the bins, but there was no doubt that he still loved Cassie too.

Did Izzy know this? Did Cassie?

I must have slept eventually. When I woke up it was six a.m. and a feeble light was filtering through the thin floral curtains. I could hear Mum moving around in her room.

I got up and found her in her red dressing gown shuffling along to the loo.

'Sorry, love,' she said. 'Did I disturb you?'

I remembered the ear plugs. I should really apologise for disturbing *her*.

'No,' I said. 'I couldn't sleep.'

'Has Chris gone?'

'Yes. Are you up for a chat?'

'Always. Just let me have my wee first.'

I made us both tea.

'A good English cuppa,' I said, which was an old joke between us.

'None of your foreign muck,' Mum joined in. I got into the bed next to her.

'Your feet are cold,' she grumbled.

'Cold feet, warm heart,' I said.

'That's hands.'

I warmed my hands on my mug. I've always loved Mum's room: the yellow walls, the flowery eiderdown, the old perfume bottles on her draped dressing table, the pictures ranging from her own oils of Greece and Turkey to embarrassing artwork from me and Sophie. The curtains were orange and the carpet red. 'My days,' said one of the carers, 'you need sunglasses in here.'

'So, what's happening?' said Mum. 'Give it to me straight. I won't tell anyone. Cross my heart and hope to die.' She gave a grim chuckle that turned into a cough.

So I told her about Gary telling Izzy that he knew who'd killed David, about Henry insisting that I was there when it happened, about Izzy's affair with Gary, about Chris mysteriously being arrested.

'And you haven't heard any more from him?'

'My phone's out of battery.' And I'd temporarily lost the charger.

'That thing's useless. Ring him from the landline.'

'I don't know the number.'

'Go round there when it's a more decent hour.'

It was nearly seven. I could hear the buses outside.

'Why do you think they've arrested Chris?' asked Mum. 'He hasn't got a motive to kill Gary or Henry. Unless he's in love with Izzy too.'

'That's not very tactful, Mum.'

'Just exploring every avenue.' The conversation seemed to have given Mum new energy. Her eyes sparkled under her red scarf, which was rakishly askew like the headdress of a 1920s flapper. I still couldn't get used seeing her without eyelashes though.

'I don't know why they've arrested him,' I said. 'I wish he'd ring.'

Chris turned up when Mum and I were having breakfast. He'd changed his clothes and looked considerably fresher than I did.

'I didn't get away until the early hours,' he said. 'So I went back to the flat to shower.'

'You could have texted.'

'I did. I bet your phone was out of battery.'

I ignored this.

'What happened?' I said, bringing him through to the kitchen. Mum was eating toast, more than I'd seen her consume for ages. She greeted Chris affectionately.

'How were the cells? Did they beat you up?'

'It wasn't too bad,' said Chris, sitting at the folding table. 'They didn't have anything on me. Linden saw that immediately.'

'How could they arrest you, then?' said Mum. 'I mean, you have rights.' She was a great one for rights. I remember being dragged along to marches for A Woman's Right to Choose and The Right To Die amongst others.

'I think DI Kaur was just chancing her arm,' said Chris. 'Wanting to see if I'd crack.'

I put a cup of coffee in front of him and refilled my mug. Mum was back to drinking hot water with lemon.

'And did you?' said Mum. 'Crack, I mean?'

'Linden told me to answer "no comment" to everything,' said

Chris. 'She wanted to see what they had, which was nothing really.'

'Did you really do one of those "no comment" interviews like on TV?' said Mum. 'Didn't that make them think you were guilty?'

'It's standard advice, apparently,' said Chris. 'But it did feel a bit awkward, especially with that Geordie policeman glowering at me.'

'Didn't DI Kaur interview you?' I asked. It was what I had been imagining.

'No. She was probably watching on a monitor somewhere. Any chance of some toast, Anna? I'm starving.'

'But why did she issue a warrant for your arrest?' I said. I thought Chris was being too breezy about the whole thing. Also, I wasn't keen on the request for toast. Just because we'd slept together, it didn't mean that I was his handmaiden. Nevertheless, I put bread in the toaster.

'Someone saw me with Gary just before he died,' said Chris. 'And an insulin syringe was found at the scene. I'm diabetic though I use a pen, not a syringe.'

I didn't know that he was diabetic. It made me wonder what other secrets Chris was keeping.

'Were you with him?' I asked.

Chris took another gulp of coffee. 'We had a brief disagreement which may have been overheard.'

'A disagreement? What about?'

Before Chris could answer, there was a knock at the front door.

'Another visitor,' said Mum. 'How exciting.'

I had been worried that all the drama would be bad for her but she looked better than she had for days, eyes sparkling like the Star of old.

'Probably just Roxy,' I said.

But Roxy, like all the carers, used the key safe. The visitor, incognito in a hat and black pashmina, was Izzy.

Feeling resigned, I took her through to the kitchen, although it was standing room only now.

'This is Izzy,' I said to Mum. 'Isabelle Istar.'

'Oh, we saw you on telly the other day,' said Mum. 'You were getting up to all sorts in a gondola.'

'And very uncomfortable it was too,' said Izzy. 'Nice to meet you, Mrs Vance.'

'It's just Star, dear. I've never been a Mrs.'

Izzy had never been to Attlee Towers before. I'd been quite defensive about it as a child. I wasn't ashamed of living in a council flat but the contrast between my home and, say, Gary's, was so huge that I was scared of becoming a debating point. 'Living conditions in Inner London still define life chances. Discuss.' Chris had visited, of course, and Henry had managed to invite himself once or twice. Funnily enough, it was Cassie who had seemed most at home here and we had spent most of the time in my room discussing the iniquity of men.

I gave Chris his toast and slid butter and marmalade towards him. Then I suggested he took his plate and we move to the sitting room. Mum used a stick when she walked now but Chris offered his arm with a courtly gesture that pleased her, I could tell. Izzy followed, pashmina trailing. I put on more coffee.

When I entered the room, Mum and Izzy were talking about films.

'Who's that actor,' Mum was saying, 'the one who looks like a tree? An evergreen?'

Izzy, understandably, looked rather baffled. Chris crunched his toast.

'So, Izzy,' I said. 'To what do we owe this honour?'

'I've got an idea,' said Izzy.

Chapter 36

Cassie

Thursday

It felt very strange to be going home, just when I'd convinced myself that I would never see my family again. It was only eleven o'clock when I let myself back into the house. I could hear Pete on the phone upstairs. For a moment, I wondered where Kevin was and then I remembered that Pete would have dropped him off with the dog walker on his way back from the school run. I stood in the kitchen staring at a letter from Lucy's school about the forthcoming ski trip. I remembered seeing it this morning and thinking, almost with relief: I won't need to worry about that, I'll be in prison. Now, all the everyday worries came flooding back, replacing the existential dread that had been with me for twenty-one years. Pete thought skiing was too dangerous and too expensive but Lucy wanted to go. I was in favour partly because I thought it would cement her friendship with Sasha and Rosie. Did I worry about this too much because I always felt like an outsider at school? What about Sam and Rhys? Would their friendship survive if Sam stopped playing football? Should I let Lucy quit the violin? Was Kevin too fat? Was I?

'Is that you, Cass?' Pete shouted down the stairs.

'Yes.' Who did he think it would be?

'Any chance of a coffee?'

I put the kettle on and spooned coffee into the cafetière. Was this my life now, making hot drinks for my husband, worrying about school trips? If I had to leave the police, there would be even less money for such things. But Harbinder hadn't said anything about firing me. She'd told me to see a therapist, mentioned PTSD, but she hadn't told me to resign. 'The David thing, it's so long ago, I can't see any merit in reopening the case.'

If Harbinder didn't think I had killed David, perhaps I hadn't?

Pete showed no sign of coming to collect his coffee so I took it up to him, feeling even more like a surrendered wife. But at least he seemed grateful. There was only one chair in the study so I leant against the door, signalling that I wasn't staying long.

'How did your meeting go?' he asked.

I'd almost forgotten about the mythical meeting.

'OK,' I said. 'I think I might be back at work soon.'

'You know, Cass,' Pete's voice was gentle, 'you don't have to go back.'

'I want to,' I said.

'How's the enquiry going?' said Pete. 'It was a real shock about Henry. I always liked him.'

'I don't know. They can't tell me.'

'But Harbinder can't suspect you of any involvement?'

I edged closer to the landing. I didn't want to get into this conversation with Pete, who knew me so well. I tried to think of something that would take his attention away from me.

'I think they're going to arrest Chris Foster,' I said.

Why did I say it was Chris? I'd always liked Chris, although he didn't take much notice of me at school. He was one of those effortlessly popular boys. He didn't have to try, not like Gary with his Lenin hat or Henry with his Machiavelli quotes. Chris could even get away with being quite geeky, playing the guitar or organising sponsored sleep-outs in aid of Shelter. He got enthusiastic about things at a time when the rest of us were pretending to be world-weary cynics at the age of eighteen. 'The circus is coming to town!' he shouted once, coming into the sixth form common room with a leaflet announcing that Mr Flight's Fantasy would soon be appearing on Clapham Common. 'You know the circus is cruel, don't you?' said Anna, hardly looking up from her book. 'And naff,' said Gary, who was writing an essay. But I think Chris went anyway.

I tried to keep in touch with Chris after we left school. It wasn't easy when he became famous. I didn't want to look like a groupie. Pete was always unselfconscious about following the Chris Foster fan page on Facebook or telling people 'Cassie went to school with him'. But I was careful. I sent Christmas cards to his London address and, occasionally, received one back. Once, I found an old photo of me, Anna and Chris taken in the music room at school. I made a copy and sent it to Chris. About a month later I received a postcard of a Jackson Pollock splatter with Chris's loopy handwriting on the back, 'Love the pic! OMG we look so young. Have you seen Anna lately?' I didn't reply to the question, which seemed almost rhetorical. In a funny way, though, the card reminded me of Anna, who used to send me pictures of strange statues when she was a student in Florence. I remember one of a naked man holding up a woman's severed head, her blood solidified into a bronze braid. 'Who sent you *that*?' Freddie asked. 'Just someone I knew at school,' I answered.

When I invited Chris to the twenty-first reunion, I added a PS. *Lots of the old gang will be there including Gary, Henry and Anna.* I knew that would get him. I also knew that Anna would come to the reunion if she thought that Chris would be there. She said that she was in London anyway, visiting her mother, but I think she would still have travelled from Italy. The lure of the twenty-first anniversary worked for most people, plus the chance to see Sonoma in her kingdom. I knew that Sonoma had invited Gary personally, which was why I was so shocked that she wasn't there.

Why was I there? You'd think that I'd have wanted to stay a million miles away from that place. But even murderers get nostalgic. I wanted to see my old friends again. For years, I couldn't see Manor Park except through the pall of David's death. Even looking at the location on a map was difficult. I once hyperventilated in Preston Manor because of the M word. But I thought that, just for one evening, I would try to forget. And I suppose I also wanted to show people that mousy little Cassie had done all right for herself. That's why I wore that top and put glitter on my shoulders.

As soon as Chris and Anna met at the reunion I knew that they still had feelings for each other. Anna was back to her brittle, bantering best. Chris just smiled goofily at her. Izzy was being quite proprietorial towards him too. It was wonderful to see everyone. I remember dancing with Henry and thinking that life was simple really. All you needed were a few friends, some cheap wine, some cheesy music. I was in such a good mood that it was a shock when, going out for some air, I saw Chris and Gary by the loos and heard Chris's voice saying, 'I'll never forgive you.' I'll never forget the venom in his voice.

Why did I tell Harbinder? I suppose I was just trying to be helpful.

Chapter 37

Harbinder

Thursday

As soon as the door shuts behind Cassie Fitzherbert, Harbinder calls Kim and Jake into her office. Briefly, she outlines Cassie's allegations against Chris Foster. She doesn't mention David Moore.

'Could Foster really be the killer?' asks Jake. The unspoken words 'but he's famous' hover in the air.

'He was in the right place for Garfield,' says Harbinder. 'He may well have had the means, an insulin syringe, and we have a credible witness who heard them arguing. I think it's worth bringing him in.'

'Arresting him?' says Kim.

'If I can get a warrant. If nothing else, that should shake him up a bit.'

'He'll get lawyered up,' says Jake, who clearly thinks this is a cool thing to say.

'Let him,' says Harbinder, trying for a bit of bluster in her turn.

'What about Henry Steep?' says Kim. 'Do you think Chris killed him too?'

'It's possible. Henry was probably on his way to meet someone he knew. Chris doesn't have an alibi for Tuesday night. We need to get hold of his phone records.'

'"I'll never forgive you",' quotes Kim. 'Any idea what that was all about?'

'No, but it certainly sounds like Chris was feeling passionate about something,' says Harbinder. 'I'll apply for a warrant. In the meantime, Jake, carry on with the MPs. Kim, you and I need to visit Paula Rice.' She overdoes the Italian accent on the first name because she knows it irritates Jake.

'Sure thing, boss,' says Kim. 'Why?'

'She wrote the bleeding heart notes,' says Harbinder, showing them handwriting sample two. 'We need to find out why.'

'Yes, I wrote them,' says Paula. She hardly seems surprised at the question. She sits very upright on her vintage sofa with a neon sign over her head saying 'Fun'.

'Why?' asks Kim.

'I knew he was seeing her. Isabelle Istar.' She hisses the sibilants like a pantomime villain. 'So many things gave him away. A different scent on his clothes, a bill from a different mobile phone company, a sudden knowledge of filming terms. I knew they were having an affair. They were childhood sweethearts, that's what Gary used to say. I was even quite impressed that he'd been to school with Isabelle Istar and Chris Foster. But, about a year ago, they must have got in contact again. Maybe at one of those bloody reunions. I've never known a school have so many reunions. In Italy, you leave school, that's it. Over. But in England, it seems, you keep reliving your schooldays for ever.'

And it was a reunion that killed Garfield Rice, thinks Harbinder.

'That must have been tough,' says Kim.

The empathy works. 'It was,' says Paula, twisting a cushion fringe. 'Gary used to go to meetings at a place called Bleeding Heart Yard. I thought, what about my bleeding heart?'

I was right, thinks Harbinder. The heart with an arrow through it. Only love is that painful.

'I sent the notes to Deborah, his agent,' says Paula. 'Gary only seemed to take notice of mail sent through her. But he never mentioned any anonymous letters to me. And he went on seeing that tart.'

Garfield had thrown the notes away, thinks Harbinder. Only Deborah took them seriously. Had Garfield taken his wife or his mistress seriously enough? She asks if Garfield kept in touch with Chris Foster.

'I don't think so. Unless they were both at one of those reunions. Boys only. Paintballing, shooting, drinking.'

'Did Gary tell you that he'd invited Chris Foster to one of his Bleeding Heart Yard lunches?'

'He never told me who he had lunch with. It was mostly boring old men. Unless it was her. Isabelle.'

Another hiss.

'Did Gary mention falling out with Chris?' Harbinder thinks it's worth another try.

'He didn't mention anything,' says Paula. 'He'd come in, pour himself a drink, watch TV and go to sleep. He never told me anything.'

Gary sounds like a husband from a 1970s sitcom, thinks Harbinder, but Paula obviously still loved him.

'What about Henry Steep?' asks Kim.

'Henry who?'

They leave it there but, on the way out, Kim has a Columbo-esque last thought. She points at one of the modern paintings in the hallway.

'Is that by Chris Foster?'

'Yes,' says Paula, with supreme lack of interest. 'Isn't it ugly? I never look at it if I can help it.'

In the car, Harbinder says, 'That was a good spot. I didn't realise you were an art expert.'

'I like art,' says Kim. 'It was my favourite subject at school, but my parents thought it was a waste of time. I remembered Chris's style from when we visited his flat. I think he's really talented.'

'Gary obviously knew Chris well enough to buy pictures from him,' says Harbinder. 'Though maybe he had an art dealer who did that for him. The house is full of weird junk that probably cost an arm and a leg.'

'There might even be an arm and a leg somewhere,' says Kim.

Harbinder laughs. She thinks back to one of the paintings in Chris Foster's penthouse. A square of blue.

'What's this one called?'

'Death of a Planet.'

'What was the title of the painting in Gary's hallway?' she says. 'Did you see?'

'Gaia in chains.'

'Gaia? That's Earth, isn't it?'

'I think so.'

'Chris Foster is obviously angry about what's happening in the world,' says Harbinder. 'Climate change and all that. I wonder what he felt when he sat down to eat with all those industrialists who were intent on destroying the planet?'

Kim gets it immediately. 'Chris told Gary that he'd never forgive him,' she says. 'Could he have been talking about Gary's attitude to the environment?'

'Possibly. But was he angry enough to kill?' says Harbinder.

Jake has also been talking about climate change. He briefs the team, legs wide apart as usual.

'Tory and I went to see James Fermoy,' he said. 'He's a Conservative MP. Old school. Very posh. Very polite.'

'I thought he was a charmer,' says Tory. Harbinder sighs.

'He was very helpful,' says Jake. 'He was at the lunch when Chris Foster was Garfield's guest and he said that Chris was furious.'

'Furious at what?' says Harbinder.

'Apparently, when the talk was going on, Foster was nodding and agreeing with everything the speaker said, about climate change, time running out and so on. Afterwards, he expected Garfield to disagree and to say it was all a myth. But, when he saw that Garfield actually believed it all but was still planning to deny it in public, he was really angry, accused him of hypocrisy and all sorts. Fermoy said it was very embarrassing. I don't think guests were meant to be so vocal.'

'We know Chris Foster feels strongly about the environment,' says Harbinder. 'But is that enough motive for murder? Cassie says she heard him say to Gary, "I'll never forgive you." That sounds more personal than political to me.'

'It does to me too,' says Jake, 'but James Fermoy said something interesting. He said that Chris's argument with Gary became very personal and Chris said something like "You were a socialist at school, I'll never forgive you for changing".'

'Very interesting,' says Harbinder. 'I think you should be the one to interview Chris Foster, Jake.'

Chapter 38

Harbinder

Thursday evening

It's nine o'clock by the time the warrant comes through. Harbinder sends two PCs to bring Chris Foster in. 'Two uniformed officers knocking on his door after dark,' she says to Jake. 'That should shake him up a bit.' 'I'm ready for him,' says Jake, as if Chris Foster is Don Corleone.

But Chris is not at home. Harbinder tells the uniforms to try Attlee Towers and isn't very surprised to learn that this is where the singer is apprehended.

'So, he is sleeping with Anna Vance,' says Jake.

'It seems so.'

Harbinder wonders why, with the penthouse at their disposal, the lovers chose Anna's single bed with its faded flowery duvet. Maybe Anna doesn't like to leave her mum at night.

It's past ten by the time Chris is booked in at the front desk. Most of the team have gone home but there are still plenty of people, police and civilian, to gawp at the famous figure in jeans and a hoodie. Chris seems quite calm, even telling Harbinder that it's good to see her again, but he's obviously come prepared. Twenty minutes later his solicitor, Linden Grey, is at the desk demanding to see her client.

Harbinder has never met the lawyer but understands immediately that she's no ordinary duty solicitor. Linden never raises her voice and is casually dressed in black leggings and a pale grey jumper that looks like cashmere. But in a few minutes she has established her ascendency. She asks to be briefed and to see Chris in private. Harbinder has to agree to both these things but she gives away as little as possible. Linden takes notes and then ushers Chris into another room.

'She'll tell him to do a no-comment interview,' Harbinder says to Jake.

'We'll break him,' says Jake.

'It's not necessary to break him,' says Harbinder. 'Just ask the questions.' As the caution goes, 'it may harm your defence if you do not mention when questioned something which you later rely on in court'. If they ask the right questions now, the prosecution can ask them in court.

Harbinder has put Jake with a DC called Patrick Connolly who, though mild-mannered in the extreme, looks intimidating. She's still operating on the theory that Chris feels more confident with women, sure that he can charm them. Patrick Connolly, six foot five of pure muscle, does not look easy to charm.

Harbinder watches via computer link as Jake reads the caution to Chris Foster.

'Do you understand?' he says.

'Yes.'

Jake then explains 'for the tape' why the interview is taking place. Chris listens with polite interest. Linden takes notes.

'Can you take us through your movements on the night of Saturday the twenty-first of September?'

'No comment,' says Chris, almost apologetically.

'Did you attend a reunion party at Manor Park school?'

'No comment.'

'Did you talk to Garfield Rice that evening?'

'No comment.'

'Did you argue with Garfield Rice that evening?'

'No comment.'

'We have a witness who heard the two of you arguing.'

'No comment.'

'Did you take an insulin syringe to the reunion? We know you're diabetic.'

'No comment.'

Jake leans back in his chair. Harbinder can't see his face but she thinks he's attempting a comradely grin.

'Look, Chris. We want to help you. We've had a credible report that you argued with Gary at the reunion. Why don't you tell us what that was about? I argue with my mates all the time. I know what it's like, especially when drink's been taken.'

What an odd phrase, thinks Harbinder. It sounds old-fashioned somehow. Maybe it's something Jake's Irish grandmother used to say. She's not that surprised when Chris answers, 'No comment.'

Harbinder would have liked to keep Chris in the cells overnight but Linden Grey is not having any of it. Even so, it's past midnight by the time that he's released without charge. She gets a lift back to the flat, which is in darkness. At this rate she will never see her flatmates in daylight. They'll think she's a vampire, like one of Buffy's mates. Harbinder makes herself some toast and eats it in the kitchen. How long ago was it that she ate Mette's chocolate on rye?

Once in bed, Harbinder finds it difficult to get to sleep. The words 'no comment' echo in her head. She doesn't think this strategy necessarily means that Chris Foster is guilty but it's frustrating, nonetheless. She thinks of the first time that she met the Manor Park alumni, the modern room with the tragic disco lights, Isabelle Istar wailing like a banshee, Cassie with her glittery shoulders. What had Chris Foster been doing? She doesn't even remember him amongst the many faces. It was the deputy head – what was his name? – who boasted that a famous pop star had been present. When Harbinder thinks of the words 'pop star', it conjures up a combination of Elton John in platform boots and Bill Nighy in *Love Actually* – a film she detests. Chris Foster just looks like an ordinary person, a rather good-looking one, true, but still someone who could pass unnoticed in Waitrose or queuing for his flight to Tuscany. Maybe this is his super-power.

Harbinder turns over and punches her pillow into shape. She needs to get a break soon, or Simon Masters will be breathing down her neck. Did she do the right thing in sending Cassie home after her confession? But, even if Cassie did push David, what good would it do to reopen the investigation, twenty-one years later? Harbinder thinks of Arthur Moore. 'He was a good boy.' David doesn't sound like a good boy but would it help his father, whose only comfort seems to be visiting family graves, to discover that now? She thinks of Margravine Cemetery, the field of tombstones visible from Arthur Moore's flat. She remembers Kim saying, 'My biggest fear is anything happening to my kids.' Cassie must have feared for her children too, when she came to tell Harbinder what happened that day by the railway tracks.

'I remember the train coming, this explosive noise, and Henry telling me to run.'

What had Henry Steep known? Why was he calling Cassie after his cosy afternoon tea with Anna Vance?

When Harbinder finally sleeps she dreams of trains in tunnels, tall penthouse apartments, the high-rise office blocks around Bleeding Heart Yard. It's all disappointingly phallic.

In the morning, both Mette and Jeanne are in the kitchen when Harbinder appears, hair wet from her shower, to grab a quick breakfast.

'Well, if it isn't the creature that walks by night,' says Mette.

'Are you having an awful time?' Jeanne asks sympathetically. 'I read about that other MP dying.'

'They're dropping like flies,' says Harbinder, putting bread in the toaster.

'Politicians are like flies,' says Mette. 'Feeding on human waste.'

'That's a nice image,' says Harbinder.

'Wish me luck,' says Jeanne, piling books into her bag. 'Year Eight first lesson.'

'Good luck,' says Harbinder. 'Want to swap with my murderers?'

'Yes please,' says Jeanne.

When Jeanne has left, Harbinder eats Marmite on toast and tries not to look at Mette striding around in cycling shorts.

'Site meeting today,' says Mette. 'They're such a bunch of shits.'

'Are they all men?' says Harbinder. 'Apart from you, I mean.'

'Mostly,' says Mette. 'Equal opportunities haven't reached the building world yet. Even the women are on the side of the patriarchy. They're not like *us*.'

What does this mean? wonders Harbinder. And does the 'us' encompass all the flatmates or just Harbinder and Mette? She's still pondering when Mette shoulders her backpack and heads for the door.

'Good luck,' says Harbinder.

'You too, Detective. Make 'em eat shit.'

Mette really hasn't mastered breakfast table conversation, thinks Harbinder.

When Harbinder gets to the station, she finds it's full of people talking about Chris Foster's late-night visit. It's going to be hard to keep this out of the papers, she thinks. Masters wants her to do another press conference later.

'I'm gutted to have missed him,' says Kim, who is eating a bagel.

'You could have talked about art,' says Harbinder.

She calls another team meeting at nine.

'Chris Foster gave a no-comment interview on his brief's orders. We need to keep digging on him. I've applied to see his phone records. If he spoke to Henry Steep on the night he died, then we have something. Chris is in a relationship with Anna Vance. Could this have been the cause of his argument with Gary? Then again, Gary was having an affair with Isabelle Istar. Chris has been seen with Isabelle at several events. Was he jealous? Is this why he couldn't forgive Gary? Then there's the political motive. James Fermoy said that Chris was really angry with Gary after the

Bleeding Heart lunch. Could this have spilled over on the night of the reunion?'

'What about the syringe?' says Kim. 'Could that have been Chris's?'

'I'm pretty sure it was Cassie's. It has her fingerprints on it and she wasn't sure if she'd taken two or three to the reunion. But Chris is a diabetic. He knows all about insulin and what it could do. I think the means points to him.'

'Henry Steep was stabbed though,' says Jake.

Alice Hunter thinks the blade was narrow and thin. 'Like a paper knife,' she told Harbinder in her schoolgirl voice. 'A jolly sharp one.'

Harbinder thinks back to the penthouse flat. There was a desk with several items of stationery. Was a paperknife among them?

'I think it was carefully planned,' says Harbinder. 'Henry's killer even armed themselves with an animal heart to set the scene. Also, if it's the same perp for Garfield Rice, his killer went to some lengths to make the death look like an overdose. But planning leaves a trail. Let's get on with tracking CCTV and house-to-house on Tuesday night. Someone must have seen something.'

The morning passes in a whirl of activity. Harbinder is grateful when Kim brings her a sandwich, oozing mayo, from one of her suppliers. She's just biting into it when Freya appears at the door.

'Sorry, Harbinder, but there's someone downstairs asking for you.'

Which of them is it? thinks Harbinder, as she descends the stairs to reception. Chris Foster come to confess? Isabelle Istar, trailing scarves, admitting to another affair?

But it's Anna Vance.

Chapter 39

Anna

Friday

We all stared at Izzy, which was just how she liked it. I was distinctly suspicious about her 'idea'. It was why she had arrived unexpectedly at Attlee Towers this morning, I realised. Why she was glowing with almost manic certainty, as if she was already in the spotlight.

'What sort of idea?' I said. Izzy was now sitting on the sofa beside Chris with her pashmina and hat thrown onto the carpet. Mum was in her usual chair, with its wide arms for all her medical paraphernalia. There was absolutely no chance of her missing this discussion.

'It occurred to me,' said Izzy, flashing her brilliant smile around the room, 'that everything goes back to David's death. You said that Henry talked about it when you saw him, Anna. The day before he died. Gary talked about it in his last phone call to me.' Her smile wavers.

'I was just saying to Anna,' said Mum, 'that I think there's been a curse on that school since that poor boy died.'

278

'I think you might be right,' Izzy said seriously. 'Everything goes back to David.'

'So, what's your idea?' I said. I took a cautious sip of coffee. I wasn't at all keen on the direction the conversation was taking.

'A reconstruction.' Again, Izzy smiled round at us. It was like a lighthouse beam. Chris actually blinked. He was beginning to look tired, as if his late night was catching up with him. I was sure that I looked like death too.

'We reconstruct the scene,' said Izzy. 'It strikes me there's a lot of buried memories. A lot of PTSD. Anna, you aren't even sure if you were there or not.'

I mumbled something. Mum turned to look at me but said nothing.

'We need to go back in time,' said Izzy. 'Reconnect with our teenage selves. What happened that day? Eighteen-year-old Anna might know.'

It was a dizzying thought. For a moment I felt as if the room was tilting, like the deck of a ship. The London skyline turned from portrait to landscape.

'Are you all right, love?' said Mum.

'I'm fine,' I said.

'Isn't there a bit of a problem?' said Chris. 'Some of the principal actors are dead.'

His dry tone made the room right itself.

'I've thought of that,' said Izzy. 'Oliver can play David.'

'Oliver?' I echoed, although I knew who she meant.

'Oliver West. My husband. Well, he *is* an actor,' said Izzy. Rather defensively, I thought.

'And Gary?' said Chris.

'I'll be Gary,' said Izzy. 'I know just the route he would have taken.'

'Cassie?' I said.

'Oh, I think Cassie can play herself, don't you?'

Izzy left shortly after this. Chris stayed until midday when it was obvious that both Mum and I were flagging.

'Shall I see you later?' he said.

'I think I want an early night.'

Chris gave me a rather rakish grin, kissed me on the cheek and shouted, 'Bye, Star.' I heard his footsteps on the stairs. The lift must be out of order again. Mum went to lie down and, after washing up the breakfast things, I retreated to my room and stared at my still-dishevelled bed. I could hardly believe that Chris and I had slept together last night. Not the eighteen-year-old Anna so cheerfully invoked by Izzy, but the middle-aged version with a saggy body and grey in her hair. It had been great too. Not at all embarrassing or over-athletic, just a lovely meeting of bodies. Slow, relaxed, fun, uninhibited.

Then, a few hours later, Chris had been arrested.

I picked up my science book. I wanted to find out what eighteen-year-old Anna had known. This time I noticed a pencil sketch on the back cover. Chris frequently drew on his friend's books as well as his own. This showed Izzy, resting her chin on her hand, her long hair flowing over her shoulders. She looked beautiful but then she *was* beautiful. *Is* beautiful. Chris was always good at getting a likeness. I opened the book.

The Heart Has Its Reasons by Anna Vance.

Some are born murderers and some have murder thrust upon them. That's how I justified it, at any rate, the day I joined the illustrious band of killers that includes Medea, Lizzie Borden and Macbeth. I didn't mean to kill Duncan but, when the moment came, it just seemed the obvious thing to do. The moment before it happened, before I stabbed him, I thought: someone has to kill him and that someone has to be me. Because I was the one who loved him.

I sat back on my heels. Several things occurred to me. The first was that, as opening paragraphs go, this wasn't too bad. It was overwritten, of course, and I was obviously very much under the influence of our set texts. We'd done the Scottish Play for GCSE and not only does Macbeth put in an appearance but Duncan as well. The first line is mangled from *Twelfth Night* and even the title comes from Pascal's *Pensées*, which we had to read in French. But, really, this Anna Vance might have a future as a writer after all. Must try harder, Anna.

Then I thought of what Izzy had said, when we were brainstorming at Chris's flat. 'That other thing you wrote, where the woman kills the man because she loves him so much.'

I got up and put on my jacket. I knocked on Mum's door. She was just a mound in the bed and, once again, the fear crept over me.

'Mum?'

'Yes?' She opened an eye.

'Just popping out. Is Anita coming today?'

'Yes. At two. Just having a little zizz.'

'You do that. See you later.' I kissed her cheek, the skin still so soft. I remember her telling me how to moisturise. 'Push the cream upwards. You don't want wrinkles at forty.' But I never bothered and now I have lines round my mouth and in the corners of my eyes. Mum was sixty-three and terminally ill but she still had smooth skin.

I let myself out quietly.

I caught the bus to West Kensington police station. I've always loved London buses. I probably even enjoyed the night bus, all those years ago. The lumbering pace, the view of the tops of bus stops and into people's sitting rooms, TVs flickering. People's lives look so cosy, seen from a distance. I was tired after my sleepless night but now that tiredness took on a pleasant, dreamlike quality. Shop windows, boarded-up doorways, a boy on one of those motorised scooters distributing leaflets. I was in such a daze that I almost forgot to get off the bus at the right stop.

The reception area was full. Two women were arguing with someone behind the counter and a homeless man was asleep across three nailed-down chairs. I took a ticket and waited my turn. I'd forgotten to bring a book and, for the first time, I wished I had a phone that could entertain me with games or those Facebook videos that my friends seem to find so amusing. The only magazine in the place was about cars and, in my desperation, I picked it up and flicked through it. I really should learn to drive one day.

'Number forty-four.'

'Can I speak to DI Kaur please?'

'What's your name?' The woman was looking at me as if I was mad. Well, maybe I was.

'Anna Vance.'

She made me repeat it twice before picking up a phone and

saying, 'Someone for DI Kaur.' Then she looked at me and said, 'Take a seat', without promising to produce Harbinder.

I sat down again and picked up *Custom Car 2017* but, only a few minutes later, I heard a voice say, 'Hallo, Anna.'

Chapter 40

Harbinder

Friday

Harbinder has time to observe Anna Vance before making herself known. She is reading a car magazine, which surprises Harbinder, who didn't have her down as a petrol head. Anna is wearing jeans and her favourite trainers, a check shirt and a blue Harrington jacket. Harbinder can see her curly head bent over the pictures of SUVs and jeeps. There's a definite streak of grey in the middle. Whatever else Anna looks like, she doesn't look like the girlfriend of an international pop star. And yet, when Harbinder conjures the image of Chris Foster in his jeans and hoodie, there is something strangely similar about the two of them. And it isn't just the shoes.

'Hallo, Anna.'

Anna puts the magazine down and stands up.

'Hallo. Thank you for seeing me.'

Harbinder offers tea or coffee which is refused. This is lucky because the vending machine is broken. She ushers Anna into a room on the ground floor. Harbinder doesn't want to take her into the custody suite but this venue is, if anything, even more depressing. The only window is a narrow slit, high in the wall, edged with spikes to deter pigeons. The room is really just a burial ground for broken chairs. Harbinder finds two of the sturdiest-looking specimens and offers one to Anna.

'Sorry about the decor.'

'It's OK.' Anna looks round as if she hadn't noticed before.

'Why did you want to see me?'

Anna crosses her legs and uncrosses them.

'You know you asked me about the death of David Moore in 1998?'

Harbinder replies, patiently, in the affirmative.

'It was so long ago,' says Anna. 'I'd almost forgotten it. Well, I hadn't really but I'd made myself forget. There was lots of other stuff around it . . . things that were hard to relive. But, when Gary died, and now Henry . . . it really seems to come back to David.'

'Does it?'

Anna looks straight at Harbinder for what feels like the first time.

'When I saw Henry at the House of Commons, he said that I was there . . . when David died. I don't think I was. I really don't. But there are parts of that day that I don't remember. I'd had a row with Chris, we broke up. I think I was in a sort of fugue state. I keep thinking, what if I was there? And Izzy says that Gary talked about it, just before he died. He said that David was murdered and he knew who did it.'

Harbinder keeps her face still. All the pigeons are coming home to roost, she thinks. Despite the spikes.

'And now Izzy wants to reconstruct the whole thing.' Anna's

voice is rising. 'She wants us to go back to the Tube station and reconstruct David's death.'

'What do you mean?'

'Izzy thinks it will help buried memories to resurface. It's obviously something she's got from all those therapy sessions. She wants us all there.'

'Why are you telling me?'

'Because I'm scared.'

'They're planning to reconstruct the crime – if it was a crime – with Isabelle Istar's husband Oliver West playing David Moore.'

'Blimey,' says Kim. 'I'd pay to see that movie.'

'You can see this one,' says Harbinder. 'I think there should be a discreet police presence. You and I should go, Kim. And I'll ask for some back-up from uniform.'

'I should be there really,' says Jake. He just, but only just, manages to avoid saying, 'You need a man on the spot.'

'You're Deputy SIO,' Harbinder reminds him. 'I need you here.'

She thought this would please him and it does. Jake smooths back his hair.

'When are they going to do it?' he asks.

'Four-thirty p.m. tomorrow, which is apparently the time of the original incident. They clearly remember it better than they claimed when we asked them about it.'

'What about Cassie?' says Kim. 'Will she be there?'

'Anna said that Isabelle was going to invite her,' says Harbinder. 'Cassie plays herself, Oliver plays David, Isabelle plays Gary.'

'Henry?' says Kim.

'Apparently Chris Foster is playing Henry.'

286

'An all-star cast,' says Kim. 'What are they hoping to achieve?'

'Retrieval of buried memories, according to Isabelle Istar,' says Harbinder. 'Anna Vance said that she was scared. I asked what she meant and she was evasive. Just said she was worried about "bringing everyone back together again". But she was obviously concerned enough to come to see me. I think she's right. You get the gang back together and who knows what will happen.'

'What do you mean?' says Jake. 'There's hardly going to be another murder in broad daylight.'

'David Moore died in broad daylight,' says Harbinder. 'But there need not be a murder, just some kind of showdown. Anna told me that Henry Steep remembered her being there that day, but she didn't think she was. Sonoma Davies said that Anna often behaved strangely, as if she was detached from reality. She more or less implied that Anna had killed Gary and Henry '

'How could you forget something like that?' says Jake.

'Anna says she was in a fugue state,' says Harbinder. 'I looked it up and it's described as dissociative disorder, a sort of temporary amnesia. People can even travel long distances and not remember how they got there.'

'Sounds like a handy defence for the courts,' says Jake. 'Roll out a tame psychiatrist and you've got a suspended sentence.'

'I do think it's interesting that Anna had this phrase to hand,' says Harbinder. 'Also, that it's described as a reversable condition. Isabelle must be planning to reverse it with her little charade tomorrow. And that's why Anna's scared.'

'But why go to the police?' says Kim. 'Doesn't that make her look guilty?'

'Maybe she's not worried about herself,' says Harbinder. 'Chris

Foster is still our chief suspect. We know he argued with Garfield Rice. He would have had access to insulin. Maybe Anna was worried about him. Maybe she's scared of him.'

'She's not scared of him,' says Kim. 'She's in love with him.'

'The two are not mutually exclusive,' says Harbinder.

Harbinder leaves work at six. She could do with an early night, she thinks. On the way home, she stops to get an Indian takeaway, although she can hear her mother's voice in her head, 'That's not authentic Punjabi. Too much cumin and not enough lemon . . .' She deliberately buys enough for her flatmates but neither of them are in. When she checks her phone she has a message from Jeanne saying that she's going to her boyfriend's for the weekend. This reminds Harbinder that it's Saturday tomorrow. A week since the old schoolfriends gathered in the library of Manor Park school.

Harbinder eats until the homesickness gets too much and she rings her parents.

'We saw you on television,' says her mother. 'You were very clear.'

'I'm eating tandoori chicken,' says Harbinder. 'It's not as good as yours.'

'No, it wouldn't be,' says her mother. 'When are you coming home, Harbi? What about coming for Sunday lunch? I could do your favourite butter chicken.'

Harbinder can taste the chicken, accompanied by naan, roti and paratha. She pushes the foil containers away from her.

'I can't, Mum,' she says. 'I'm working.'

'Even on a Sunday?' says Bibi. 'Your father's shouting that you shouldn't have to work at weekends. I don't think that's right. Isn't there a union?'

'As soon as I crack the case, I'll be home,' says Harbinder. 'I promise.'

'Oh, you'll crack it,' says Bibi. 'It's always the least obvious person. Now Deepak's shouting that I've got it all wrong. I don't know who made him Hercule Poirot all of a sudden.'

When Harbinder has said goodbye, she puts the remaining dishes in the fridge. As she does so she hears the sound of the shower. If Jeanne is with Bob, that must be Mette. An image comes into Harbinder's head of Mette striding to the bathroom, wearing only her headphones. 'Don't go there,' she tells herself. She washes up her plate and gets out an old London A–Z which she found at the station. She wants to find the exact spot on the map where the so-called reconstruction will take place tomorrow. She thinks of Anna saying, 'Izzy thinks it will help buried memories to resurface. She wants us all there.' Anna also said that she was scared. Of what?

The shower has stopped and Harbinder hears Mette padding along the landing. Harbinder bends her head over the book. It's a strange, dense little publication. Did people really use this instead of Google maps? The orange and yellow streets merge in front of her, the thick blue line of the Thames below. So many roads, so many houses, so many people. Harbinder thinks of the view from Chris Foster's penthouse, that same grid laid out for his delight. Isabelle Istar's townhouse, Anna Vance's council flat, Cassie's noisy family home. So many different lives, now converging at this point on the map.

Imperial Station is no longer marked on the map but Manor Park is shown by the letters SCH. Harbinder traces the route along the smaller white roads, some with red one-way arrows, to the place where the locked Tube station still stands. The footbridge doesn't feature but Harbinder can see that the street can be accessed from two sides. Did Cassie say that there were warehouses overlooking the platform?

'Good book?' Mette materialises, hair wet, dressed in a black trouser suit and red shirt.

'It's an A–Z,' says Harbinder. 'A map.'

'We have maps in Denmark too,' says Mette.

'There's food in the fridge,' says Harbinder. 'Lamb bhuna gosht, tandoori chicken, sag aloo and rice.'

'I love Indian food,' says Mette. 'But I'm going out to dinner. A work event. How do I look?'

'Great,' says Harbinder, rather hoarsely.

Mette leans over. Harbinder can smell her perfume, something lemony and sharp.

'I'm working near there,' she says. 'Luxury flats. None of them big enough to swing a cat. Have I got that right? Seems a strange phrase.'

'No, it's right,' says Harbinder, who is finding it hard to string her words together. 'Swing a cat. Very odd.'

'Imperial Quay, it's called. Though it's nowhere near the river.'

'There used to be a Tube station called Imperial near there.'

'That must be why. I'd better go. Pat's picking me up.'

And she whisks away. Leaving Harbinder with an urgent desire to know if Pat is Patricia or Patrick.

Chapter 41

Cassie

Friday

It was almost as if I was expecting Izzy. Ever since the reunion, I'd had an idea that she would make contact. And there she was, in a green coat with a stripy scarf wrapped several times round her neck.

'Hallo, Cassie. Can I come in?'

The kids were still at school and Pete was at a client meeting. Kevin frisked up to Izzy and I had to pull him back before his paws made contact with the coat.

'Cute dog,' said Izzy, backing away.

'He'll be OK when we sit down,' I said. I'd had another morning of frenzied tidying but, when we went into the sitting room, I thought how tatty it still looked; the marks on the walls from indoor football, the place where Kevin had chewed the rug, Sam's Lego tower still on the window seat because I didn't dare move it.

'What a lovely family room,' said Izzy. It must be even scruffier than I'd thought.

In sixth form I'd thought of Izzy as my best friend. I'd desperately wanted a best friend and had somehow failed to acquire one all through primary and secondary school. Oh, I had friends. In fact, I was often described as 'popular' but I didn't have that one special companion, the repository of secrets, the kindred spirit. I didn't want a sidekick; I was happy to be in the subordinate position. I just wanted company.

It was in the sixth form – smaller classes, self-selected studious types – that The Group started to take shape. Of my previous friendship group, two left after GCSEs and two did different subjects. I knew Izzy a little because I'd been in a couple of school plays. I like acting and, once again, was quite happy with the sidekick roles. It was always understood that Izzy would be the lead. I was Bet in *Oliver!* and Celia in *As You Like It*. In the lower sixth we did *The Crucible*. Izzy was Abigail, the scheming temptress that gets to do the screaming, but I was Mary Warren, a more interesting part to my mind. The one who gets to choose between her friends and the truth. Izzy and I started to 'go around together' as we called it at Manor Park. When Izzy decided that she fancied Gary, I was the person she talked to about him. Either she didn't know that I'd been out with him in Year 10 (I remembered Harbinder's unkind crack about that, asking me if I'd dated David in Year 10 too) or she didn't care.

As I said, we drifted apart after school. Izzy came to my wedding with her then boyfriend, a striking black guy whom I've since seen on TV. I saw her a few times after that, and we exchanged Christmas cards, but as she became more famous, the contact withered and died. But when I saw her at the reunion, trying desperately not to catch Gary's eye, I knew I'd see her again.

I offered tea and coffee, which Izzy refused, putting a hand to her waistline for some reason. Kevin hunted around and brought her a piece of rope he'd been keeping for a special occasion. Izzy edged away from him.

'I wanted to see you,' she said. 'Isn't it mad about Henry? Isn't it awful?'

'I still can't quite believe it,' I said, truthfully.

'And Gary.' Izzy's eyes actually fill with tears. Is she acting? I can't tell any more.

'You must have been really upset about Gary,' I said.

'Did you know?' says Izzy, stroking Kevin, who closes his eyes in ecstasy. 'I expect you guessed.'

'Were you seeing each other again?' I had guessed.

'We were in love,' said Izzy and I remembered her propensity for the grand statement. I'm leaving school. I abhor Sociology. 'We had never stopped being in love, really. It was just like being eighteen again, the passion and the horror of it. You know.'

'I know.'

'And now he's dead. I can't stop thinking about it. And I think it all goes back to that day when we were all eighteen. The day David died.'

I said nothing. I thought of the moment when I'd confessed to Harbinder and had, momentarily, thought I'd laid David to rest. I might have known that he'd come rising up from the grave, the way he used to do in my dreams, his face caked with blood and mud and worse.

'I want us to reconstruct it,' said Izzy, apparently taking my silence for approval. 'Oliver can be David. But I need you to be you.'

'No,' I said.

'Please, Cassie. It's a part in a play. I remember what a great actress you are.'

I couldn't resist a slight glow of satisfaction at hearing those words come out of the mouth of BAFTA-winning Isabelle Istar. And I did like acting, even if it was in those murder mystery dinner party plays. But to relive the worst moment of my life before an audience of my old schoolmates? I couldn't do it.

'Chris has agreed. And Anna.'

I thought of what I'd said to Harbinder, about hearing Chris argue with Gary. I wasn't wild about the thought of facing Chris again.

'I can't,' I said.

'Cassie.' Izzy leant forward, giving me the benefit of those mesmeric eyes. 'You need to do this. We have to lay the ghost.'

I thought of a quotation from *The Tempest*, our A level play. I'd done very badly on my second English paper. But then, I'd had other things on my mind.

'Hell is empty and all the devils are here.'

Chapter 42

Anna

Friday

Roxy was with Mum when I got back from the police station. I could hear them chatting about *Strictly* in the kitchen but, when Mum went to lie down, Roxy knocked on my door before leaving.

'Star seems a bit tired today. Did she have a bad night?'

What should I say? We had a disturbed night because I slept with my ex-boyfriend and then he was arrested for murder? We were just having breakfast when another old friend turned up and wanted us to reconstruct a suspicious death that happened twenty-one years ago?

'We were both a bit wakeful,' I said.

'You know you can contact the Macmillan nurse – what's her name? Anita? – about getting Mum some sleeping pills.'

'Thank you,' I said. 'I might do that.'

Roxy looked at me kindly. She was a youngish woman with tattoos all over her arms. Mum admired them exorbitantly. She has a dolphin tattooed on her bottom and a star on her shoulder. It's always been a slight disappointment to her that Sophie and I don't have any ink on our bodies.

'It's tough, I know,' said Roxy. 'But maybe it's time to think about the hospice . . .'

'I'll contact Anita,' I said.

When Roxy had left, I went to find my phone, which was still charging, but couldn't bring myself to make the call. Mum might talk about St Xavier's as if it were a luxury spa but I knew that, when she entered those landscaped grounds adorned with calming water features, she wouldn't be coming home again. It's the tiredness, I told myself, as tears came to my eyes. I picked up my phone again and, to my surprise, an unknown number popped onto the tiny, cracked screen.

'Hi. Is that Anna?'

'Yes.'

'This is Aisha. Aisha Mitri,' she added, after a pause. 'From the reunion.'

I remembered. The woman whose tone I had liked. The doctor who had pronounced Gary dead at the scene.

'I know this sounds a bit strange,' said Aisha, 'but I'm in a café near you. Would you be able to meet me for a chat?'

Many things came into my mind. How did Aisha know where I lived? What could she possibly want to talk about? How did she get my number? But then I thought of an evening alone in my room, worrying about Mum.

'Where are you?' I said.

★

Aisha was in a café that had been colonised by people working on laptops whilst eking out giant cups of coffee. The place had a strange sadness to it, despite the sanded floors and trendy French posters. It was a waiting room, an in-between place, a limbo. Or maybe I was just over-tired.

Aisha was drinking still water. I splashed out on a Diet Coke, thinking that I needed the caffeine.

'I know this is a bit odd,' she said, 'but I got your number from Cassie.'

Of course she did.

'The police took my statement after Gary died,' she said, 'but I didn't hear any more. I gathered that he didn't die from a drug overdose though. It's a murder enquiry now.'

'That's right,' I said. My nerves were jangling. Every time the door opened to admit another laptop owner, I jumped a mile.

'And now Henry's dead too.'

'Yes,' I said. 'It's awful.'

'It really is,' said Aisha. 'Did the police interview you after the reunion?'

'Yes,' I said. 'I used to be quite friendly with Gary at school.'

'I remember,' said Aisha. 'You were part of The Group.'

She made it sound both sinister and rather ridiculous.

'We were all in awe of The Group,' she said. 'Especially Gary. Everyone thought he was so brilliant. I kept telling myself that my grades were as good as his but the teachers only had eyes for him. Him and Sonoma. They got all the prizes, didn't they? Studying medicine at UCL was nothing compared to PPE at Oxford.'

'It seems much more useful to me.'

'Well, it does to me too.' Aisha gave me a sudden grin that

seemed to take the bitterness out of her words. I felt myself relaxing slightly.

'But I didn't get you here to reminisce,' said Aisha. 'Or for a post-mortem on why I didn't win the sixth form prize. It's because I had a surprise visitor today. Isabelle Istar. She actually came to the hospital. You know I'm a consultant at Charing Cross?'

'I didn't. You definitely should have won that prize.'

Another grin. 'I know, right? Well, Isabelle swans in, wearing a bright green coat.'

'I know the one.'

'All the students were staring at her. I remember she played a doctor in a TV series a few years back. Completely unbelievable. She never once tied up her hair. Anyway, Isabelle asked to see me. I was very busy but curiosity got the better of me. Isabelle came into my office and told me that a group of you are going to re-enact the death of that poor boy who fell on the train tracks.'

'That's right,' I said. I wondered if I could make it sound any less weird and decided I couldn't.

'I have so many questions,' said Aisha. '*What the hell are you thinking of?* is the main one. But what worried me was that Isabelle seemed to think I should be there in case someone got hurt. I need you to tell me, is someone going to fall onto the line tomorrow? Do I need to go to the police? I gather Cassie's on leave at the moment.'

'Why are you asking me?'

'Because the other members of The Group are either dead or mad.'

Chris wasn't either of those things, I thought, but I could see why Aisha didn't feel she could contact him. Fame is its own protection sometimes.

'Izzy thinks that we need to re-enact the scene to find out what really happened,' I said.

'Is there some question mark about what happened?' said Aisha. 'I thought the boy . . . what was his name? . . . David? . . . I thought he fell onto the tracks because he was drunk or high.'

It sounded so simple put like that. So simple and so tragic. I remember reading about it in the papers, just days after it happened, and thinking: this is the story I want to believe.

I looked at Aisha. She was regarding me with such a steady, compassionate gaze that I felt able to say, 'There are some question marks. For example, Henry said that I was there, at the scene, but I can't remember it. I mean,' I added, rather desperately, 'you're a doctor, you know about these things, you can't forget something that actually happened, can you? Or invent something that didn't?'

Aisha paused before replying, 'It's not my field but I read something about false memories recently. And, actually, it's perfectly possible to convince someone they experienced something they didn't.'

'Do you mean through hypnosis?'

'Not at all. Apparently, all that's necessary is for someone you trust to tell you that you did something and you start to believe it. In the case I read about, a psychologist called Elizabeth Loftus succeeded in planting false memories in people, quite traumatic things like getting lost as a child or even being under demonic possession. All the subjects believed they had had those experiences. Memory is a dynamic thing, it's constantly being updated.'

As Aisha said this, I had a sudden vision of myself standing on the platform at Imperial station. David was walking towards me, smiling.

'Are you all right?' said Aisha.

'I'm fine,' I said. 'I'm just a bit tired. I'm looking after my mum. She has terminal cancer.'

'I'm sorry,' said Aisha but didn't say more. I supposed that she had heard similar words many times before.

After another pause, she said, 'If you are going to do this crazy thing, please be careful. Don't let anyone get hurt.'

'I will,' I said. Though I had absolutely no idea how this was possible.

Chapter 43

Anna

Saturday

I nearly said that I couldn't make it. Mum had had a bad night and was sick in the morning. I called Anita who said it was probably a reaction to the latest round of chemo.

'I'll pop round with some anti-sickness medication,' she said, 'but really she probably needs to rest. Have you two been having wild parties?'

I forced a laugh. 'No, but I did have a couple of friends over yesterday. That could have been it.'

'I'm sure Star loved that, though. She's loved having you home.'

'Thank you.' I was worried that I was going to cry.

Anita said, very gently, 'We could always admit her to the hospice now.'

'No,' I said. 'Not yet.'

I made Mum hot water with some lemon in it and she managed

to drink it. Then I rang Sophie. 'I've got to go out this afternoon. Could you sit with Mum?'

'Are you going out with Chris?' said Sophie. Mum had obviously been keeping her updated.

'Amongst others.'

'I've got to take the girls to football, but I'll be round at two-ish.'

'That would be great. She's not having a good morning.'

Sophie's jolly soccer-mum voice faltered slightly. 'Maybe she's just tired.'

'That's what Anita said.'

'We'll have a cosy afternoon. Watch a film or something.'

'Thanks, Soph.'

Chris offered me a lift, but I thought I'd prefer to walk. It was Saturday and the shops were busy, their windows already full of pumpkins and Hallowe'en paraphernalia, although it wasn't even October yet. Hallowe'en is not such a big deal in Italy, where many people still celebrate All Saints' Day instead. As I walked, I began to find the skeletons and tombstones rather oppressive. I didn't want to think about death. When I neared Manor Park, the streets became quieter. It's in a residential area, flanked by large houses set back from the road. I seem to remember the residents continually complaining about the noise from the school but, at weekends and holidays, it's as quiet as the grave. There I go again.

I looked up at the many windows of the school, the iron walkways, the posters for dance recitals and performances of *Oliver!*. It's an unprepossessing building really. I couldn't imagine singing a school song or becoming tearful about its playing fields but those ugly brick walls contained such a wealth of memories, good and bad, that I thought it was a wonder they didn't spontaneously combust, like those houses in horror films built on ancient burial grounds. I remembered, on the night of the reunion, having a flashback to my teenage self, entering through the gates. Now I saw myself leaving them, eyes streaming with tears, on the day of that last exam.

Had I walked this way that day? Past the sweet shop with the notice ONLY TWO MANOR PARK PUPILS AT ANY ONE TIME that had been there since my day. Past the pub where the sixth formers used to drink and where, shamefully – August birthday again – I was once denied entry. Past the house with a statue of a dog in its garden, memorial to a much-loved pet, past the flats with mirror windows that could dazzle, past the shops where I'd seen Izzy at the chemist's, past the wall that concealed the old station entrance.

It was different now. The old warehouse was covered with scaffolding and a sign announced that Milford and Haze, architects, were converting the building into 250 luxury flats. And, most surprisingly, the door in the wall was open, popped ajar with a brick. It felt like something from a fairy tale. *Alice in Wonderland*. Eat me. Drink me. I went closer and a voice said, 'It's as if someone was expecting us.'

It was Chris, wearing his baseball cap disguise again. I felt wrong-footed. Why was the door open? Was it to do with my visit to DI Kaur yesterday? But there was no sign of her or of any police presence. Before I could answer, though, Izzy appeared, arm in arm with a man I recognised as Oliver West. He was smaller than he looked on TV but pleasant enough, with reddish hair and heavy spectacles, presumably to hide the famous blue eyes.

'Where's Cassie?' I said.

'I'm here.' She'd been standing behind Izzy and Oliver. Had she arrived with them? I wasn't sure how the dynamic worked.

Izzy looked at her watch. 'OK, Anna. You need to be in the flats opposite.'

'It'll be locked,' I said, aware that I was sounding pathetic. 'There'll be CCTV.'

'I popped across just now,' said Izzy. 'There are some builders there and they said it would be fine for you to go up to the first floor. Just say I sent you. They were really very sweet to me.'

I bet they were.

'Chris, you need to go down onto the platform.' For a moment, none of us realised she meant 'at once'. Chris shrugged and moved to go through the door. Then he turned back. 'Here, Anna.' He passed me his hat. 'You used to wear a cap.' I put it on my head. Chris winked at me and then we heard his footsteps descending the stairs.

'I'm going to the footbridge,' said Izzy. 'Ollie and Cassie, you give me and Anna enough time to get into place and then you go down to join Chris.'

'How do you want me to play it?' said Oliver, apparently seriously.

'Just be a prize creep,' said Izzy. 'Then you'll be fine. OK, Cassie?'

'Fine,' said Cassie. It was the first time I'd seen Cassie since the reunion, and I was shocked at how thin and pale she looked. She was wearing an oversized jumper with the sleeves rolled back and her wrists were skinny and frail-looking.

'OK, Anna,' said Izzy. 'Action stations.' I started to walk away when I heard her call, 'Be careful', and I remembered that Izzy had wanted a doctor to be present.

I wasn't surprised when the builders greeted me like an old friend. Some of Izzy's stardust had evidently rubbed off. 'Mind where you walk,' said one of them. There were plastic sheets on the floor and bunches of wires protruding from the walls but you could see that the flats were talking shape. The staircase swept upwards with the words 'Imperial Quay' on each riser. The corridor was empty, but I could hear a sound on the floor above, hard to identify, a metallic hum like cogs whirring. For a moment, I thought of Izzy's ghost story about the empty warehouse, the caretaker who fell to his death and thereafter stalked the empty corridors, lamp in hand, calling out in spectral tones, 'Who goes there?' It was like a *Scooby Doo* story, I had thought then, one designed to stop children venturing into the so-called haunted house that was actually a counterfeiters' den. But today's sound was probably just builders at work on the conversion.

Even so, I looked nervously over my shoulder as I walked along the corridor, which had a vaguely art-deco design running along the dado rail. It made me think of the *Titanic*, or at least of the film version, and of my dream the night I had slept with Chris in my childhood bed. I walked until I found an open door. I thought of *Alice in Wonderland* again, the tiny door that led to the secret garden. Of *Brideshead Revisited* and the low door in the wall, the gateway to another way of life. I went in.

There was a small hallway, smelling of fresh paint. In front of me was a choice of three doors, like a video game. I chose the middle one and it led into an empty room, presumably the sitting room. It

305

struck me that the luxury flats were really very small. Mum's front room was bigger. But there was a large sash window and, walking over to it, I saw that it overlooked the old station. I raised the sash slightly and traffic noises filtered in. I could see the metal canopy, the yellow lines along the platform, even the faded posters. *No, no, no to underarm O.* Once again, I had that topsy-turvy feeling. Had I really stepped back in time? Would I see a soldier striding along or a woman in a 1930s coat, her hair in a smooth roll on her shoulders?

But what I saw was Chris, his suspiciously blonde hair gleaming. He looked in my direction but I'm not sure if he saw me. At any rate, he didn't respond to my wave. Then I saw Cassie and Oliver. He was laughing, obviously indulging in a bit of method acting. Cassie backed away from him. Was she acting too or was this real?

Like Chris, Cassie looked in my direction.

And then she screamed.

Chapter 44

Harbinder

Saturday

Harbinder decides to visit Imperial station on her way to work. That way, she can see where the land lies and prepare for the afternoon's big show. To test herself, she follows the A–Z and not her phone and, to her surprise, finds the place quite easily. There's a shopping parade on one side, the upmarket sort with two estate agents, a chemist and a florist but no Tesco Metro. Opposite is a high wall where the word Imperial is still visible, alongside the ghostly outline of the London Underground logo. The circle with the line through it, like the heart pierced with an arrow. Behind this is a huge scaffolded building bearing signs for Milford and Haze, a name that Harbinder has seen on Mette's high-viz jacket. There's a door in the wall. Harbinder tries the handle. Locked. She'll have to get on to the council to open it.

Harbinder circles the wall and finds an alleyway in front of the old warehouse. This, in turn, leads to a footbridge. This must have been the place where Garfield Rice watched David Moore fall onto the tracks. Had he thought, at the time, that it was an accident or had he seen Cassie give the fatal push? *Did* Cassie give the push? Harbinder isn't sure even after hearing her account. What is certain is that Gary later saw something that made him reconsider the events of that day. And Gary is now dead.

Harbinder looks across at the station platform, deserted apart from a large rat who appears from the gutter and sits insolently washing his whiskers. Gary would certainly have had a good view from here. Harbinder turns. She can see the flats too, some of their windows still covered in plastic. Of course, the building was an empty warehouse in 1998. Harbinder wonders what the owners of the luxury apartments will think of the view. Deserted Tube station, complete with rat. She leans over and looks at the tracks below; still live, still deadly. The railing shudders and, seconds later, a train rushes past underneath. The noise is, momentarily, shocking. Harbinder hopes that Mette's flats are soundproofed.

The footpath leads to another alleyway which opens out onto a busy street. She'd better get to work. A black cab stops at the lights and Harbinder raises a hand to hail it. She can never do this without feeling as if she's in a film.

At the station, the team is with Trish, the civilian officer. There's excitement over a new piece of CCTV film. It shows Henry Steep talking to a man in Ely Place, just yards from Bleeding Heart Yard, at twelve minutes past midnight on Wednesday the twenty-fifth. At least, they think it's a man. The figure is indistinct but towers over Henry, who was, in Harbinder's estimate, about five foot seven. This seems to rule out Anna Vance, who isn't much taller than

Harbinder. She remembers Mette talking about a bishops' palace at Ely Place. There's no sign of it in the image, which is obtained from a jeweller's shop called Diamonds are Forever. Hearts and diamonds, thinks Harbinder. She's not a fan of card games but she can see a pattern here.

'Can't we get a better image?' Harbinder asks Trish.

'I've enlarged it as much as I can,' she says. 'But he's overshadowed by the porch of the shop. I'll see if there's anything else from the surrounding area.'

Harbinder calls a brief team meeting.

'We've now got a pretty good idea of Henry Steep's movements after he left the House of Commons at eight p.m. on Tuesday the twenty-fourth,' she says. 'He left the House, got a cab on Westminster Bridge which took him to a pub on the corner of the Strand and Aldwych. Later that evening he walked to an all-night café near Temple Tube station, where he met Sonoma Davies. At eleven he texted his husband to say goodnight. At eleven-forty-five he set out from Temple, apparently planning to walk to Bleeding Heart Yard. This latest CCTV shows him very near there at twelve minutes past midnight. Is he talking to his murderer? It's a possibility.'

'I've got something too, boss.' Harbinder thinks that Jake has been waiting for his moment. He stands up and assembles his legs. 'I spoke to the head waiter at the Houses of Parliament restaurant. He served afternoon tea to Henry Steep and a woman who answers Anna Vance's description. The waiter remembers them having a heated discussion and the lady leaving in a hurry.'

'Really?' says Harbinder. 'Did he hear what they were arguing about?'

'No,' says Jake. 'Though I'm guessing it wasn't for lack of trying.

But he did hear Henry saying, "Don't go." But Anna left. In the waiter's words, "She flounced off in a huff."'

'Typical,' says Kim. 'A man loses his temper, but a woman goes off in a huff.'

'I don't make the rules, Blondie,' says Jake.

'Arguably, you do,' says Harbinder. 'As part of the patriarchy. But let's concentrate on the facts. Henry and Anna argued. Anna certainly didn't tell us that at first. She gave the impression that they just had a cosy chat, catching up on old times. But, when she came to see me yesterday, she said that Henry claimed that she was there the day that David died. I guess that could have made her quite heated.'

'We'll see if anything happens this afternoon,' says Kim. 'The gunfight at the OK Corral.'

Kim often references cowboy films. It reminds Harbinder of her father, who loves them, despite finding the phrase 'Cowboys and Indians' offensive.

At four o'clock, when Harbinder is about to leave for the OK Corral, Trish knocks on her door. Harbinder knows at once that she's got something good.

'You know you asked us to look for CCTV around Attlee Towers?'

'Yes.' It was one of Harbinder's first actions after Henry was found dead. She wanted to check the movements of all the surviving members of The Group: Anna, Chris, Sonoma and Izzy. So far, all they have is a grainy picture of Izzy having supper with her agent. This looks like it will be more promising.

'It's from a garage on the Sutton Estate.' This is very near Anna's mum's flat. Harbinder leans in closer.

'Taken at one a.m. on the morning of Wednesday the twenty-fifth.'

The picture shows a woman walking. She is wearing jeans and a hoodie and her head is down. But it's definitely Anna Vance. Harbinder calls Kim and Jake into her office.

'Anna could have killed Henry at a quarter past midnight,' says Jake, 'and then walked this far. Or got the night bus.'

'I just can't see Anna leaving her mum, going off to stab Henry and then walking back,' says Kim. 'Most likely she just popped out for some ciggies. This is just around the corner from their flat.' Kim says the word 'ciggies' almost wistfully. She told Harbinder that she gave up smoking ten years ago, but she still talks about it a lot.

'Anna argued with Henry at the House of Commons,' says Jake. 'She could have arranged to meet him later. It explains why he went so willingly. He didn't think he was in danger. Anna confronted him at BH Yard and she stabbed him. Maybe she was in – what was it again? – a fugue state.'

'Maybe,' says Harbinder. 'We certainly need to question her about this. Anna led us to believe that she slept soundly all night, then went jaunting off to Brighton with Chris Foster. We'll talk to her when this charade is over. Come on, Kim. Time we were off. Let's wear our vests, just to be on the safe side.' The vests destroy their cover, but they are bulletproof and also come with handcuffs, flashlights and body cam.

'I'll keep an eye on things here,' says Jake. Unnecessarily, in Harbinder's opinion.

The squad car has to break the speed limit, and a few one-way restrictions, to get them to Imperial on time. When they arrive, the door to the old Tube station is open. Did the council do it or is this the work of one of The Group? Harbinder can't be sure. Across the road, looking in the window of an estate agents, Harbinder recognises a plain-clothes surveillance officer. Otherwise the street is deserted. The theme tune from *High Noon* arrives, unbidden, in Harbinder's head. 'Do not forsake me, oh my darling.' Wrong Western, she thinks. Another favourite of her dad's, though.

'You go down to the platform,' she tells Kim. 'I'll take the warehouse.'

She circles round the boarded-up station and crosses the alleyway to the scaffolded multi-storey building. Two builders are standing, apparently aimlessly, by the entrance.

'Don't tell me,' says one. 'Marilyn Monroe sent you.'

'It's our day for entertaining beautiful women,' says the other.

Harbinder has had enough. 'Police,' she says, pointing to the badge on her vest. 'Did someone else just come in?'

'Yes,' says the first man, now sounding rather dazed. 'A woman. First floor.'

Harbinder takes the curved staircase two at a time. The corridor seems to stretch to infinity – just how big is this apartment block? – but there's an open door a few metres away. It leads into a hallway smelling of paint and new carpet and opening out into an empty room. Anna Vance is standing by the open window, looking out. Something about her stance makes it look as if she's on the point of collapse, one hand is over her mouth, the other clutching the window frame.

'Anna?' says Harbinder.

Anna turns and a look of surprise transforms, nightmarishly, into one of complete horror.

Harbinder is about to speak when something cold and metallic is pressed against her head. Despite never having had this experience before, even in training exercises, she knows what it is.

'Throw down your phone,' says a man's voice. He sounds vaguely familiar, but Anna supplies the name in an anguished whisper, 'Pete.'

Harbinder puts down her phone and, in doing so, turns slightly. Cassie's husband is facing her, wearing dark clothes and a baseball cap, and holding a handgun in an uncomfortably professional way.

Several things become clear to Harbinder in that second. Including the words that had puzzled her in Cassie's account of David's death.

'I remember the train coming, this explosive noise, and Henry telling me to run.'

'You shot him, didn't you?' says Harbinder. 'You shot David Moore. Probably from this very spot. Cassie heard the gunshot, but she didn't realise what it was.'

'I killed him to protect her,' says Pete, in the same pleasant tones that had discussed Mario Kart and joked about a spaniel called Kevin. 'I knew it was the last day of exams, so I came down from Loughborough to see Cassie. I followed her and David to the station and I watched them from this window. I *surveilled* them. When I saw them struggling, I shot him.'

Anna starts to move, and Pete turns to point the gun at her. 'Over by the wall, both of you, where I can see you.'

Harbinder wonders if she should rush at Pete, try to knock him off-balance. But he's armed and the bulletproof vest would not protect her at this range. Besides, there's a civilian present. Harbinder's priority has to be to preserve life.

'Do what he says,' Harbinder tells Anna.

Anna and Harbinder stand against the wall. The decorators will be furious, thinks Harbinder, if we get blood all over their nice white wall.

'Did you kill Gary and Henry too?' Anna asks Pete. Keep him talking, Harbinder sends her a thought message. It's too risky to shout out, even if the chatty builders are still downstairs. But, surely, the more time they take, the more likely it is that help will come?

'Yes,' says Pete carelessly. 'Gary worked it out – I don't know how – on the day of the rugby club reunion. I heard him telling Izzy on the phone. Henry too. He rang Cassie and left a message. I listened and then deleted it. Henry said that he'd worked it out. He had looked up that day and seen someone in the window wearing a cap.'

'He thought it was me.' Anna sounds on the verge of hysteria. 'He thought it was me wearing my butcher boy cap.' She's wearing a baseball cap today. It states – erroneously, Harbinder is sure – that it's the property of the NYPD.

Harbinder remembers that the rugby club reunion was actually a day spent clay pigeon shooting. Although a shotgun is very different from a handgun, it must have been the sight of Pete holding the weapon that had triggered Gary's memory. Izzy was right about buried memories, whatever else she had got wrong.

'It was easy to kill Gary.' Pete is quite chatty now. 'I took one of Cassie's syringes. I wore gloves, of course. Gary was standing by the loos talking on his phone. I knocked him out and then injected him, right in the backside. Then I rolled him onto his back and put some coke round his nostrils. It wasn't hard to get hold of. You can buy cocaine anywhere in London. It's disgusting.'

Is the man really lecturing them about the dangers of drugs?

'What did you do next?' asks Harbinder.

'Threw the syringe in the bin and went back to join the party.'

Harbinder remembers her first sight of Pete, sitting with the other ex-students in the library, the way he had looked at the floor as if trying not to be sick. She had thought he was just drunk.

'How did you kill Henry?' asks Anna.

'Stabbed him,' says Pete. 'I sent him a text from Cassie's phone saying that I'd got his message and wanted to talk. I suggested Bleeding Heart Yard because Gary said he met his Tory mates there. Misdirection, isn't that what you call it? I thought the cow's heart was a nice touch. We buy them for Kevin.'

Before Anna can ask another killer question, there's a thunderous roar from outside. The train, thinks Harbinder. The open window. Pete is momentarily distracted. Harbinder grabs Anna's hand. Anna doesn't need it spelt out for her. They race for the door, across the hallway and into the corridor. 'The stairs!' pants Harbinder, tripping over plastic sheeting. She pushes Anna ahead of her. But Pete isn't far behind. A shot rings through the air, shattering glass somewhere in the building. He won't miss twice. They are nearly at the stairs but Pete is taller, stronger, fitter. Harbinder turns. He is right behind them, levelling the gun. And then, like a dream, a blonde Valkyrie on a bicycle appears at the end of the corridor. In a blur of wheels Pete is thrown sprawling to the ground and drops the gun. Harbinder grabs it, just as voices are heard on the floor below.

Chapter 45

Harbinder

Harbinder thanks the genderless god that she has her body cam on because everything is a bit hazy after that. She stands over the still-prone Pete Fitzherbert, cuffs him and reads him his rights. Kim appears, accompanied by a uniformed PC. Harbinder thinks the builders are there too, and Chris Foster, who is hugging Anna. She sees Mette's wheels still spinning and realises that she is holding her flatmate's hand. She drops it hastily.

Then they are descending the stairs. Pete is pushed into the squad car and Kim goes with him. Anna and Harbinder follow in the next car, with Mette and Chris Foster too. Cassie, Izzy and Oliver are still at the old Tube station, in the care of a woman police officer. Helen, the family liaison officer, is on her way. It will be her job to tell Cassie what her husband has done.

'What about your bike?' says Harbinder to Mette. 'What about Sven?'

'I'll pick him up tomorrow,' says Mette. 'You know, this is only the second time I've been arrested.'

'You're not being arrested,' says Harbinder, wondering about the first time. 'You're a witness. You're a hero.'

'You are,' says Anna. 'You saved our lives.'

Harbinder hasn't introduced Mette so she supposes she really does seem like a superhero to the others. Bicycle Woman. Architect Girl. Was Mette in the building for work or because she knew Harbinder would be there?

Chris says, 'I can't believe it of Pete. I always thought he was such a good guy.'

'I thought he was just a meat-head who loved Cassie,' says Anna. 'But that's what all this is about. He was obsessed with Cassie. He killed David that day to protect her.'

'Love is a violent thing,' says Chris.

Harbinder speaks quickly because she has a horrible feeling that they are about to start kissing. 'We'll need statements from all of you. Anna, how are you feeling? Do you need to see a doctor?'

'I feel wonderful,' says Anna. Hysteria again, thinks Harbinder.

'What about Cassie?' says Chris. 'Is someone with her?'

'My colleague said she left Cassie with Isabelle and her husband,' says Harbinder. 'I'll send a family liaison officer round to her house later.'

'Poor Cassie,' says Chris. 'All these years she thought she was a murderer and it was her own husband all along.'

'I know a little about how that feels,' says Anna. 'Ever since I saw Henry I've wondered if I was there that day. Even if I killed David. It was horrible. Henry thought it was me at the window but that was just because the person – Pete – was wearing a cap.'

'You and your butcher boy cap,' says Chris, so fondly that Harbinder is glad they have arrived at the station.

★

Pete is being booked in at the custody desk. Harbinder has time to go upstairs to the incident room and is amazed to be met by a round of applause.

'Well done, Blondie and Suzi,' shouts someone.

Kim grins at Harbinder who raises a hand to acknowledge the ovation. 'Thanks, guys,' she says. 'Still a lot to do but we've made an arrest. The suspect also made a confession which was filmed on my body cam. We need to interview him now and I expect he'll ask for a brief. Jake, can you take the lead on that?'

'Sure thing, boss.' Jake puffs out his chest.

'Let's talk interview strategy,' says Harbinder. 'Jake, Kim, can you come into my office? Great work, everyone.'

She feels amazing, like Jane Tennison or some other TV cop who has succeeded against all the odds and delivered a result before the ten o'clock news. It hardly needs the phone call from Simon Masters, 'Super work, Harbinder. Can you put out a statement tonight? Great to have some good news for a change.'

Harbinder relays this word for word and tells Jake and Kim what happened in the old warehouse, soon to be Imperial Quay Apartments. Freya brings in coffee and one of the team contributes some biscuits.

'So, your flatmate just appeared out of nowhere?' Jake is having trouble.

'She's an architect working in the building,' says Harbinder carefully. 'But she certainly appeared at the right time.'

'She was very cool, I thought,' says Kim. 'Six foot tall, Swedish blonde.'

'Sounds just my type,' says Jake.

'She's Danish,' says Harbinder. 'And she's not your type. She's my type.'

She doesn't wait to see how Jake takes this.

Harbinder uploads the film from her body cam. 'It's all here,' she says. 'It'll be hard for him to backtrack, but we obviously need a proper forensic interview. I know I can leave that to you, Jake.'

'You can,' says Jake. 'I'll take Tory with me. I think it might be good to have a woman in the room.'

'Your call,' says Harbinder. She supposes that Tory, especially if she does her wide-eyed thing, might lull Pete into a false sense of security.

'At the rugby reunion, Pete overheard Gary phoning Isabelle and telling her that he knew who killed David. It seems that Gary told quite a few people this, including Sonoma Davies. I think it was because, when they were out clay pigeon shooting, Gary saw Pete with a gun. That must have triggered a memory of seeing him in the old warehouse that day. Pete killed Gary to keep him quiet. He was quite matter-of-fact about it. Said that he killed Gary with one of Cassie's syringes after knocking him out first.'

'Then injected him in the arse,' says Jake. 'Nice.'

'Then Pete put coke round Gary's nostrils, chucked the syringe away and calmly went back to the party. I'm betting we find his DNA on the syringe. Or on Garfield's body. It hasn't been released to the family yet.' Although Paula is clamouring for this every day.

'What about Henry?' says Kim, taking a biscuit. They are the classy sort, from M&S.

'Henry left a voice message on Cassie's phone. In it he said he knew who killed David. He'd seen a figure in the old warehouse that day and initially thought it was Anna. Something about a hat,

319

I didn't follow it all. But, sometime on the Tuesday night, he must have realised it was Pete. Maybe he remembered Pete holding a gun too. He was there at the clay pigeon shoot. Pete listened to the message on Cassie's phone, deleted it, then texted Henry, pretending to be Cassie. He arranged to meet him at Bleeding Heart Yard. My guess is that Pete's the man seen talking to Henry on CCTV.'

'Cassie slept on the sofa that night,' said Kim. 'God help me, I thought that pointed to her.'

'Me too,' says Harbinder. 'But actually, it meant that Pete could sneak out, kill Henry, and be back in time for breakfast.'

'Cassie often took sleeping pills too,' says Kim. 'I remember her telling me once.'

'OK,' says Harbinder. 'Let's get as much detail from Pete as possible. We also need witness statements from Anna Vance and from Mette, my flatmate.'

'Anna must be quite traumatised,' says Kim.

'Actually, she seems in good shape,' says Harbinder. 'She was really brave.'

'She was holding hands with Chris Foster when I saw them downstairs,' says Jake. 'Are they an item?'

'Who says "an item"?' laughs Kim. 'Are you a hundred years old, Anton?'

'I think so,' says Harbinder. 'They certainly seem very close. I think they're both shocked about Pete.'

'I am too,' says Kim. 'He seemed so nice, so reliable. Cassie will be shattered.'

'She'll need a lot of support,' agrees Harbinder. 'You know, she thought she'd killed David Moore?'

'Really?' says Kim. 'Did she tell you that?'

'Yes. She said she thought she'd pushed him under the train. I wasn't sure at the time if it was a reliable account. There seemed to be a lot of holes in it. And Cassie described this explosive noise, which didn't sound like a Tube train to me. It must have been the gunshot. Pete travelled down from uni to see Cassie on the last day of the exams. He followed Cassie and David from the school to the station, "*surveilled* them", in his words, and, when he saw them struggling on the platform, he shot David. I don't know where he got the gun but I'm guessing that Pete has quite a collection at home. I'll request a search warrant.'

'Pete injected Gary with insulin and stabbed Henry,' says Jake. 'Must be a cold-blooded bastard.'

'I think he must be,' says Harbinder, remembering the clinically tidy study and the way Pete had suddenly appeared in the doorway. She'd been slightly frightened of him then, she realised.

'Let's get a confession recorded,' she says.

Jake heads off to find Tory but Harbinder calls Kim back.

'Did I hear someone call me Susie just now?'

'Yes. It's your nickname. Didn't you know?'

'Why Suzi?' says Harbinder. If it's racist, she thinks, she'll sue.

'After Suzi Quatro. Because you wear a leather jacket. Shows the average age of people around here.'

Harbinder is not, strictly speaking, displeased to be compared to the iconic rock singer.

'They call me Suzi at work,' Harbinder tells Mette. 'After Suzi Quatro.'

'Down in Devil Gate Drive,' sings Mette. 'That's very cool.'

They are lying on Mette's bed. Outside, the lights of London twinkle and promise. Pete Fitzherbert has admitted to the murders of David Moore, Garfield Rice and Henry Steep. Harbinder has issued a statement saying that a forty-two-year-old male (always male, never man, in police parlance) has been arrested. The Sunday papers will lead with the story. Harbinder is going to visit her parents tomorrow and will read the *Observer* on the train. She's slightly hoping to be recognised.

Mette plays with a strand of Harbinder's hair. 'Finally,' she says. 'Finally we're in bed together.'

'Have you wanted to be, then?' says Harbinder.

'Have I wanted to? I've given enough signals. Asking you out to the pub, wandering around naked, saying that I liked the lesbian character in *Buffy*.'

'I didn't realise you were gay,' says Harbinder. 'I just thought you were being Scandinavian.'

Mette laughs, a rich full sound that chases away any remaining demons. 'You're the only person in the world who didn't realise. My workmates knew immediately. Even the builders yesterday knew.'

'They said it was their day for seeing beautiful women,' says Harbinder. 'I might have known they meant you. It was so amazing,' she says, not for the first time, 'when you appeared like that.'

'I always ride my bike along the corridors,' says Mette. 'It's quicker and easier. When I heard a gunshot, I just went in that direction.'

'You were very brave,' says Harbinder. 'You saved my life.'

'Let's make the most of it,' says Mette.

Chapter 46

Cassie

One of the uniforms drove Izzy, Oliver and me to the station. 'We'll need to take statements from all of you,' said Terry, the desk sergeant, 'and then you'll be free to go.' He looked at me very kindly. 'Are you OK, Smoothie?' I didn't think he knew the whole story but he obviously realised that something was up. 'I'm fine,' I said. 'Do you want me to stay with you?' asked Helen, the FLO, as Izzy and Oliver were ushered away. 'No,' I said, 'I'll be OK.' I've worked with Helen on a few cases and she's nice enough but I didn't think I could face her looking at me with professional pity. I imagined her gossiping with her colleagues later. 'Who would have guessed it of Cassie's husband? Mind you, I always thought he was a bit weird. She must have suspected too, don't you think? Maybe they were in it together.'

I didn't recognise the DC who took my statement and I was grateful for that. But, afterwards, Harbinder came into the interview suite and asked if I wanted to see Pete. Her face was suitably serious but I knew that inside she was glowing with the satisfaction of a job well done. She'd got a result. Upstairs the team would be celebrating. There might even be Champagne. There would certainly be biscuits from M&S. I wished, more than anything, that I could be with them, that I'd never heard of Pete Fitzherbert, or been lifted over his head to see one of the Spice Girls. But, without Pete, I wouldn't have my children and I couldn't wish them away.

Pete was in one of the holding cells. Harbinder left us alone together, which was certainly stretching the rules.

'Are you all right?' I said. There was a bruise on his face. I'd heard someone say that Harbinder's flatmate had knocked him down with a bicycle but you can never believe anything you hear in a police station.

'I'm sorry,' he said. And he looked so the same, large and dependable, his big hands on his knees, that I was almost tempted to forgive him. But then I remembered; this man had killed three people, two of them my friends.

'Why did you do it?' I said. Harbinder told me that he had made a full confession.

'They knew about David,' he said. 'They knew I'd killed him. All those years ago.'

'Why did you kill him?' I said.

'I was protecting you,' he said. 'I saw you struggling with David on the platform. So I shot him.'

'Why were you even there?' I said. It was hard to equate this version of events with the one that had lived in my head for so long. David and I had struggled. My push hadn't sent David to his death. He had, apparently, been dispatched by a bullet.

'I came to see you,' he said. 'I knew it was the last day of exams.

I wanted to talk to you, to tell you that I loved you. Then I saw you leaving the school with David. So I followed you.'

I remembered the feeling I had, when I was walking to the Tube station with David, that I was being followed by an angel who would protect me. Except that it wasn't an angel.

'Why did you have a gun with you?'

'I often used to carry a gun in those days,' said Pete casually 'It was one of my dad's.'

I knew that Pete's father had a gun, a relic of his army service. He often boasted about it, adding that it was properly licensed and that he 'knew how to handle himself.' But it seemed that he had failed in the first requirement of gun ownership. He hadn't locked the weapon away.

'It was lucky I had it,' Pete continued. 'I was able to act when he assaulted you.'

Lucky was not the word I would have used.

'What about Gary?' I said. 'Why did you kill him?'

'He knew,' said Pete. 'I heard him telling Izzy on the phone after the clay pigeon shoot. He said he knew who'd killed David. So I injected him with your syringe. He was no loss. He thought he was so wonderful but he was just another corrupt politician. Besides, I always thought he was after you.'

Pete always had been jealous of Gary. He would call him 'your boyfriend' in that tone of voice, remembered how we had gone out together at school, when we were in Year 10 and Pete was in the sixth form. I thought that Pete and Gary might have bonded at all those rugby and football reunions, but I think, on some level, Pete was just biding his time. 'He didn't love me,' I said. 'I think he always loved Izzy.' Saying those words filled me with a great sadness. Perhaps Izzy and Gary should always have been together. Anna and Chris too. How many lives had we ruined that afternoon at the abandoned Tube station?

'What about you?' said Pete.

'I loved you,' I said, realising that this was true. I had thought that, on some level, I was still in love with Gary but really I had loved the life I had built with Pete, even though that turned out to be based on a whole foundation of lies.

'I'm going now,' I said.

'Will you come back?'

'I don't think so,' I said.

Izzy and Oliver were waiting in the reception area. They were both very kind. Izzy hugged me. 'Do you want to come back to our house tonight? We could pick the children up on the way.' Lucy and Sam were at a friend's birthday party. I remembered making the arrangement, writing it smugly on the Mummy Pig calendar, pleased to have them both occupied for the afternoon.

'No, thank you,' I said. 'I just want to go home.'

I didn't tell Lucy and Sam. Let them have one more night of not knowing, I thought. I didn't tell my parents either. Or Pete's. After the kids were in bed, I sat in the kitchen with Kevin and drank the best part of a bottle of wine. Pete didn't like me to drink too much. It was one of a whole series of restraints, offered subtly in the form of caring, designed to form me into his perfect wife. On our first date when he lifted me into the air, I'd chosen to see this as romantic but was he really just displaying his superior strength? Pete was certainly never violent but, in his soft-spoken way, he undermined me all the time. You should get promotion, your boss is younger than you, take your sleeping pills, don't eat your crusts, stay at home and look after me. And I let him do it because, deep down, I didn't feel I deserved any better.

It's funny, when I confessed to Harbinder, I thought I was ending my life. I thought I might go to prison, that I'd never see the children again. When Harbinder gave me absolution, I wasn't sure what to do with myself. I went home feeling like a whole new person, a clean slate, a white page. I didn't tell Pete though. I wonder why now.

But then, the next day, Izzy appeared on my doorstep with the crazy idea of reconstructing the events leading up to David's death. We should lay the ghost, she said, sitting there wet-eyed, talking about how much she had loved Gary. Why did I agree to it? I suppose I wanted to know. Harbinder had made me doubt myself. Izzy talked about buried memories and I thought: what have I buried alongside David in that grim Baron's Court cemetery? Because I had visited the grave many times. *David Nathaniel Moore 1980–1998. Beloved Son.* Once Arthur found me there, laying some flowers, which confirmed my angelic status in his eyes.

I used to think about *Sliding Doors*, the film I'd seen with David. Gwyneth Paltrow misses her Tube train and the film shows what would have happened if she'd caught it, how her whole life would have been different because of that one small detail. David said that I looked a bit like Gwyneth but then he pounced on me and the rest of the story is a bit of a blur. I used to wonder what would have happened if I hadn't gone to Imperial that day, if I hadn't killed a man.

When I saw the station again, the door propped open, I was

surprised how calm I felt. Because it wasn't the same. I wasn't an eighteen-year-old who had just failed to answer coherently about *The Tempest*. I was a middle-aged woman in one of my husband's jumpers. Oliver wasn't David, he was the man in that TV series about a cop who doesn't seem to have heard the word 'procedure'. Even when we went down those still foul-smelling steps, it wasn't the same. But then, on the platform, Oliver said something like, 'Give us a kiss, darling.' It was such an obvious piece of acting that Chris, lurking in the background, laughed. But it jolted me. I looked up. And I saw a figure staring out from the building opposite. A figure wearing a dark cap.

And I remembered.

Chapter 47

Anna

Even though, this time, I was a witness and not a suspect, it was still scary being interviewed by the police.

'Just tell us what you remember,' said Kim, all sympathy, leaning forward in her chair. There was another officer there too. A large man who said very little. 'Just tell us what happened today, Anna. In your own words.'

What did I remember? 'Memory is dynamic,' Aisha had said. But I had to try to pin down what had actually happened before my imagination started adding extra detail. I remembered entering the apartment block, the builders' badinage, feeling self-conscious as I walked away from them. I remembered finding the open door, the hallway with the smell of paint, the wires sprouting like fungus in the corner of the room. I remembered opening the window, looking down on the station platform, seeing Oliver and Cassie walking along like extras in a film. Oliver moving forward, Cassie stepping back, Cassie looking up, Cassie screaming.

After that, it was more difficult. The voice saying 'Anna?' that I didn't immediately recognise. Turning to see Harbinder with a gun to her head. The gunman resolving himself into Pete, my friend's husband, the man whose wedding I had attended. Asking him questions, the need to know temporarily stronger than the instinct for survival. Harbinder warning me to do what he said, her voice reminding me how serious the situation was. Harbinder touching my hand, silently telling me to run. The corridor, stretching for ever like something from *The Shining*, the gunshot. And then the gleaming figure on the bike, Pete sprawled on the ground, Harbinder saying, 'Pete Fitzherbert, I'm arresting you . . .' Suddenly Chris was there, holding my hand, and I could have sworn that Harbinder was holding the cyclist's hand too. I didn't add this last bit.

'I do need to ask you something, Anna. Just to dot the i's and cross the t's.' What's coming now? I wondered. Kim continued, almost apologetically, 'We have a CCTV image of you walking past a garage on the Sutton Estate in the early hours of Wednesday the twenty-fifth of September.'

I remembered. After that meeting with Henry, when he told me that I'd seen a murder, I hadn't been able to sleep. I'd got up, dressed and had walked to the garage to buy some chocolate. In the end, I hadn't even gone in. The lighted forecourt was enough to remind me that life, in all its messy glory, was still going on. The tarmac had shimmered with a petrol rainbow. A taxi driver was leaning against his cab, drinking a cup of coffee. I told all this to Kim, as best I could.

'I thought you'd popped out to buy cigarettes,' she said.

'I don't smoke.'

'Very wise.' But I thought she sounded slightly disappointed in me.

When Kim read my statement back, it sounded fantastical, less believable than anything I'd written in my unfinished crime novel. But I agreed that this was what happened and signed at the bottom of the page.

Once again, Chris was waiting outside.

'They're giving us an escort home,' he said. 'We must be the good guys at last.'

I realised that the last time Chris was in this building, he was being arrested on suspicion of murder. He seemed remarkably sanguine about the whole thing. 'They thought I'd killed Gary because I was so angry about global warming,' he told me afterwards. 'It was quite flattering really, that they thought I was that much of an eco-warrior. Apparently, someone – probably Cassie – heard me arguing with Gary at the reunion. We did argue. I told him I'd never forgive him for selling out the way he had. Being a Tory was one thing but pretending to be a climate change denier because it suited his business interests? That was unforgivable. I think I really hated Gary when I said those words. But it wasn't much to build a case on.'

I was surprised to find that it was still light when we went outside. It felt like years had passed since I'd walked to Manor Park, reliving my past. But now it was seven o'clock and the shadows were starting to lengthen. London looked incredibly beautiful as we drove the short distance to Attlee Towers. Even the brutalist 1960s flats looked mellow in the soft blue light. As Chris and I climbed the stairs, the setting sun blazed in through the landing windows, making golden shapes on the lino.

Mum and Sophie were watching an Ava Gardner film. Sophie jumped when she saw Chris and looked accusingly at me, obviously wishing that she'd had time to put make-up on. But the glow enveloped her too and I thought she looked beautiful in her old hockey hoodie, hair pulled back in a careless ponytail. Mum's dressing gown gleamed crimson in the half light and the cranberry juice in her glass looked like a magic potion.

The film seemed strange and surreal, involving bull fighters, archaeologists and the *Flying Dutchman*. Chris and I were quite content to sit, sharing an armchair, until it was finished.

'Your friend Izzy looks a bit like Ava Gardner,' said Mum.

'She really does,' I said.

We told Mum and Sophie what had happened, with many recaps to keep Sophie up to speed. Mum followed remarkably well. 'Poor Cassie,' she said. 'She always had bad luck with men, ever since that awful incident with the boy at school.' I hadn't realised that Mum had known what Cassie and I were talking about, when we shut ourselves into my bedroom. She hadn't known, though, that Cassie's attacker was the 'poor boy' whose death had, supposedly, brought the curse down on the school.

'I'm glad it was all resolved before you had to go back to Italy,' said Mum.

'I wish you hadn't got to go back,' said Sophie.

I looked at Chris. 'I might stay for a while longer,' I said.

The heart has its reasons.

Epilogue

'I'm nervous,' says Mette.

'Don't be,' says Harbinder. 'My parents are dying to meet you.'

And, although she doesn't say it, this is the problem. Harbinder's parents are both delighted and apprehensive at the thought of meeting their daughter's first official girlfriend. 'I'll make smorgasbord,' Bibi said to Harbinder on the phone, 'that's what they have in Denmark. I've been reading about it.' 'She likes Indian food, Mum,' said Harbinder. 'It's the only reason she's going out with me.' She had laughed to show this was a joke.

'I'm not worried about your parents,' said Mette. She was sitting opposite Harbinder on the train, clutching a bouquet of yellow roses. 'I'm worried about your friends.'

Harbinder is planning to meet up with her friends Benedict, Natalka and Edwin after lunch. It will be the first time they've met one of her girlfriends and she knows that they will be curious (Edwin), emotional (Benedict) and embarrassingly direct (Natalka).

'They'll love you,' says Harbinder. 'Though you're right to be nervous. Benedict will probably cry and Edwin will tell you long stories about the BBC.'

'And Natalka?'

'Natalka will probably ask if you're a spy. She thinks everyone's a spy. Especially since she's started her detective agency.'

Natalka, once a carer, once a dealer in crypto-currency, has recently started her own private investigation firm. Eighty-one-year-old Edwin is one of her best sleuths. Benedict, Natalka's partner, an ex-monk who owns a coffee shop, provides refreshments.

The train moves slowly, on Saturday wheels, through south London. Harbinder thinks of the day after the events at the old Tube station, when she travelled on this route to visit her parents. 'MP Deaths,' screamed the headlines. 'Police make arrest.' The *Observer* had called her 'hot-shot DI Harbinder Kaur, one of the new breed of Met detectives.' This was a roundabout way of saying that she was one of the few women of colour at that rank. Nevertheless, Harbinder had cut out the article. Her mother keeps a scrapbook.

Two days earlier Harbinder had received an email from Anna Vance saying that her mother had died. 'She was still at home and I was glad that Sophie and I could be with her at the end.' Harbinder had replied with condolences and asked when Anna was returning to Italy. 'I'm staying in England for a bit,' was the answer. 'I want to take a break from teaching. I might even write that book!' Harbinder felt that the exclamation mark disguised a wealth of feeling, including embarrassment at such a clichéd ambition and a conviction that she would succeed. Harbinder wished Anna luck and asked if she would be living at Attlee Towers. 'No. The council have only given us a week to move out all Mum's stuff. I might stay at Chris's for a bit.'

'I might stay at Chris's for a bit.' That told Harbinder all she needed to know. Anna is back with the man she has loved since she was eighteen. Harbinder wishes them well. She thinks they are well-suited, whatever the tabloids might say. And, if Anna wants to return to Italy, Chris can buy her a Tuscan villa. Hell, he can probably buy Tuscany.

Cassie has been in touch too. These have been hard weeks for her. Harbinder can't begin to imagine it, having to tell your children that their father is a triple murderer, facing the fact that you lived with this man for years, that you built a life together. Cassie is currently on compassionate leave and has taken the children to visit her parents in Tenerife. Harbinder is slightly surprised that Cassie is determined to return to her old job. 'I'm a police officer,' she said, rather defiantly. 'It's what I do.' Smoothie is evidently tougher than she seems.

Isabelle Istar is starring in a new adaptation of *Zuleika Dobson*. 'The original femme fatale.' Oliver West, in a fat suit, is playing Zeus.

Sonoma Davies is still patrolling her domain, no doubt wearing a red power suit.

'Who will be there today?' asks Mette.

'Mum and Dad,' says Harbinder. 'My brothers Khushwant and Abhey. Their wives. Their children. Oh, and my parents' mad dog, Starsky.'

'Just a few people then.'

'You're lucky they haven't invited all the aunties from the gurdwara.'

'I think it's great,' says Mette. 'I've always wanted to be part of a big family. It's just me and my parents. No siblings or cousins.'

Harbinder thinks about this all the way to Shoreham.

In the end, lunch is a success. Bibi tries to talk to Mette about architecture but gives up because she can't remember if Renzo Piano is an architect or an opera singer. Luckily, they get on to TV and discover they both love *Downton Abbey*. 'That Mr Bates is so lovely,' says Bibi. 'He's a psychopath,' growls Harbinder, who is not a fan of the period drama.

Mette talks easily to the children about school and football. They are all excited to hear that she once played semi-professionally. 'Sis here can't kick a ball,' says Abhey, disloyally. But I can kick you, thinks Harbinder, and does so, under the table. Starsky barks. Deepak makes them all laugh with his experiences as a touch-line grandfather. 'It's very competitive. To be really successful you need a beer gut and an England shirt.'

Harbinder helps her mother take out the numerous dishes. In the kitchen, Bibi whispers, 'I like Mette.'

'So do I, Mum,' Harbinder gives her a hug.

'She's very tall, isn't she?' says Bibi, loading a plate with kala jamun and Jaffa Cakes.

'Is she?' says Harbinder. 'I hadn't noticed.'

After lunch they walk along the promenade and meet Benedict, Natalka and Edwin outside Benedict's Coffee Shack. It's a beautiful autumn day, the sea sparkling like a postcard.

'I'm so happy to meet you.' Benedict gives Mette a hug but, thankfully, refrains from tears. He makes them all coffees although the Shack is officially closed. Benedict likes to observe Sunday as a day of rest.

'I once went to a fascinating conference in Copenhagen,' says Edwin. 'It was in this amazing hotel in the middle of an amusement park.'

'The Nimh Hotel in Tivoli Gardens,' says Mette. 'I've never stayed there but it is beautiful. There's a lovely Christmas market in Tivoli Gardens,' she tells Harbinder. 'We must go this year.'

'Being an architect would be the perfect cover story for a spy,' says Natalka, but her heart's not in it.

They all raise their cups to toast Harbinder's success in the MP murder case.

'To crime,' says Edwin, who loves a good murder mystery.

'To love,' says Benedict, moist-eyed.

'To detection,' says Natalka.

'To us.' Mette smiles at Harbinder.

'To the future,' says Harbinder.

Acknowledgements

Bleeding Heart Yard is a real place, as are all the other wonderful London street names on Mette's list. It was a real pleasure to write about London, where I was born and where I have lived for long periods of my life. However, all the characters and events in this book are entirely imaginary. Manor Park School is also fictional, as are all its pupils, past and present. Imperial is fictional but there are several such 'ghost' tube stations in London.

Thanks, as ever, to my wonderful editor, Jane Wood, and to all at Quercus. It takes a team to produce a book and Team Elly is the best in the business. Thanks to Joe Christie, Bethan Ferguson, Florence Hare, David Murphy, Ellie Nightingale, Hannah Robinson, Hannah Winter and everyone else involved. Thanks to Liz Hatherell for her meticulous copy-editing and to Chris Shamwana for the truly stunning cover. Thanks to my fabulous agent, Rebecca Carter, and all at Janklow and Nesbit. Thanks also to Kirby Kim at Janklow US and to Nicole Angeloro and all at Mariner Books.

Thanks to Graham Bartlett for the advice on policing. Any mistakes are mine alone. Thanks to Harpreet Kaur and Balwinder Kaur Grewal for their insights into Harbinder's home life. Thanks to Lesley Thomson for her constant support and knowledge of the A–Z. Thanks to my friends, and ex-publishing colleagues, Paul Cherry and Kate Harris, for introducing me to Bleeding Heart Yard.

This book is dedicated to the memory of my much-loved father-in-law, John Maxted. John was particularly fond of the lines from *The Tempest* quoted by Anna at the Houses of Parliament. Love and thanks always to my husband Andy and our (now grown-up) children, Alex and Juliet. I couldn't do it without you.

Elly Griffiths
September 2022